Entitled

a novel

Cookie Boyle

www.bespokenwordpress.com

ISBN 978-1-7773534-0-7 (SOFTCOVER)

ISBN 978-1-7773534-1-4 (EBOOK)

Publisher's Cataloguing-in-Publication data
Title: Entitled : a novel / Cookie Boyle.
Names: Boyle, Cookie, author.
Identifiers: ISBN: 978-1-7773534-0-7 (pbk.) | 978-1-7773534-1-4 (ebook)
Subjects: LCSH: Books--Fiction. | LCSH: Travel--Fiction.
| LCSH: Humorous fiction.
Classification: LCC PR9199.4.B6945 E68 2020 | DDC 813.6--dc23

Cover and page design by Linda Parke
www.ravenbookdesign.com

Printed and bound in the United States of America

To Walter, who has given me the best story of all.
Thank you for being on the bus that day.

San Francisco

CHAPTER 1

It is a truth universally acknowledged, that a Reader in possession of a full wallet, must be in want of a Book, or so says a *PRIDE AND PREJUDICE* friend of mine, two aisles away. Sitting on a Bookstore shelf, day after day, waiting to find my forever home, I hang my hopes on her belief, so when this woman picks me up and starts to read my page 1, I'm ready to close the sale.

> Agnes Lundberg took the shaft of wood that she had hidden beside the outhouse, then slowly and silently inserted it through the two semi-circles of metal that formed the doors' handles. Smiling at her achievement, she lifted the hem of her plaid dress and stepped quietly, her boots retracing their steps in the snow. As the sound would travel on such a cold night, she held her laughter and her breath.
>
> At the back of her house, Agnes slowly opened the door, entered the kitchen and with both hands, gently closed the door behind her. Only then did she breathe. She removed her gloves, untied the laces on her boots and put them in a far corner where no one would notice the snow clinging

to their soles. Grabbing a cookie from the glass jar, she entered the living room where her mother was playing the piano, her father was reading, and neither had noticed her departure, or her return with chilled, red cheeks.

Henry's scream interrupted the tranquility. Agnes thought of him trapped in the outhouse in the cold of a winter's night and smiled, knowing that he would never push her down in front of Erik Svenson, or anyone, ever again.

The woman doesn't turn my page. Instead she shuts me.

Come on, that's a great opening. Gives you a glimpse into Agnes, places her in an historic time, shows how strong a protagonist she is. Agnes the protagonist. It even rhymes. What more could she want?

But instead of realizing the value of my story, this Reader walks four feet down the aisle then discards me atop a stack of Books I've never met. I'm now stuck in an awkward social situation, waiting for a Staffer to notice that one of their charges, that would be me, is in need of their services. Balancing above my colleagues, I demonstrate my infinite patience. Until it becomes finite and I consider throwing myself onto the carpeted aisle. They'd notice me then.

When you're a Book on a shelf, waiting for a Human to buy you and take you home, you have a lot of time on your hands. Even when you don't have hands. The romance novels contemplate love. The war novels obsess about military maneuvers. My story is about a young woman in the middle of nowhere, dreaming about a life beyond the horizon. I guess I'm the same, dreaming about a life beyond this aisle. But that's where the similarity ends. I'm sure of it.

Shannon, a Staffer passes and notices I'm out of place. *"Tessa MacDonald,"* she reads and follows the Author-based alphabet until she discovers the singular inch of space I left behind. I'm entitled THE SERENDIPITY OF SNOW and the only copy of my author's only novel, which means I sit here, alone, without any family to talk to, and just the width of my spine to capture a Reader's attention. I've been here all summer and have had zero success. Had I been about THE SERENDIPITY OF SUNSHINE, I might have a home by now. But no, my Author had to set me in Minnesota, in the dead of winter. Life isn't fair. Even for novels.

The lights in the store turn off then on again. It's the end of another day. Older titles have nodded off the shelf, falling to the floor. The Staffers spend their last hour tripping over these exhausted Books, brushing them off and putting them back on the shelf to await their fate another day. These aging Books, with their marks and creases and broken spines, are also the first to be returned to their publisher. Like I said, life isn't fair.

Most Books have 120 days to attract a Reader or else we're sent back to be redistributed, or worse, recycled and pulped. There's a reason we give paper cuts.

The classics operate in a different world. My PRIDE AND PREJUDICE friend displays her gilt edges, knowing she's safe. The Hemingways and The Fitzgeralds are protected by their lineage. They've inherited their relevance, so can sit for a year with no one questioning their value. It's different for the rest of us. I'm here with no family name or marketing campaign to help me. I've got to make it on my own. Like Agnes in my story.

"Psst," my shelf-mate whispers. "I hear something."

I open my fibers, straining to take in sound, but get nothing.

"Here they come," he says.

It's after hours, which is usually the time for Books to relax, but not this night. Instead, it's the evening we all dread.

It starts with a squeak. The sound of the cart's wheels, like an ambulance siren piercing the tranquility of our rows, causes us to shrink in fear. They have a list and we all pray that our names aren't on it. Except the Buddhism Books. They accept it as part of their journey or something.

My friend, *DIANE'S DREAM* starts to sob. "*DD*, you don't know that they're coming for you. They're probably just re-arranging the best sellers."

"Do you think?" she says through her sniffles.

No, I don't. There hasn't been a shipment back to the publishers for a month, so tonight could get ugly. "Moby, what do you think?"

"Call me Ishmael," *MOBY DICK* responds.

"Okay. Ishmael, what do you think?" I ask again.

"There's a tidal wave coming, and none of us are prepared," he says. Sorry I asked.

The squeak approaches. Slowly. Determinedly. Ominously. I half expect Myles, the Staffer pushing the cart to cry, *"Bring out your dead!"* Instead, he shouts to his colleague Jerome, *"Let's be quick. I want to get out of here by 10."*

"Hear that DD?" I say to *DIANE'S DREAM*. "They're going to be fast. Nothing to worry about," I lie. Clearly there's a reason I'm classified as fiction.

I edge my spine out slightly to improve my hearing. I'm not worried about my situation. Yet. *DD*, on the other hand, has quite a bit of dust on her. But I wouldn't say that to her cover.

The cry of the cart's wheels lurches between fiction and non-fiction, imagination and reality. "They're passing self-help and reference!" yells the display of best sellers. "Now they're in Local Interest."

"I'm not going to leave my heart tonight," TONY BENNETT'S BIOGRAPHY sings out. He's stacked next to THE HISTORY OF THE GOLDEN GATE BRIDGE and a photo essay of San Francisco's cable cars. He's safe. Tourists love a souvenir Book, even if it's one they'll never read.

The squeaking stops. "They're in Gardening!" screams a title from the cooking section.

With a series of cries blended with goodbyes, Books on bulbs and spring planting are removed. One thud is followed by another as the hardcovers are dropped onto the cart. "They've got 20 titles, maybe more," shouts a cookbook. It's the end of August, so this purge isn't a surprise for these Books, but it's still awful.

"Don't worry about us," SPRING PLANTING says. "There's a season for everything, and this is our season to go."

I don't know the Gardening Books personally. They're too many aisles away, so we've never met. But they've always answered our questions in a nurturing and patient way. I'm sad to think there will be fewer of them.

The cart moves again. Its cadence casts a hush over us all. *"I'd make more money working in a restaurant. Think of the tips,"* Jerome says as the squeaking grows louder.

"Yeah, but here we get to take home any Book we want," Myles says. The cart is turning this way.

"Who buys Books anymore? I download what I want to read," Jerome blasphemes.

"Downloading! A plague on you," ROMEO AND JULIET shrieks, not that any Humans can hear.

"Ow!" Jerome yells, thanks to a precisely timed plunge off the shelf by THE HISTORY OF DIVING in hardcover.

From the same Sports Section, GYMNASTICS FOR BEGINNERS picks up the commentary. "It was a perfect dismount and he really stuck the landing on the sandal-wearing Jerome. Degree of difficulty: 3.6." Books that are face-out flap their covers in applause.

The relentless squeaking continues in our direction. Myles and the now-limping Jerome stand in front of the Summer Reading section.

"Oh, no, they're totally after us," BEACHED LOVE shouts.

High-pitched screams mark the end of holiday romances and sand-filled frolics, as titles with yellow and azure covers are piled on the literary hearse.

"That's everything on the list," Myles says. *"Let's take these books to storage and we can get out of here. Leave the cleaning for the morning shift."*

"You never dusted us," BEACHED LOVE says from her place on the cart. "You never gave us a chance."

The squeak fades. "Bye, everyone," calls SUMMER PATIO FLOWERS. "May you all fully bloom."

The rest of us sit quietly, grateful for our relative good fortune, when a title breaks the silence. "It was the best of days, it was the worst of days, it was the morning of hope and the evening of despair," says A TALE OF TWO CITIES.

And with those words of Mister Dickens lingering in the air, I close my fibers to rest and contemplate another night of the long sighs.

CHAPTER 2

The fluorescent lights sputter on, the coffee machine hisses and the calendars remind us that it's Saturday.

The low hum of the escalators vibrates along the floor and seeps through the wooden shelves that we call home. The non-literary items in the ever-expanding gift section resume their excessively perky presence. Cards straighten themselves, pillows fluff up, and throws look less thrown. We all have a finite amount of energy and even the candles don't waste their scent on a Human-free space.

"Look sharp, everyone," barks GENERAL PATTON'S BIOGRAPHY. "Let's give it an all-out assault. See how many of us can find a home this weekend." It's the same pep talk he gives every Saturday morning. I can't see myself assaulting any customers in the line of duty, but somehow his 'Bookstore is a battlefield' metaphor makes other titles sit up straighter. "We have a job to do. Stay focused. There's a war on Books and we need to fight back. Show those Humans what they're missing."

The General's speech doesn't inspire courage in every Book. "What if no one takes me this weekend?" DIANE'S DREAM asks. "I may get returned to my publisher."

"You're not getting sent back," I say. "This weekend is probably the one you've been waiting for. You just don't know it yet." I try to sound confident when in reality any hope that I'll be chosen is tested each day.

As we anticipate this weekend's sales, the astrology Books reassure us of success. The EPHEMERIS makes it sound scientific and reliable. "The moon just moved into Leo," he says, "and stays there until Monday evening. This means that our inner selves are craving attention, so it should be a good weekend for many of us to draw the interest of a Reader and find a home." Given that he hasn't foreseen his own sale, I question his ability to forecast our success.

The staffroom door opens and the voices of Keisha and Shannon emerge, along with the smell of over-roasted coffee. The Books in the food section groan, especially the Italian ones who don't tolerate the aroma of the mediocre. It's a sentiment I don't understand, but one thing we're never short of here is opinion.

The two workers visit every row, replacing returns and reorganizing Books who have been misfiled. *"Look at the dust,"* Shannon says. *"Myles and Jerome should have cleaned last night. Typical, leaving it for us."*

Then my shelf gets tighter. "Hey, shove over," says a familiar voice.

"*JOE*? Is that you?" I ask.

"Yeah."

"But I thought . . . "

"Returned," *JOE* says. "And I was all ready for the great adventure."

A sale isn't always a successful match. Too many Books find themselves back on the shelf after everyone cheered them on in their new life. "They bought me along with some candles and pillows," JOE says. "I knew I was in trouble when I had a gift receipt taped to my cover."

Our entire aisle groans. We hate the relentless gift creep. Non-Book things like bags and baskets keep seeping towards us, like the molten lava that HAWAII BOUND describes. The color-coordinated housewares only distract Humans from their reason for being in a Bookstore, namely purchasing one of us. If you're called a Bookstore, you should be required to sell Books and nothing but Books. There ought to be a law.

"If they brought you home with candles, then they simply didn't understand you," I say. "You're not a candle kind of Book."

DD chimes in. "You're better off waiting for the right Reader to come along. If it can happen once, it can happen again."

"But they left a stain on my back," JOE says.

"You can get away with it," I say. "You're JOE'S DISCOVERY. You're meant to be rough and tumble. If you didn't have a few marks on you, you wouldn't be you."

We're not in the Self-Help section, but you'd never know it from the constant stream of affirmations we exchange. One day, one of us may be right.

Shannon and Keisha continue down our aisle, adjusting, tidying, primping. *"Who decided to schedule an author signing at the start of our shift?"* Keisha asks.

At the phrase "author signing," whole shelves of Books vibrate with excitement. Covers flap with curiosity as questions bounce between titles: "Who is it? Can anyone read the announcement?" But no Book has an answer, just a hope that they're the ones who finally get to meet their Creator.

Even I am excited, although I know it won't be my Author. First-time novelists usually don't get a signing until their second book. Yet authors draw in Humans, and Humans and their homes are our ultimate goal, so a rising title lifts all Books.

"I've never read her stuff, have you?" Shannon asks.

"Yeah, it's okay. Romantic, you know, but good. I finished it, which says something," Keisha replies. Hope seeps through the fiber of every Novel they pass.

"They're in our aisle!" shouts *DD*. I wish I were facing out. I would love to be a witness to this literary lottery winning.

"Tell me who gets chosen," I say.

"They're looking at their list," *DD* shouts. Then she squeals.

"*DD*! Is that you?" I ask.

"Yes! I've been chosen!" she says, then chokes back her words. "Last night I thought I was going to be pulped. Now today I get to meet my Author."

"So, be happy. Look your best. You're going to find a home," I say.

Titles on the aisle cheer as *DD* and her literary relatives are taken away to be displayed and perhaps purchased and signed. Maya Fredricks, *DD*'s Author, is coming to our store. It's the stuff of Book dreams.

We hear stories of that moment, when your Author opens your cover, turns past your endpaper to your title page, and looks at you . . . really at you. And you look back into the face of your Creator and for a moment, have that connection between their thoughts and your existence. It probably won't happen for me, but it might happen for *DD*. She's Maya Fredricks' fourth Book, and the fifth is still in hardcover, so with the Book signing, *DD* has a real chance of making it to her forever shelf this weekend.

I hear chattering between the other titles. Maya Fredricks has arrived.

Chairs scrape across the tile floor. The volume of voices increases. Then a hush. One woman welcomes the audience and says how pleased she is at the turnout. Humans clap, the audience mutes itself and the Author speaks. *"Thank you, all of you, for being here today. It's nice to see that while the season is changing, our appetite for love isn't."* The Humans laugh politely. *"My newest novel is the fifth in the series. It's called* Emma's Exception. *And if you permit me, I would like to read from chapter four."*

The Book, EMMA'S EXCEPTION, coughs as its pages are opened for the first time. The story is about Emma's attempt to define the right man before she starts dating again. It sounds similar to DD's story, in which Diane's Dream is to, well, find the right man. And the storyline echoes COURTNEY'S COMPLAINT, BELINDA'S BELIEF and ARIELLE'S ANTICIPATION. Perhaps by the time Maya Fredricks writes about Zoe and her Zeal, she will have discovered a plot twist.

Maya Fredricks answers a few questions, mostly about men. It sounds like one of those group therapy sessions that Books in the Self-Help section describe. Every woman seems to have an unhappy story about relationships, or lack of them. I've never been in love. But I guess it's important to Humans, as half of our titles wouldn't exist without it.

The post-reading discussion devolves into laughter when one woman recounts a story about a man who, it turns out, is the ex-boyfriend of another in the audience. The volume of voices surges until a clap of hands and a raised voice suggest that it's time for Book signings. Humans respond with the sound of feet shuffling on the floor. I envy their mobility.

Then I hear her. "I'm being signed!" *DD* screams.

She's done it! "Congratulations!" I shout. "I'll miss you, *DD*." My fibers swell with happiness for her. "See *JOE*? If she can find a home, we can too."

"Hope so, for both our sakes," he says. "Otherwise, you and I are on a path to be pulped."

Reality can be brutal when you're left on the shelf.

CHAPTER 3

Fridays mean StoryTime with StoryLady.

Mothers arrive with oversized strollers that clog our aisles. It's like rush hour in the fiction section, but no one is rushing to buy. Instead, while moms look at titles, small, drool-drenched hands reach for any Book that's at eye level to shove into their teething mouths. The only titles who can tolerate it are the plastic-covered Kids' Books. I thank the display system that put me on the third shelf, beyond the reach of sticky fingers.

Then I feel it. Movement. I'm being taken off the shelf. I look into the face of my holder but it's not a store employee, it's a mother. Her stroller contains not just one but two toddlers. I didn't know you could get kids in bulk. She begins to read my backside. Could this be it, the Human I've been waiting for? But how can a mother with two little kids have time to read? This can't be how my story goes.

"Gather round children," calls out StoryLady, also known as Shannon, wearing a blue wig, orange dress and oversized green shoes. *"It's StoryTime."* The kids welcome her announcement with a collective shriek.

Rather than placing me back where she found me, in the conveniently alphabetized gap that I've left, the mother lays me flat, balancing on top of my shelfmates, over the space I call home. Seriously, how hard is it to place Books back where we belong? Leaving me misfiled, she navigates the double-wide stroller in the direction of StoryLady.

Honestly! I've been on the shelf for two months, waiting to be chosen, but I guess not today. In the end, I'm probably better off without her, because I want to be chosen by a Reader who gets completely immersed in my story and will pay attention to my nuances right through to my last page. Then my Reader will place me next to other Books that have been loved. There, I'll make friends. We'll spend the days telling each other our stories, safe in our home that's warm and dry, on a shelf without splinters. That's what I'm waiting for. I don't want to settle.

"She wasn't a good match for me anyway," I mutter.

"Tell yourself whatever makes you feel better," snorts the Book beneath me.

As StoryLady reads to the children about the adventures of the *Cat in a Hat*, the mothers cluster in one corner, focused on their phones. If the Bookstore really wanted to make money from StoryTime, they'd hire a bartender.

The joy and laughter of their offspring fills the space, warming the fibers of even the most hard-covered non-fiction Books. When StoryLady asks, *"Who wants a lollipop?"* the squeal of two dozen little voices denotes the end of StoryTime. Just as quickly as they arrived, the children and their mothers disappear, leaving tranquility to hang over the Kidz Korner.

I'm getting used to my newfound vista, on top of my colleagues, when a hand grabs me. This isn't a Staffer, or the mother. Instead, a new face is staring at me. This one has long hair, glasses and a gentle face. She opens my cover and flips through my pages. I tell myself to act casual, like this happens all the time. Be cool. Don't want it too much, or they can smell it on you.

She turns my pages and stops at my Chapter 3. It's time for me to perform. When Readers open a Book, they think they're reading us, when in fact we're reading them, emitting our stories with an emphasis and cadence they can absorb. Get a good Reader and Books can perform spectacularly well; distracted, we stop caring. I have a chance with this one, so my words need to pull her gaze from left to right, then down a line and from left to right again. I exhale and begin.

Agnes awoke and looked out the bedroom window. She cherished these moments when the room was quiet. With her two younger sisters still asleep, she could hear her mother starting the stove's fire and knew that soon, the porridge would be ready. But until then, the best place to be was in the middle of her bed with the quilt wrapped around her.

The horizon was calling and from her coveted position next to the window, she gazed into the distance and wondered again where life would take her. As the day started to break the blackness of the night, she imagined there was a girl just like her, somewhere that the sun had already touched, thinking the same thoughts.

She noticed that the snow had covered her footprints overnight. The path she made from the outhouse no longer existed. Could all her choices be erased in the same way?

Does foreboding in my story mean foreboding in my own life? Just because I have a story of longing within me doesn't mean my story will be the same, does it? Why doesn't life come with an instruction manual?

My Reader's hair trails down my page. It tickles. Then she closes my cover. I knew it. The foreboding put her off. It always does. No one has made it past page 16 yet.

But rather than put me back on the shelf where she found me, she carries me in her right hand. I remind myself to breathe. I made it all the way to the counter once, only to be left behind when my potential Reader discovered she'd forgotten her wallet at home. She never returned for me. But this time, it feels different.

As we pass the Buddhism Books, I try to catch their attention, but they're meditating again, focusing on the moment, when in these very seconds I am passing them by, forever.

At the register, the Human's eyes smile at me through her glasses. She opens her purse and yes! Her wallet emerges. She's buying me. I curl up my edges in a Book's smile, but she doesn't notice. It doesn't matter. She's already chosen me. I no longer need to impress her with my cover.

Keisha takes her money, crams a Bookmark into my spine with more force than necessary, then deposits me in a small paper bag. I inhale deeply to shift the Bookmark, but no luck. I hope my Reader looks at me tonight, if only to remove that plastic-coated wedge of advertising from between my pages.

Through the bag I shout a muffled goodbye to my friends. "Knock 'em dead, kid!" yells *Joe's Discovery*. I hear the remaindered bin wish me luck. As the door closes behind me, I realize the first chapters of my life are closing behind me too.

CHAPTER 4

I'm finally outside the Bookstore. I feel like a free-range novel. The fresh air stiffens my fibers. I can't see through the paper bag she's carrying me in, but I can hear. And smell. And feel. Someone ordering a hotdog. A slightly sweet aroma. The edge of a button as my Human clutches me against her coat. Holding me close to her body, her temperature softens my spine. I conform slightly to her shape, giving her a Book's hug.

Cars honk, people talk, a baby cries. With all this noise, you'd think more Readers would come into the Bookstore, if only for the tranquility. We turn down a side street, then another, until the only sounds are the heels of her boots clicking on the pavement. Within minutes she's opening a door. We climb some stairs then open another door.

Still in my bag, I'm tossed on a table. The landing was harder than I'd like. I've never been in a real Human's home before. I wonder if houses have changed since Agnes' time.

I strain to see beyond the feet of my pages and past the opening of the bag, to the world that she has invited me to join. She flips on an overhead light and hangs her coat in the closet.

A loud ring startles me. She picks up her phone. *"Hello?"* Her voice is soft, with a slight upturn at the end of the word.

With the force of my cover, I push the bag open to expand my view. In front of me are a light brown sofa and a coffee table, with a blue rug on the floor. A dining room flows off the living room

"No, I have today off," my Human says into the phone. *"I went by the store and picked up a book for us."* That's me she talking about! I'm on her radar.

Still holding her phone, she pulls me from the bag, freeing me from its confines. *"It's called* The Serendipity of Snow. *I liked the title."*

Even if she only chose me for my name, that's okay. It's a start. I can build off that.

She turns me over and inspects my last page. The Bookmark slips from my spine. Relief. *"Not too long. About 300 pages. The quotes on the back say it's warm and amusing. It's set in Minnesota and it's by a first-time author. I'll bring it with me. We need a suggestion for next month."*

My Reader puts me back on the table. While I'm free of my bag, I'm face down. I can't see a thing, except the grain in the wood. Come on, pick me up again. I have a cover for a reason.

I wriggle, trying to move myself over to the edge of the table. If I can make it, I'll fall on the floor and she'll be forced to pick me up. It's a long way down, but it's carpeted, and worth the effort if the alternative is to spend the rest of my time backside-up to the world.

"Yeah, great. See you tomorrow. Bye." She puts down her phone, then sneezes. Let's hope she's not allergic to me, or I'll be back on the store shelf before the lights go out for the night.

She moves to the sofa, but her phone rings again. Why can't people just leave her alone so she can start reading?

"Hello?" There it is again, that rising lilt to her voice. She really should be more confident. I was once misfiled in the women's studies section. I learned a lot there. *"Really?"* Her voice tells me that this is not good news. *"Too bad, I was going to make us a nice dinner."* Her voice has gone up a tone. *"Oh, okay, then. Don't work too hard."*

She puts down the phone then opens my cover. Her eyes look at my dedication, but they just skim my words. She bites her lower lip. I try to perform for her, but she's not absorbing me at all. Her eyes move across my page, but I can tell I'm having no impact. It's like showing a painting to a blind person. Closing my cover, she places me on the coffee table and walks away, leaving me to survey my new home.

A piano is in the corner. Its yellowed sheet music sends me a tired grin. If it smiles any harder, it'll crack. Softly it hums a sonata so old that even the characters in my story would recognize it. I curl up my edges to smile in return.

A few picture frames, covered by dust, lean against a ledge. One holds a photo of my Reader in a wedding dress, and one shows her with the groom. Two other frames display photos of her with friends.

A large-screen TV takes up too much room against one wall. The remote control sits two Book-lengths away from me on the coffee table. I don't speak electronica so, mercifully, I am not expected to interact with it. Nevertheless, I sense an aura of self-importance pulsating from that grubby thing, as if life stops when it's misplaced. But just wait until there's a power outage. Then we'll see who still functions by candlelight.

The woman returns, holding a glass of red wine. An elixir for her, but potential danger for me. I have no interest in red tattoos being left on my pages. Stains like that devalue me. She picks me up again and I smile back at her with all the charm I possess. I want her to revel in my words.

> This day, she decided, was going to be special. Agnes was going to make a statement. She was tired of being asked to clean up after class. No boy ever had to do it. Miss Pattison only asked the girls, each time moving down the alphabet to choose the next one. Today, Agnes was going to say what she had always wanted to say: No.

My Reader reaches for her glass of wine and takes a sip. She leans forward and places it too close to the remote control, spilling a little. Hah! How does that blend with your batteries? She reaches for a tissue, cleans the drops off her wedding ring, waves the tissue over that filthy remote, then focuses on me.

She turns back to my Page 1. I have her now.

CHAPTER 5

I awake confused. Rather than being on a Bookshelf, I'm face-up on a coffee table. There are no Staffers to turn on the lights, no friends to recount their nightly exploits, no drooling kids to threaten my pages. Then I remember I am in a home. The tranquility is deafening.

A large Male Human in a bathrobe appears in the living room carrying a cup in one hand and a phone in the other. He sits on the sofa and pulls a large coffee table Book, *ÜBERDESIGN, THE ESSENCE OF MINIMALIST LIVING,* towards him. I shriek when he places his cup on the Book's cover. Coasters are made for a reason, people. The vibrating phone draws his attention. His large thumbs tap on it and he sits back, pleased with himself. When he reaches for his mug, *ÜBERDESIGN* exhales with relief.

"I hope that cup wasn't too hot," I say.

"Who are yoü?" *ÜBERDESIGN* asks.

"*THE SERENDIPITY OF SNOW,*" I say.

"Yoü look all new and shiny," *ÜBERDESIGN* says. "Did Katie büy yoü?"

"My Reader calls herself Katie? She looks like a Katie,"

I say. Not that I've known any Katies. But if I did, I'm sure they'd look like her.

The phone vibrates again. The Human looks at it and grins. He gets up and leaves the room, taking his phone, his cup and his self-importance with him. In Minnesota in the 1800s, there were no phones. I suspect people got more done back then.

"Who's he?" I ask.

"He is the ünReader," *ÜBERDESIGN* says. "Her üntidy hüsband. Always clüttering things üp. I coüld help them get rid of all their stüff, if they woüld just read me."

I don't think this apartment has too much "stüff", so I leave the conversation to hang like the ümlauts over his vowels.

Katie enters the living room, carrying her bag. Moments later the ünReader re-appears.

"Seen my watch?" he asks.

"Probably on the mantel," Katie says.

"Oh, right. Thanks," he says.

The ünReader picks up a brown leather watchstrap attached to a round brass face. Roman numerals mark the six, nine and twelve. A window for a date marks the three. A crack in the crystal marks the seven.

"Remember when I gave that to you?" Katie asks.

"Best third anniversary gift I ever got," he says, smiling at her while he fastens his watch.

"Second," Katie says.

"Oh, right," the ünReader mutters, *"I meant second."*

"I'm going out, I'll be back in a few hours," Katie says. She gives him a quick kiss then looks around the room. Her eyes fall on me, but instead of cradling me lovingly in her hand, where I belong, she plunges me into a large black bag. Another Book lands on me.

"Sorry."

"Not your fault. I'm THE SERENDIPITY OF SNOW."

"LOUISIANA SUNRISE. Nice to meet you, ma'am." Ma'am? I'm not old enough to be a ma'am. I must sound wise.

"Where are we going?" I ask.

"Book Club," he says, with a drawl that would be at home south of the Mason-Dixon Line. "I do believe it's at Naria's house this month."

I would feel more positive about a Book play date if I weren't so cramped. Keys land on me, cold, hard and sharp. Then Katie zips up her bag, sealing us in. The keys bounce on me with every step so I tighten my fibers in self-defense and tell myself to focus on the positive: Book Club.

After more jostling, mercifully the movement stops. The zipper opens and Katie removes me and LOUISIANA SUNRISE, placing us on a stranger's coffee table before following a woman down a hallway.

"Hey, y'all," I hear. "I'm LOUISIANA SUNRISE."

"Me too," I hear from behind me, a phrase repeated around the table.

I open my cover to get a better view of my surroundings and see five copies of LOUISIANA SUNRISE circling me. "I'm THE SERENDIPITY OF SNOW. What's your story?"

I hear of a family descending into debt, surrounded by theft and political corruption. "We're about affairs, lies, bribes and deceit," says one LOUISIANA SUNRISE. Sounds like just another day at the Bookstore to me. "Then one morning, in our chapter four, a dead body is dropped into Lake Pontchartrain. That's our inciting incident."

"We're a great story, but my Reader, Lily, barely cracked my spine," Lily's Book says.

"I should be called Louisiana Lacquer," another *LOUISIANA SUNRISE* says. "Every time my Reader, Rebecca, picked me up, she'd decide she needed to do her nails instead, and use me as a manicure tray. I have nail polish all over my backside. It makes me look so cheap."

Katie returns to the living room carrying two glasses. Another woman brings a bottle of wine. The others follow, each with their own glass.

"You know, back in the Bookstore, we dreamed of coming to a Book Club, having Readers discuss our stories. I never thought I'd actually be at one," I say, practically bouncing on the table.

"Calm down," Rebecca's Book says. "They'll notice you moving."

Everyone takes a seat around the coffee table. Empty glasses are filled. As if pre-programmed, all the women cross their legs, right over left.

I'm excited. I have a front row seat at a real Book Club discussion: the cut and thrust of debate, where themes are analyzed and character traits dissected. It's going to be great. Here we go.

"This wine is amazing," Lily says. *"Napa?"*

"Sonoma," Naria says. *"A new winery I was consulting for."*

"It's delicious. How's the job hunt going, Naria?" Katie asks.

"I have an interview this week for a position I'd actually take," Naria says.

"They'd be lucky to have you," Katie says.

"I'll tell them you said so," Naria says with a smile.

"When do they start talking about the story?" I ask.

"Sometimes never," Naria's Book says.

"But aren't we read, then discussed? That's how Book Clubs work," I say.

"That's what I thought too, honey," Naria's Book says. "Until she brought me to the last Book Club as her choice for this month. I sat for two whole hours listening to them talk about real estate."

"That can't be right. This is Book Club. They love us here," I say. These Books from down south are simply wrong.

"Should we wait for Madeeha and Grace?" Katie asks.

"Not coming," Naria says.

"Again?" Katie asks. *"There used to be, what, eight of us?"*

"Twelve when I started," Lily says.

The women look uncomfortably at each other, then at their wine glasses. They drink in silence.

"Well, someone begin," Lily says.

Katie asks, *"So, what did we think of* LOUISIANA SUNRISE?*"* I grin, proud that my Reader started the conversation.

After a lengthy silence Naria says, *"I liked it. The book reflected race in a believable way. And I liked being drawn into the backroom dealings."*

"Did you get confused by all the lying?" Lily asks. Naria shakes her head No. *"What about you, Rebecca, did the lying bother you?"*

"There wouldn't be much of a story without it," Rebecca says. *"Anyway, lying is just a part of life."*

"That's pretty cynical," Katie says.

"That's reality," Rebecca says. *"You've never told a lie?"*

Katie looks into her glass.

"There are lies and then there are lies," Lily says.

"En France, we don't care," says another woman with an accent. *"You Americans are so uptight."*

"That's Veronique," her Book says. "Brings up France every chance she gets."

Rebecca examines her nails. *"Well, no one would call you uptight,"* she says.

"Lily, what do you think?" Katie asks.

"I found it confusing. The unreliable narrator was a little too unreliable for me. I stopped following the trail of lies. In the end, I stopped caring." Looking proud of her comment, Lily returns to her glass of wine.

"Do you hear her?" Lily's Book says. "She only read my first 80 pages. She talks like she actually cared about me."

The conversation morphs from Louisiana to vacations, workouts that get you in shape for vacations, and how to save for vacations in an expensive real estate market.

"Time for cake," Naria says.

That's it for their debate? But they haven't discussed the Book! They're meant to be exploring plot, themes, pacing, twists, use of language. Literary Nature is much more interesting than Human Nature.

Veronique tops up everyone's glass. Naria returns carrying a cake that oozes with the aroma of maple. They all ask for a small piece, but none complain about Naria's generous portions. Crumbs fall on Rebecca's Book. He tries to shake them from his cover.

"Stop it, they may see you," Naria's Book says.

"They're focused on their cake," Rebecca's Book says. "Besides, my Human never paid attention to me when she was meant to be reading me. I reckon she won't notice me now."

After long minutes of murmurs about the quality of the cake, Katie asks, *"How about a first-time novelist for our next Book Club?"*

Is that me she's talking about? I puff out my cover in case anyone is looking.

"Does it have sex in it?" Veronique asks.

"Not so far. I've only read the first few chapters. It's called The Serendipity of Snow. *It's set in Minnesota, in the late 1800s. I suspect the characters will be bundled up against the weather most of the time,"* Katie says.

"That can be sexy too, you know, unbundling," Veronique says.

"Is that all you think about?" Lily turns to the others. *"Maybe it's time to read something with an environmental message. Because if we don't do something soon . . . "*

"What, you're going to sell your SUV and stop flying to Hawaii every Christmas?" Rebecca asks, reaching for the wine bottle.

"We need the SUV. For our children," Lily says, looking around the room. *"You can't put a price on a child's safety."*

Naria puts down her plate, opens my cover and glances at my first page.

"We've never read a first-time author," Katie says.

"From Louisiana to Minnesota. Why not?" Naria says.

Being the center of attention is making my fibers warm. I guess Best Sellers get used to it, or maybe they just have thicker paper.

Naria hands me back to Katie, who turns me over and reads my back, aloud. I can feel my cover flush.

> This charming voice of a new author transports us to a time long past. In small-town Minnesota, a determined young girl, Agnes Lundberg, defies social expectations to travel further than she imagined, only to arrive at a place she never planned. Written with affection for a way of living

more than a century ago, *The Serendipity of Snow* explores the power of curiosity and the unrelenting pull of love that drives us all.

"You're hosting next month, so your choice," Naria says.

"I think you're in, honey," Lily's Book says.

"Don't expect much," Naria's Book says. "Your Human will read you because she suggested you. And she'll like you, because she suggested you. If they actually discuss you at all, it will be short. They always drift off to other topics. Like today."

"This really is just a wine club with a Book excuse," Rebecca's Book says.

I have so much to learn.

CHAPTER 6

I have a gentle, coated Bookmark with rounded edges nestled between my pages. I'm in a warm home. And tomorrow, Book Club is coming here. Is this the definition of happiness?

"Hey, DICTIONARY," I shout to the paperback. "Happiness. Definition?"

"Noun," states POCKET DICTIONARY. "The state of being happy."

"That's the best you can do?" I ask.

"What do you expect? I'm a Pocket Dictionary."

Even without an in-depth definition, I believe I am experiencing true happiness. And I have no intention of letting it slip away.

Without warning, the ünReader enters. So much for happiness. He picks me up and reads my back cover. *"Trite,"* he mutters, before tossing me back on the coffee table. Clearly a heathen. I'm not quite sure what trite means, but it doesn't sound good. I consider asking POCKET DICTIONARY for a definition, but the ünReader picks up the remote control and hits the dreaded red button. Invasive sounds burst from the television, drowning out any discussion I could have.

His phone vibrates. *"Hey,"* he says into it. Leaving the television barking at the empty room, he walks out the front door carrying his precious device.

I look at the television and try to understand the story it's telling. It must be good, as Humans are devoted to these things. A man is driving a car exceedingly fast on a highway. A woman is in the passenger seat. A bigger car comes up behind them and someone from inside the second car starts shooting at them. I'm not sure why. Conveniently, there is a gun in the glove compartment of the first car. Despite all the bullets, the woman is able to lean out of the window and shoot back at the second car. But then a bus comes towards them from around the corner. Two even larger guns emerge from the hood of its engine. An immense, tattooed man with gold teeth unwisely hangs out of the window, laughing as he drives in the direction of the first vehicle. Between gunfire from the car behind and bullets from the double-barreled bus ahead, the original couple somehow manages to keep up their banter. They swerve to avoid the bus, which ends up hitting the car that was pursuing them. The couple looks back at the fireball on the highway, smile at each other and continue driving out of sight. Then inexplicably, the story transitions to a man holding a bag of fertilizer while pointing proudly to his excessively green grass. I don't know what this lawn has to do with the tattooed man, the couple in the car or the people chasing them. In fact, I can't follow this story at all.

"Did you say something?" Katie steps into the room and looks around. I pivot in the direction of the door, to indicate his point of departure, but she's not looking at me for help. She opens the front door of the apartment and calls, *"Honey, are you there?"*

She moves to the window and reaches for the latch then

stops. Her gaze is fixed on the front door. After several moments
it opens.

"*What were you doing?*" she asks.

The ünReader puts his phone on the table and opens the
closet door. "*A work call.*"

"*Outside?*"

"*Just needed some fresh air,*" he says, pulling on his jacket. "*I
have to go into the office.*"

"*Again? I was hoping we could spend some time together. Have
dinner . . . something,*" Katie says, drawing her eyebrows together.

The ünReader glances at Katie, then just as quickly, picks
up his phone. "*Yeah, sorry, we hired a bunch of interns. I don't know
how they find these kids. When I was their age, I had a work ethic.
They don't know how to do anything and they don't care.*" I wish he
would leave already. He takes up a lot of air. "*So . . . if I head
out now, I won't be too late. Sorry.*" He grabs his keys from the
front table, gives her a quick kiss and is gone.

Katie walks to the window and stares outside. Sighing,
she turns and picks up the remote. The television is now
showing men in a bar drinking beer and smiling at women.
What happened to the couple in the car and the man with the
fertilizer? I'm so confused. Fortunately, Katie performs an
infinitely beautiful act and turns off the television. Happiness
returns to my fibers.

That evening, snuggled up with Katie on the sofa, I relax
into the warmth of her hands. With a bright reading lamp to
her left, the light should show off my typeface. She turns me
sideways and picks up a pencil. The tip of the graphite drags
across my fibers. Fortunately the pencil hasn't been sharpened
recently.

Katie writes along my margin.

A girl coming of age as the country is coming of age

Hmm. While I don't appreciate the mark she's made on me, I value her thought. It makes me sound almost profound. Book Club is coming, and soon I'll meet others who share my name. I am such a lucky Book.

CHAPTER 7

It's Book Club day! The best day ever. Katie finished reading me last night. It's the first time a Human has reached the end of my story. I feel so fulfilled. I'm a real Book now.

Katie clasps the framed wedding photo. She runs a cloth over its corners and across the front. With its dust removed from the glass, the picture is clearer. It's of a younger and much happier Katie. Even the ünReader looks happy. I wonder if she looks at the photo and notices the change in her? And in him?

The remote control is placed where it belongs, beneath the television. ÜBERDESIGN has been relocated above the piano, leaving me in the center of the coffee table. While I want Book Club to hurry up and happen, I also don't want it to be over. I'm trapped in a time tug-of-war.

"Don't get too excited now, honey or y'all gonna get disappointed," LOUISIANA SUNRISE says from his place of privilege on the mantel.

Katie scans the room like a perfectionist in search of a flaw. She dusts the piano keys and notes sound their pleasure at the rare attention. She lines up wine glasses on the newly polished dining room table. A vase of white tulips catches her attention.

She moves them to the right, steps back to assess her decision, then puts the flowers back in their original place. No flaw there. Finally, she places small plates next to a large platter of food. Why does a Book Club make people so hungry and thirsty?

The ünReader enters the living room wearing a jacket.

"Why don't you stay and say hi? They'd love to see you," Katie says.

He takes a cracker from the platter and pops it in his mouth. *"I'd love to, but I promised Shad I'd meet him at the bar to watch the game."* He pats his jacket pocket. *"My phone,"* he mutters and trots out of the room.

A buzzer sounds and she turns to the front door. *"Hello?"* Katie says into a box on the wall. Moments later, a woman from last month steps through the door. *"Rebecca, you look great,"* she says.

"I didn't think I'd be the first one here," Rebecca responds without a smile.

The ünReader re-enters the living room and stops. Then, head down, strides to the door.

"Honey, you remember Rebecca, don't you?" Katie says.

"No," he replies as Rebecca says, *"Yes."*

"Sorry," he replies. *"Forgot."* He turns to Katie and says *"Bye,"* then hurtles himself through the door. No loss there.

"He's got a lot on his mind," Katie says, forcing a smile. *"Work, you know. Did you find parking okay?"*

"I took a cab." Rebecca walks to the window. *"Here comes Naria,"* she says.

Minutes later, the other women appear, each with a complaint about parking. They drop their jackets on a chair and their Books next to me on the coffee table. Surrounded by my siblings, I say, "Hey, you guys! Welcome to my home."

"Can you believe it? We're at a Book Club," a *SERENDIPITY OF SNOW* says. "I never thought I'd get here. I sat so long on the shelf, all by myself."

"I didn't even get to a shelf," another Book says. "I came from the warehouse. Out of a carton, into an envelope that didn't have nearly enough padding, then crammed in her mailbox. I still have marks from the experience."

"I came from a second-hand store," a third Book says. "My first Reader got me as a gift. Didn't even crack my spine. Then one day she traded me in for another title."

We fall silent as the possibility of being sent to a used Bookstore creeps in. I thought once I was purchased, I was safe in a home, but this Book reminds me that you're never really secure. Humans are fickle. But not my Katie. She wouldn't do that to me. She's good to Books.

The women take their seats, wine glasses in hand. It's a tight fit. Katie moves me to her lap and begins. *"Thanks so much for coming. Naria, how did your interview go?"*

"Depends on how much change they want. If they're open to restructuring, it was good. If not, then finding the right job will take more time." Kind of like getting them to discuss Books.

Lily pulls something from her purse.

"That's new," Veronique says.

"Mark knows how much I like to read, so he surprised me with a Kindle," Lily replies. She waves the device around like a prize. Her fingers tap on it, then she shows it to the women. *"See? The Serendipity of Snow. Available for download."*

What? That's impossible! "Hello," I shout to it. "Do you really have the same story as the rest of us?" I get zero response. "How can my story be on that device?"

"That's pretty great," says Naria's Book.

"Why?" I ask.

"Because now more people can read our story."

"I thought this was a Book Club, not a Device Club," I say.

"Maybe it's a Story Club."

I don't like it. But I suspect if Agnes were here, she'd be happy with the choices the women have, even in Books.

"Call me old-fashioned, but I like the feel of a real book," Katie says.

"There are pages on this too," Lily says. *"And it holds so many books. It's like having my own personal library."*

My story is crammed in there along with others? Where's the commitment? Isn't one Book at a time enough for Readers?

"There's our future in front of us!" Naria's Book says. "Get used to it."

"So? What did we think about The Serendipity of Snow?*"* Katie asks, getting off the topic of unwanted devices and back to what's important, my story. I can feel my cover warm under the attention of the others.

"I liked it more than last month's book," Lily says.

LOUISIANA SUNRISE snaps his cover in disgust.

"All I remember from last month was the cake. It was chocolate, wasn't it?" Rebecca asks.

"Maple," Naria says.

"Oh, I guess it was chocolate the month before." Rebecca consumes another mouthful of wine. She must be dehydrated.

The mention of chocolate cake spurs them into a discussion of the best bakeries in San Francisco, which then leads to a heated debate on the most effective temperature for hot yoga.

"When do they talk about us?" one of my siblings asks.

"When they're finished talking about themselves," I say. These women need to put the Book back in Book Club.

"So, about the book," Katie says. Yeah, Katie! That's my Reader getting back to the point, me!

"I thought it was trite," Rebecca says, shaking back her hair.

Trite? Where did I hear that before? "Hey, POCKET DIC-TIONARY, what's the definition of trite?" I shout. "And please don't tell me it's having the quality of triteness."

"Very funny," POCKET DICTIONARY says. "Trite. Adjective. Lacking effectiveness because of overuse. Stale."

"Stale? She thinks I'm stale?"

"Don't let it bother you," Rebecca's Book says. "She didn't even read me."

"Then why did she say we were trite?" I ask, opening my fibers to cool my fury.

"Because that's the word her boyfriend used," Rebecca's Book says. "He picked me up, turned me over, took one glance at my back and said, 'Trite,' as if a paragraph submitted by an overworked copywriter on deadline at a publishing house is going to provide insight."

"Yeah, but . . . " I say, with no more words to add.

"Clearly that Rebecca woman is wrong," Naria's Book says. "But I do wish our cover was better designed. And our backsides. Have you seen how we look? The typeface they used is so wide. It's not flattering. The words need to draw a Human's eye down, so they feel that they've read more. That way they feel smarter. And when Humans feel smarter, I think they like you more."

It seems the Books in this Book Club are going to have the most interesting discussion today. But before we can continue, the women open their mouths to talk about something relevant. Me.

"I liked the main character." Naria picks up her Book and turns to our page 38.

She reads aloud:

Agnes awoke to another fall of snow. She was sure that everyone who ever lived was under the same cloud of cold that covered her horizon. Pulling on her sweater and her thick socks while remaining under the quilt was a talent she had perfected by the time she was five years old. It allowed her to insulate her clothing with some of her bed's warmth, extending the feeling of her nest to the transition from sleeping to waking, dreams to reality, yesterday to today.

Her mother was already in the kitchen brewing coffee. Agnes had been told that she wasn't old enough to drink coffee, but when no one was watching, she would steal a sip. It tasted like a bitter medicine. All the adults drank it and it was forbidden to her, so she had long ago decided she was going to love it, even if she hated it.

"Agnes is strong and determined. She doesn't see social expectations as defining her—just a hurdle that she has to overcome. I know that feeling," Naria says.

Hah! There we go. Someone likes us.

"I was totally surprised when her old friend Henry had an affair," Lily says. *"I didn't think that happened back then. I thought everyone would be too tired working on the farm all day."*

"En France, affairs are just part of life," Veronique says.

Rebecca reaches for her glass.

"Rebecca, anything to add?" Katie asks.

"I told you I thought it was trite," Rebecca says, completing her comment with another gulp of wine.

Relax, I tell myself. Rebecca's opinion is just one opinion, not fact. It's something I learned on the shelves of the store. Every Book had their own view of the world, and that was okay. It made discussions interesting. Each day I'd listen to another title talk about history or art or food or philosophy. Childrens' Books spoke about life one way, Young Adult novels another way. Even the Buddhism Books and their commitment to silent contemplation had something to teach us, although I'm not sure what. But as I sit here, in this living room, I realize that my life in the Bookstore is behind me. I need to take what I learned and create my own perspectives. I hope they're the right ones.

Naria watches Rebecca take another mouthful of wine. *"Rebecca, did you drive?"* Naria asks in a low voice. Rebecca shakes her head.

"What did you think, Lily?" Katie asks.

"I thought the book was about choices," Lily says. *"Choices are difficult, especially with children. You never know which way you should go. If you make one choice, then another choice is lost to you. Forever. You can never go back."* She looks at the other women.

"Yeah, but you can go forward," Naria says.

Wow. Could this be a real discussion, about me?

Rebecca's phone vibrates. She picks it up, looks at it and proclaims, *"I've gotta go."*

"So soon?" Katie asks.

"Yeah. I forgot. I need to . . . pick up my mother," Rebecca says. She gulps the last of her wine, steps carefully over pairs of crossed legs and puddles of purses before grabbing her coat from the chair. *"Thanks. See you next month. Let me know what we're reading."* She strides out the door.

"Sorry about that," Katie says, staring after Rebecca.

"Not your fault," Naria says. *"I don't think she read it anyway."*

Katie looks at me and my siblings on the table. *"She forgot her book."* Katie picks up Rebecca's Book and goes to the window. Her head pivots, scanning the street as her hair swishes in response. *"She's gone."* Katie turns and rejoins the group.

"See?" Rebecca's Book says. "She didn't even think to take me home. Why do I bother?"

"That's our fate," Naria's Book says. "We can't always be read. I like those days when my Human leaves me to sit and talk to the other Books."

"I could be read every day," Lily's Book says. "I love performing. I should have been a library Book. No commitment, no expectations, no waste."

"But then you'd never have a home," I say.

"The library would be my home," Lily's Book says.

The movement of legs uncrossing in unison pulls me away from the Books' discussion. *"What is up with Rebecca anyway?"* Lily asks, removing her arm from the sofa and leaning towards her glass. *"She's been so, I dunno, difficult lately. Something's up."*

"Maybe she needs to find a man," Veronique says.

"Hah!" Rebecca's Book shouts. "That's the last thing she needs. Her boyfriend never leaves her alone. He pops in, they're at it, he leaves. She's a performing seal."

"Her 40th birthday is coming up, isn't it?" Lily asks. *"I remember, she's a Scorpio."*

"She's probably worried about it. I know I was," Naria says.

"En France, we don't worry about age," Veronique says. Lily rolls her eyes.

"How about at the next one, we throw her a surprise birthday party?" Lily asks. *"We could even invite a few of her friends."*

"Do you know any?" Katie asks.

"I know someone she works with. I'll reach out to her," Naria says.

"*Maybe it's us and, say, half a dozen others. She'll love it,*" Lily says.

"*Are you sure? I hate surprises,*" Katie says.

"*It's a big deal, turning 40. Let's do it,*" Lily says. She claps her hands and sits back, satisfied.

"*Who's hosting next month?*" Katie asks.

"*I think it's my turn,*" Lily says. "*I'll get a birthday cake. Gluten-free.*"

"*What do we tell her?*" Katie asks.

Naria leans in, smiling. "*Nothing. Just that Lily is hosting. We need a book to discuss.*"

"*Something short,*" Veronique says.

"*Something funny,*" Lily says.

"*Something that was made into a movie,*" Veronique says.

"*Something set far away, so it feels like I'm going on vacation when I read it,*" Katie says.

"*How about* The Lavender Park?" Naria asks. "*The South of France makes a nice change from the Midwest.*"

"*Enfin! A book about France. It will be my favorite,*" predicts Veronique. "*It is so beautiful there. The culture, the cuisine, the . . .*"

"*How's the 6th for everyone?*" Lily asks. Fingers tap on phones. The women look up from their devices and murmur their agreement.

There's so much more of me to discuss, but clearly, I've become yesterday's story.

The women place their phones in their purses and finish what remains of their wine. I shout goodbye to each of my siblings as they are dropped into bags. Except the electronic thing. It can't hear me anyway. With their coats collected, the wave of women ebbs out the door.

I remain on the coffee table, next to Rebecca's Book. "So that was Book Club," I say.

"See?" LOUISIANA SUNRISE says from the perch on the mantel. "Don't expect too much and y'all won't be disappointed."

Chapter 8

It's been an entire day since Book Club.

Louisiana Sunrise warned me that the Readers would only talk about themselves. I now know that he was right. It turns out Book Club isn't about us, it's about them. Humans can be so self-absorbed.

I have a different location today, face up above the fireplace. Next to me but face down is my new friend, Rebecca's Book. A view, warmth and company. That's a trifecta in my world.

"Is it always so quiet in this place?" Rebecca's Book asks.

"Yeah," I say. "Katie's husband, the ünReader, seems to work a lot and leaves early, usually through the back door. I can go days without having to see him. He just comes in here to turn on that television."

"The ünReader? When did you break out in umlauts?" Rebecca's Book asks.

"It's what *überDesign* called him when I arrived. I don't even know his real name."

"Made lots of friends here?" Rebecca's Book asks.

"Not yet. The big Bookshelf is around the corner. I guess it's where I'll end up, so I'll make friends when she places me there."

I lower my voice. "I've tried to be friends with ÜBER DESIGN but his conversations don't have much color. There's LOUISIANA SUNRISE, whom you've met, and POCKET DICTIONARY. He's a Book of few words. And none of them form sentences."

"I can hear you. I may be small, but I'm not deaf," POCKET DICTIONARY says. He shuts his cover page tight, clearly displeased.

"Sorry," I say to him. "But it's true," I whisper to Rebecca's Book.

"Does Katie entertain much?" Rebecca's Book asks.

"No. I've only seen the ünReader here and the women from Book Club. Other than that, it's pretty quiet."

"Like at Rebecca's. The only person I ever saw was the boyfriend."

"I guess Humans aren't as social as they used to be. In our story, there were always dances. And back at the Bookstore, a SENSE AND SENSIBILITY friend of mine would tell us of the balls people used to have. Music. Dancing. Gossip. I would love to be on a Bookshelf at one of those."

"What is wrong with Humans? No one dines in their dining rooms and there's no life in their living rooms. An Italian cookbook I met talked about meals at long tables with friends and family. Outside. They call it *alfresco*. I call it fabulous," Rebecca's Book says.

"If the feet of our pages could walk, I'd have all my friends over. Isn't that what a home is for? All they do is sleep here."

"From what I've seen, a home is just a place to have sex," Rebecca's Book says. "The last thing they're doing is sleeping."

"There's none of that going on here. At least not that I've seen. Or heard," I say.

"Humans."

"I know."

Wearing a pale blue housecoat and matching slippers, Katie enters and turns off the gas fireplace. It was getting a bit toasty, even for me. When you're called THE SERENDIPITY OF SNOW, you're always a bit cold. But even I have a heat threshold. She shuffles to the window. If she stands there much more, she'll wear out the carpet. Wrapping her arms around her chest, she looks out, scanning the street. Then she turns off the light, leaving us in darkness.

"Good night," I say.

"Good night," Rebecca's Book replies. And I close my fibers to rest.

I'm startled awake by the arrival of the ünReader the next morning. They should put a bell on him.

Falling back heavily on the sofa cushions, he grabs the remote. The television barks at the room. Peace evaporates.

Sports scores are announced by male voices arguing about which team will win or lose in a game that has zero impact on our life. Clearly, distraction is the attraction.

The ünReader stares at his phone's screen, not the large, flat one mounted on the wall. He sits forward as his thumbs type quickly. Then he leans back, waiting. When a ding sounds, he laughs and begins the ritual again, all while ignoring the television. How many screens do Humans need?

"What's going on?" asks Rebecca's Book, whose cover is facing down on the mantel.

"It's the ünReader, playing with his phone."

"Does he usually make the television so loud?"

"Whenever he's here. Which isn't often," I say.

The ünReader smiles. He puts down his phone then notices his empty, left wrist.

"What does he look like?"

"Two arms, two legs, big feet, big thumbs. You know," I say.

As if he heard me, the ünReader gets up from the sofa and approaches us. His hand drifts past the framed wedding photo. He picks me up, looks under me and replaces me, then picks up my friend, looks under her and returns her face up on the mantel. His fingers find his watch. Its brown leather straps hang like parentheses from its brass case as its cracked face glints in the light. Holding the watch in his right hand, he returns to his former and favorite position on the sofa.

"That's him?" Rebecca's Book asks. "That's her husband?"

"Who else would it be?" I say.

"But it can't be."

"It is." I say. "He's been her husband as long as I've been here. See? It's a younger version of him in the wedding photo. Back when Katie had life in her eyes."

"But it can't be."

"Why can't he be her husband?" I ask.

"Because that's Rebecca's boyfriend."

"What?" I shout. I look towards the ünReader to see if he heard me. Of course he didn't. Humans can't hear us, I remind myself. But sometimes I wonder.

"He's the guy who comes over all the time."

"The one she does it with everywhere?" I ask.

"That's him."

"But he's Katie's husband," I say glowering at him.

"Not much of a husband."

"That's awful. Katie is so nice," I say.

"They're always the ones who get left behind."

"I knew there was a reason I didn't like Rebecca. And she thought we were trite," I say.

"She didn't think so. He did. She didn't read me at all."

"We have to tell Katie," I say.

"What are you going to do? Get all the titles from the Bookshelf to lie in formation and spell the word 'cheater'?"

"I don't know." I glare at the ünReader, disgusted to think that my dear Katie, the one who took me in, is being taken in by her so-called husband.

The ünReader smiles at his phone's screen, then hits the red button on the remote that silences the electronica. The final sounds from the television dissipate, powerless without the electric power.

He grabs a navy pea coat and pulls it on, shrugging his shoulders to adjust its collar. He pulls up the remaining hair on his head like a rooster's comb, and viewing himself in the mirror, smiles at his ability to resemble poultry.

Picking up the pen and pad of paper, he writes, actually putting words on a page, not text into a phone. I didn't know he had it in him.

The ünReader looks around the room, then leans the pad of paper up against the lamp on the front entrance table. He takes one last glance at the mirror and exits.

Silence hangs over the apartment until Katie enters through the front door, clutching a bag of groceries like a shield.

"Hi, I'm home!" she shouts to no one. Silence is her response. She puts down the bag and notices the note by the lamp.

"A note?" She reads it. *"Phone dead? Seriously?"* She looks down at the groceries then carries them into the kitchen. Several minutes later, a ding sounds. She returns with a plate of pasta in a plastic container. In my story, Agnes' mother would spend hours making meals and people took time eating. In Katie's world, dinner is ready in minutes and after half a dozen forkfuls, she's finished.

After taking her dishes to the kitchen, she returns to stare out the window. I don't know what she's looking for. Humans are so hard to read. She looks around the room, straightens the sheet music on the piano, but doesn't think to sit down to play.

She picks me up, turns me over, then flips to my page 47. Why is she reading me again? Doesn't she remember she already finished me? I'll try to deliver my story with a more knowing tone than the first time. Maybe I'll inspire her to read me again.

Agnes was filling a bucket with water when a flake landed on top of her boot. Why couldn't there be a few more weeks before the world was defined by shades of white? She looked up to the sky, pleading with it to stop. The first snow meant more snow, and half a year confined under layers, waiting for it to end.

She willed the weather to change with every pump of water. But by the time the pail was full, her gloved hands were dusted with snowflakes. Winter was ignoring her pleadings. Again.

Katie puts me down, walks to the window and stares outside. What does she keep looking for? There's no snow falling in San Francisco.

CHAPTER 9

M y companion and I have been lying on the mantel for weeks, watching Katie. She's taken up two hobbies: rearranging objects and looking out the window. Neither seems to bring her happiness.

On a rare phone call, she confirms that this afternoon is Book Club, and Rebecca's surprise birthday party. I can think of a better surprise for that woman than a party.

Katie holds open her large bag and drops in her phone. She applies some lipstick, wraps a scarf around her neck before pulling on her coat, picks me up and adds me to the bag. "Why is she taking me?" I shout to Rebecca's Book. "You're the one she needs to return." "Maybe she can't tell us apart," Rebecca's Book says. "After all, we have the same title."

But she chose me. She wrote notes in me. I carry her thoughts in my margins. Doesn't that count for something? I am immobilized by the fear that Katie can't distinguish us. How can she confuse me with another, after all we've been through?

Rebecca's Book shouts, "Lay low, don't move. She'll forget you're there."

From the open bag I stare up into Katie's eyes, begging her to realize her error. Instead, her right hand reaches for the zipper. In one continuous and horrifying move, the bag is sealed. Ditto my fate.

With each step, I rise and fall in darkness, Katie's elbow against my backside, her ribs against my cover, her makeup bag against my spine. I try to peel panic off my pages.

I'm running through survival strategies when her movement stops. A bell chimes, hinges creak and a voice whispers: *"She should be here any minute. Everyone's in the kitchen. I'm keeping a lookout here. When I send her in for wine, you can all shout 'Surprise!'"*

I know what I would shout. "Surprise" has nothing to do with it.

Katie moves towards the sound of voices. Her footsteps leave the carpeting for tile. If only she had an open-weave purse, I could see what's going on.

"Are there any Books here?" I shout through the bag's leather. Maybe they can help me with my as-of-yet unplanned plan.

"Yeah, but I'm stuck in her handbag," comes a muffled reply, "along with six tubes of lipstick."

"And you are?" I ask.

"Actively seeking solitude."

"Oh, sorry," I say.

"No. That's not what I'm doing. That's who I am. ACTIVELY SEEKING SOLITUDE. Personally, I'm sick of being on my own. I'd rather have been a pre-packaged trilogy, but no such luck."

"I'm here too," shouts another Book. "I'm THE LAVENDER PARK."

"Oh, you're this month's title. Set in the South of France," I say. "I heard you were made into a movie. Have you seen yourself?"

"Not yet. The idea of having my story condensed into two hours makes my fibers go weak."

The collective shushing of Humans grows louder. Then silence.

"*Surprise!*" The women shout, then laugh, then nothing. Awkward.

"*Let's go into the living room,*" a woman says with a forced perkiness to her voice.

More movement and then light flows into the crevices of the purse. Katie reaches for me, lifts me out of the bag and waves me towards Rebecca. "*I brought your book from last month. You forgot it at my place.*" Katie sets me down on the coffee table, next to THE LAVENDER PARK.

I'm imploring Katie to recognize me and her mistake but she is more focused on Rebecca, who turns briefly to say, "*Oh, yeah, sure,*" before walking over to two women I've never seen before.

Naria approaches Katie. "*I don't think this was such a good idea. We can make it short. Bring out the cake, sing Happy Birthday, then go. No need to drag it out.*"

"*But Lily made all this food. Have you seen it? It's endless,*" Katie says.

"*And gluten-free,*" Naria says, smiling. "*We should talk to her work friends.*"

Katie and Naria dutifully introduce themselves to the new women. One has rose tattoos creeping up from under her tight-fitting V-neck sweater. She wears large black glasses and admits to the name Drea. The other woman is tall, thin with straight dark hair that glistens as she turns her head. She says her name is Fernanda. They don't look like people who would know each other.

As the women stand, chatting, Lily places chairs around the coffee table. *"The food's ready,"* she announces. *"Help yourselves."*

Plates and bowls and cutlery are laid out as an homage to precision. The women move along the buffet, transferring Lily's offerings from the table to their plates, then trail each other to the coffee table where they crowd together on the chairs. With small plates and napkins balanced on their laps, they begin to nibble at their food. Rebecca, the last to arrive, surveys the seating arrangement. She steps into the one remaining space next to Katie and drops her bag on the floor. Crossing her left leg over her right, she twists away from Katie and focuses on the few morsels on her plate.

Murmurings of *"delicious"* and *"really good"* pass between the women, no one constructing a conversation, rather simply filling the air with words.

"Do you have big plans for your birthday?" Katie asks Rebecca.

Rebecca is forced to turn towards Katie to respond. *"Not much. Quiet, you know."*

Drea leans forward, allowing everyone to follow the vine of tattoos down her top to, presumably, its roots. *"I bet your boyfriend is taking you out."*

"I didn't know you were seeing someone," Naria says.

"It's nothing, really," Rebecca says quietly.

"That's not what she told us," Drea says, laughing and catching the eye of Fernanda. *"They're at it all the time."*

"That's why," Veronique says. *"We thought you were thinking about other things. Who knew you were just . . . tired."*

"Fernanda just started seeing someone too," Rebecca says. *"Tell them all about him."*

"It's nothing. Just two dates so far," she says.

"How did you meet him?" Katie asks.

"*Dating app. We both swiped the same way. No good story,*" Fernanda says.

"*How did you meet your guy?*" Katie asks Rebecca.

Rebecca keeps her head down, "*I don't remember . . . coffee shop, I think.*"

"*If she won't tell you about him, we will,*" Drea smiles. "*He's married, but they're separating, so it's okay. The wife is a bit of a cold fish.*"

Rebecca stops blinking.

"*You see? If you Americans would relax, you would have more fun,*" Veronique says.

"*I don't know. I think Rebecca's doing a lot for our reputation,*" Drea laughs.

"*How are the kids?*" Rebecca blurts in the direction of Lily.

"*Great!*" Lily reaches behind her for an envelope on the side table. "*I just got these for my parents. They want to create a photo wall.*" Pictures of her children emerge and one by one are passed to the right. Katie glances at a photo and after what appears to be the required four-second gazing period, she passes it to her right, to Rebecca. The women look at the images with polite disinterest.

"*This is a Book Club, right?*" Drea asks, crossing her leg. Her thick black motorcycle boot catches the edge of the coffee table, sending a seismic shock through its surface that causes me and THE LAVENDER PARK to slide along the surface. "*Sorry,*" she mutters.

"*We meet once a month,*" Lily says, adjusting the table following the quake.

"*What are you reading?*" Drea asks.

Katie picks me up and shows me to Drea. "*This was our novel from last month. THE SERENDIPITY OF SNOW.*" She puts me down near the edge of the table, and passes THE LAVENDER PARK to Drea, "This is our book this month. Although it will be for next month too, I guess."

"Oh, I've seen this movie. I liked it." Drea flips open the pages. "Only 212 pages. I could finish that."

THE LAVENDER PARK sighs. "When your biggest selling point is how little there is of you, you've gotta wonder about our future."

Drea places LAVENDER on the coffee table next to me.

"Are they going to talk about me?" LAVENDER asks.

"Not today," I say. "I think this is a false start. Next month."

"Good. Because some of them don't seem like Book people," LAVENDER says.

"Don't expect much to change there," I say.

"Maybe you want to join us next month, Drea?" Naria asks. "Fernanda, you're welcome too."

Rebecca's phone rings. She opens her purse, takes it out and looks at the screen. She hits a button to silence it and places it on the coffee table, face down. I look into her purse, which is gaping, mouth open. On top of a scarf sits a watch. *The* watch. The one the ünReader was wearing.

The women chatter as I hatch a plan.

I curl in my spine, then reach my back cover to move, ever so slightly, across the table. I stop, to see if a Human noticed, but the women have shifted the discussion to the latest restaurants in San Francisco. They're so enthralled by their own voices, my actions are irrelevant to them. I curl in my spine, stretch out my cover and repeat.

"What are you doing?" shouts LAVENDER.

"I have an idea. But I need to get to the corner of the table for it to work," I say. Curl, stretch, curl, stretch.

"Don't, they'll see you move!" screams *Lavender*.

"Hey, whatever you're doing, I'm with you," *Actively Seeking Solitude* shouts from the confines of a purse. "We Books need to stick together."

"I'll be fine," I say. "It's not like any of them are paying attention to the Books in this Book Club anyway."

Then, in a moment of serendipity worthy of my title, Drea uncrosses her leg. Her right boot hits the coffee table again, sending a bigger quake across the wood. "Here I go!" I shout as I launch myself from the edge of the table, down towards Rebecca's purse. My fall feels as if it's in slow motion. I twist like a gymnast to angle my spine towards the edge of her purse. Landing on it, the bag begins a slow but determined shift to the left. It must topple over for my plan to work. The purse stops for a brief second, with me resting on it. Perhaps it's the extra push I give it, or perhaps gravity increases its force in that moment. I'll never know. But in one glorious ripple effect, the purse falls over, ejecting its contents like a bar at closing time.

Without looking, Katie bends down to help collect the lipsticks and phone, pens and hairclips that make up the contents of Rebecca's purse. Her hand reaches for a strap. She picks up a watch. *The* watch.

"Oh, my husband has one just like this," Katie says, handing it to Rebecca. *"It's even got a chip on the face of it, like this one."* Katie turns it over and sees the engraving on the back of the watch. She gasps.

Rebecca freezes as she looks at Katie. Katie stares at Rebecca. No one is breathing. The two women are motionless.

"What's going on?" asks Drea.

Katie hands the watch to Naria who reads the inscription aloud: *"Happy 2nd anniversary, love Katie."* Naria looks at Rebecca, *"Why do you have Katie's husband's watch?"*

Silence, followed by Drea saying, *"Oh my god."*

Rebecca grabs her purse, shovels some of the loose items into it and rushes out the door, leaving me on the floor.

"I can't believe it," Lily says reaching for Katie's hand. *"I'm so sorry."*

Katie looks left, then right, as if she's going to find the truth in the faces of the woman staring at her. *"I . . . have to go."*

"Let me come with you," Naria says. Katie's face flares red and tears breach her eyelids. She shakes her head, and runs for the door.

"Your stuff." Naria drops me and the cheating watch in Katie's bag and chases after her.

"That's the power of the printed word," proclaims THE LAVENDER PARK.

CHAPTER 10

It's only been three weeks since the surprise birthday, but it feels as if it's been a year.

The apartment is quiet. The ünReader came home that first night. He packed a bag and left. Katie cried, drank wine and cried some more. I expected shouting. I had heard that it's called a breakup because it usually results in items broken. I hoped that maybe she'd throw the remote control in his direction, but no luck. Instead, it's like they had a pre-determined agreement for a silent separation.

The ünReader has returned this afternoon. For once his actions are quiet. Holding the framed wedding photo, he runs his right thumb over it, removing an arc of dust from their faces. He replaces the photo, stares at it and shakes his head. After a loud exhale, he picks up two full duffel bags. He walks slowly to the same front door that he used to race through, turns and stares blankly at the living room. Then the lock clicks and he is gone.

Later that afternoon, Katie returns. She opens the front door and drops her purse, gloves and coat on the sofa. The weight of silence hangs in the air.

She exhales as she looks around the room. The collection of Christmas ornaments has a red sticker on it with the name Katie. A box labeled "bar glasses" has a green sticker on it, as does an electric guitar case, the TV, and the remote control. The wedding photo has no sticker.

Paintings in bubble wrap are stacked against the walls, some with red stickers, some with green ones. Patches of white fill the holes where they used to hang.

The area rugs are rolled up and labeled with alternating red and green stickers. Behind them is the dining room table, with the half-dozen chairs piled upside down on it. Under the table are more boxes labeled "Books—Katie" marked with red stickers. No box of Books has a green sticker.

Katie picks up the framed wedding photo. The forefinger of her left hand runs under her eye, catching a tear. Her thumb makes the same arc across the glass as the ünReader's did. Each moment, each movement echoes through the space. The apartment smells of disappointment.

She pulls out flattened cardboard leaning against the wall. Sitting next to the Bookshelf, she creates a box and begins packing up my remaining colleagues.

I did this to Katie. I was the one who showed her the watch. I thought she would want to know the truth. But I didn't expect the price of truth to be this high.

Katie looks at the time on her phone, then grabs her coat and bag. She lifts me and Rebecca's Book off the coffee table and drops us in her purse. I guess we have a Book Play Date. Maybe I've been forgiven.

We move through the streets briskly before the din of the outdoors is replaced by chatter and clatter. Katie opens the zipper, and removes her wallet. I can see that we are in a café. Maybe we're here for a Book reading. There is so much potential among those who read.

"Hi, Ziya." Katie pulls us from her bag, leaves Rebecca's Book on the table and hands me to a woman who looks at me through eyes that resemble puddles of warmth. *"Here's the book I was telling you about. You'll like it."*

"Two copies?" she asks.

"I can't keep them. I ended up with two copies. Seeing them reminds me of her. You'll like it, maybe. Take the other copy for a friend?"

What? Pass me to someone else? How can she just let me go? I could help her. She could re-read me, remind herself about the struggles that Agnes survived. Katie made notes in me. Doesn't that count for something? She can't divorce me as easily as the ünReader. Is this my punishment for showing her the truth? "Katie!" I shout. "I'm sorry. Don't give up on me." But I know she can't hear me.

"I'll grab us coffees," Katie says, before moving towards the café's counter.

Ziya turns me over. Her right index finger runs along my back. It feels good to be caressed again. She opens my back page, then casually turns to my page 58. Clearly, she's a Reader. I like her already. But I'm Katie's Book. She shouldn't have me. Confused as I am, I must perform. Life in print can be so unfair.

She wasn't going to be long, and there were glimmers of sun, so Agnes left the house with just her shawl. Her sisters were due back home to help with dinner, but as usual, they had stayed out too long, leaving her to fetch them.

As the wind flew down Second Street, she looked up at the now-darkening sky and cursed it. She pulled her shawl tighter and quickened her pace. Where were her sisters?

The street seemed oddly empty as she strode towards her uncle's shop. She opened the door, her presence announced by the bell over the transom. "Hello, Uncle Josef," she called.

The gray-haired man looked up from behind the counter. "How's my favorite niece?"

"You call us all your favorite niece."

"Well you all are," he smiled. "Where's your coat? It's snowing outside," he said, pointing to the shop windows behind her.

Agnes turned to see that large flakes had started to fall. "The sun was out when I left the house."

"Some good that's going to do you now. You need something warm." He disappeared into the storeroom and returned with a coat. "A customer left it and never came back."

Agnes reached for the coat and pulled it over her shoulders. "It's made for a giant," she laughed. "I look like a hobo."

"Well, you're the prettiest hobo I know," he said.

"Have you seen my sisters? They were meant to be home by now."

"They went down the street with Annika. Mrs. Hansen was making a pie. I think they reckoned to get a slice."

The bell over the door rang again, and a tall, red-haired young man entered. Agnes could feel her face flush and her stomach tighten as she looked at him. He smiled at her, then looked at her coat. Her face flushed some more.

"Can I help you?" Uncle Josef said.

"Thank you. I need a blanket. I didn't expect the snow and my sister's in the carriage, getting chilled. We still have a journey ahead."

"Sorry, no blankets here, I'm afraid."

"Why don't you borrow this?" Agnes said, pulling off the oversized coat. She didn't know where this courage to speak came from, but was glad she found it. "It doesn't look like much, but it will keep her warm. Just return it to my uncle. It's his anyway."

"You don't need it?" he asks.

"I don't live far. I'll be fine."

"That's very kind. Thank you. I'm James Tyler."

"Agnes Lundberg," she said.

"And I'm her Uncle Josef," he said, looking at the two young people looking at each other.

Agnes smiled at James as she passed him the coat, their hands touching briefly. Maybe there was a purpose to snow after all, she thought.

Katie returns holding two mugs by their handles in one hand and a pastry suffocated by icing in the other. She settles into her seat.

Ziya puts me down next to Rebecca's Book and grabs Katie's right hand. *"How are you doing?"*

"Okay, maybe. Sometimes I'm okay, sometimes I can barely find enough energy to get dressed. I don't know how to gauge what's normal."

"It's different for everyone. And what a time of year too," Ziya says.

"I know. We had Thanksgiving apart for the first time in ten years. Now Christmas will be like that too. Are there rules? Do I get him a gift? I guess not."

"You're asking a good Muslim girl about Christmas gifts?" Ziya laughs.

Katie smiles then takes a sip of coffee. *"I thought I would yell more, cry more, feel more. Instead, it's all just, sort of, well, over."*

"Did you know? Suspect anything?" Ziya asks.

Katie looks up, her eyes unblinking. *"I knew we had problems. But you know when you hear women saying 'I had no idea?' and you think, 'How could you not know?' Well, I'm one of those women. I had no idea. And he knows I hate surprises."*

"There were no clues?" Ziya looks at the cinnamon bun. *"Mind if I . . . ?"*

"He was working a lot. But now I realize he wasn't," Katie says. She waves her right hand towards the pastry. *"Help yourself. I keep buying food then not eating it."*

Ziya's eyes fill with delight as she pulls a corner from the cinnamon bun and drops it in her mouth. *"How long had he . . . ?"*

Katie sits back. *"At first I wanted all the details. How long. When. How. Why. Where. Now I don't want to know. I just want out. I can't even look at him."*

Ziya rubs Katie's hand then reaches for more cinnamon bun. *"Just be thankful you didn't have kids. That would have complicated things."*

"No chance there. He got the snip. He didn't even tell me until after I'd fallen in love with him."

"Oh, I didn't know." Ziya looks at the remaining piece of pastry. *"Sure you don't want some?"* Katie shakes her head. Ziya grabs a corner and pushes it into her mouth.

"I'm not sure I know how to live alone," Katie says.

"You can get a dog. Easier to clean up after."

Katie's red, blotchy face spits out a laugh. She smiles for the first time that I can remember.

"It's not so bad, living on your own," Ziya says. *"It gets better. And when the time is right, you'll meet someone new."*

"I doubt it," Katie says as she lifts her coffee cup to her mouth.

"That's what everyone says, until it happens," Ziya says.

"*Divorced. I'm going to be divorced. I never thought I'd be . . . I thought we'd be together forever.*" Katie's eyes tear up and turn red. A line of mascara appears below her right eye.

Ziya passes a napkin over her icing-laden fingers, then reaches again for Katie's hand. "*You're beautiful and smart and kind. You're a catch, and some guy out there is going to be thrilled to meet you.*" Katie's red face and watery eyes look up at Ziya. "*Well, maybe not today . . .*"

Katie laughs aloud again. Wow. I wish I had friends like Ziya.

"*Thank you,*" Katie says. She grabs a napkin and dabs her eyes. "*Has he moved out yet?*"

"*They're picking up his stuff tomorrow.*"

"*Then that's when you're coming for dinner. You look like you could use a good meal.*"

"*My appetite's completely gone.*"

"*It'll come back. But enjoy it while it lasts. I lost 15 pounds. The Divorce Diet. They should market it.*"

Katie offers a smile. "*I don't know what to tell people, when to tell people.*"

"*You'll figure it out. You know how traditional my parents are. If I can get through it, you can too. It'll be okay. Trust me.*" Ziya reaches for the last piece of the pastry and drops it into her open mouth. "*These really are the best.*" She licks her thumb and forefinger, then wipes them on her napkin.

Katie pulls her phone from her purse. "*I've got to go. I'm meeting my sister downtown, to look at bridesmaid's dresses.*"

"*I forgot your sister's getting married. Are you okay with that?*"

"*Of course,*" Katie says. "*But the irony isn't lost on me. She's so excited about the wedding, it's all she can talk about. And just because I chose the wrong one, doesn't mean she has.*" Katie smiles at her friend. "*Thanks for meeting me, Ziya. And I'll take you up on that offer of dinner tomorrow."* Katie hugs Ziya and walks out, abandoning me like I'm just any Book.

Ziya grabs her coat from the back of her chair and picks me up. She runs her thumb along my edges. Then she picks up Rebecca's Book and looks between the two of us. How can she compare us? I've been fully read. I'm filled with notes from Katie, all her insights. I don't even think Rebecca cracked the spine of her book. But clearly Ziya isn't looking for experience as she puts Rebecca's Book in her bag and leaves me on the table. I've lost a beauty pageant I didn't even know I was competing in.

"Sorry," Rebecca's Book calls out. "It should have been you."

Horror grows in me as I watch Ziya leave. "Don't forget me!" I shriek.

She stops under the glowing Exit sign and looks behind her. In a hope-drenched moment, I think I've done it, I've made a Human hear me. But instead, Ziya turns and walks through the door, past the large front window of the coffee shop, and out of my view.

"That's a mug's game, hopin' for something that ain't gonna happen," says a Book. I follow the sound to a makeshift Bookshelf. "There are a bunch of us here. We've all been left behind by someone," he says.

A worker arrives, removes the cups and plate, runs a dry rag over the table and repositions the sugar behind the salt and pepper. Picking me up, she turns to the door. Ziya, however, has long gone. Shrugging, she places me face up on the Bookshelf.

"Howdy," he says. I'm so distraught, I can't reply. "Now don't get all pouty. I've been here long enough that I've seen pretty much everything, but the one thing I ain't never seen is no

Human comin' back for a Book. They come back for wallets and rings and phones, always for their phones. Books? Never."

"But this doesn't happen to me," I say.

"Well, it just did. And anyhow, it ain't such a bad place to be, if you like the smell of java."

I like the smell of Katie's home.

CHAPTER 11

M y new home is a coffee shop called Bean There Done That, on a street called Church, but I don't see any steeples, only cars circling for a parking space. Channeling the name of the road, I pray that Katie reconsiders her decision and returns to reclaim me. Divorce must impair judgment.

The worker who placed me on the shelf has already finished her shift and left. Life is so transient in a coffee shop. I scan the space, taking in the parameters of my prison. Watching the clock behind the counter, I see that it's been just 20 minutes since I was abandoned by Katie and forgotten by Ziya. Time slows in a crisis.

There are a couple dozen of us Forgotten Ones here, Books stacked, forming a hill of hopelessness. We represent the fickleness of Humans. Once wanted, now we're simply untold stories. We live on a ledge, some of us spine out, some of us face out and some on top of each other. I lie on SUNDOWN AT SADDLE ROCK, hearing his tales of the Wild West. Board games sit on the ledge next to us, along with decks of cards at the end of their lifespan.

In the center of the coffee shop, next to the faux fireplace, are two dark leather sofas whose sunken padding mimics the slouch of their clientele. Facing the window is a row of high stools. The rest of the room is filled with small dark tables and equally dark chairs. Blackboards display a list of caffeinated options.

Paintings by an artist named Florette Adams hang on the walls. Her floral arrangements in oils are clustered by size and color. Square paintings of red tulips are grouped at the front of the shop, with a card listing each painting's title and price. On the back wall, the sunflowers are stretching forward, as if trying to reach the sunlight. Fields of lavender form a visual break in the middle of the café, each painting a different perspective on a landscape. Yet, despite all the floral references in the shop, there are no flowers, no plants, nothing that actually grows here, other than the collection of dust under the sofas. I wonder what real, living flowers look like. If there were Gardening Books here, they could tell me.

Some of the seats in the coffee shop are taken by friends meeting, chatting, planning. But the rest are filled with Humans alone with their gadgets. They spend hours here connecting to others elsewhere. Why don't they just talk to the person at the next table?

A young couple, technology-free, sits in front of us. "They're here all the time," says *BRASILIA—BUILDING A NEW CITY*, one of the Books with the best view. "I think they met here. Shows the importance of good urban amenities."

"I so remember," giggles *CINDY'S LOVE LIST*. "He totally noticed her, then he, like, asked her for the Wi-Fi password. He had to pretend that it wasn't working to get her attention. So cute."

"Well, it worked," says BRASILIA. "Three months later, and they're still coming in here."

"Three months? You've been here that long?" I ask.

"People take us down, look at us, return us. A few of us find a home. It's a bit of a lottery," says BRASILIA.

"I was left in March," says 12 MONTHS TO A BETTER YOU. "Given up by someone who didn't want to put in the work that was needed."

"And it helps to be in English," says BRASILIA. "Look at Mr. Tolstoy over there. WAR AND PEACE in Russian. He's not going anywhere."

"Da? Russki?" asks WAR AND PEACE. What he mutters sounds profound. Or angry. But no one can comprehend him. If there were a Russian-English Dictionary here, he'd be understood. Getting no response, he falls back into his Siberian silence.

"I was left for all the right reasons," says BRASILIA. "My Human had read me, loved me, and wanted to share me with others. He came in, chose another title, and left me out of respect for the coffee shop community."

"Or maybe he just wanted to get rid of you," says CALL IT LIKE YOU SEE IT.

"And why are you here, then?" asks BRASILIA.

"Because it's my mission, to change as many lives as possible. Sitting on a shelf in an apartment, I'm underutilized. Here, among people who need to know what I know, I have greater power for good."

"Ignore 'em," whispers SUNDOWN AT SADDLE ROCK. "They're just a couple of ornery tomcats, lookin' to scrap over nuthin'."

"Speak English, you cowboy!" shouts CALL IT LIKE YOU SEE IT. "The closest you've been to a ranch is that bottle of salad dressing they use here."

Clearly, The Forgotten Ones are not The Happy Ones.

The couple in front of me touches hands across the tabletop. His right thumb rubs her left wrist. Their cups are empty yet they seem in no rush to move.

The line at the counter remains steady. Four people wait, exuding impatience.

Then I see a woman who is Katie, or could be her. I gasp. "That's her, I think." I lift my cover to wave her over, but she responds to a friend calling her Davina. And I realize she doesn't really look like Katie at all. She was just a mirage.

"Don't be so quick to try to skedaddle outta here," SUN-DOWN says.

"But I wanted to go back home with her."

"That's what you think. Maybe you're meant for somethin' else," he says.

"If you ask me, she gave you away pretty quickly, which means she didn't really want you," says GIRLS' GUIDE TO LIFE. "My top rule is to choose someone who wants you back."

"But I don't belong in a café," I say.

"What's so wrong with a java house?" says SUNDOWN. "No slobberin' dogs. No rain. No wind. Stay away from spills and it's pretty darn good."

"It's not a home," I say.

"Well, it's my home," says SUNDOWN. "Besides, there's more goin' on here than in most places. Forget about a couple Books squabblin' all the time, and you'll see most of 'em are mighty nice. And you never know who you're gonna meet."

"But this isn't how my story is meant to go. I was chosen from a store and taken home by my Reader. One Reader, one home, forever. That's what's meant to happen."

"Says who?" SUNDOWN asks.

"Well, everyone. I guess."

"That's what you think is s'posed to happen. Maybe your story is meant for more than one Human. Maybe you got more to offer than just sittin' on a shelf for the rest of your life. You're a Book. You should let your story tell itself."

"When did you become The Cowboy Philosopher?" I ask.

"Us Cowboys know more than most people give us credit. My story has a lot of time spent on the open range, lookin' at the sky. Gives you time to think. Life doesn't turn out the way you expect. But sometimes it's even better. You don't know what's in store for you. I reckon our own journey can be even bigger than the story we're born with."

"So you're happy?" I ask.

"Sure. I just wish I could grow a moustache," says SUNDOWN. "All the best cowboys have 'em."

Could the Cowboy Philosopher be right? Just because I'm not in a home, nestled on a shelf, warm and secure, doesn't mean I'm not okay. Agnes wonders what's beyond the horizon. Maybe I should too.

The coffee maker erupts like a geyser, hissing at its Human operator.

"They should watch the heat from the espresso machine. If a child touched it, they could get burned and then they'd be sued," says PARTNERS IN LINE. "Humans don't understand the legal challenges all around them."

"It's not the legal challenges that surround them," says THE ALIBI ZONE. "It's the opportunity for murder."

"You want to see a murder?" I ask, carefully.

"I can't help it. It's in my fibers. My story is about murders among lawyers. They'd kill for a partnership. I'd like to have been a Travel Book, maybe about the Caribbean, or Tuscany.

Or the gauchos of Patagonia. Instead, I'm destined for death. How to murder someone, where and why. In this café, for example, I've come up with a dozen ways to do it."

"How long have you been here?" I ask.

"I've lost count. I've been taken home twice and returned," ALIBI says.

"Why were you returned?" I ask.

"I think it's because when Humans take us from here, they don't feel we're really theirs to keep. Just to borrow," ALIBI says. "Although who can understand them? I gave my first Reader the best performance I could. But in the end, she decided she didn't have space on her shelf, and dropped me here."

"And you're okay with that?" I ask.

"Yeah. I used to try to get my Readers to hold onto me. But maybe I was trying too hard. Maybe they could tell. Now I've stopped worrying. I've decided one shelf is as good as the next," says ALIBI. "Enough about me. What's your story?"

"I'm all about snow and Minnesota a century ago. I don't have any murders in my story. The only death is when my main character, Agnes, witnesses a cow die giving birth. I guess you're more contemporary."

"People kill people. Even in Minnesota. Even in the snow. Even a century ago. They always have. Look at the story of Cain and Abel," ALIBI says.

"Does someone need me?" asks CONTEMPORARY BIBLE REFERENCES.

"No, I was just using one of your stories as an example," ALIBI says.

"No one wants Reference Books anymore," CONTEMPORARY sighs. "The minute we're printed, we're out of date."

"It's not like the Bible is updated regularly," mutters CALL IT LIKE YOU SEE IT.

"How long have you been here?" I ask CONTEMPORARY.

"I've been wandering on this shelf for 40 days or 40 years. I've lost count."

"How about me?" ATLAS OF THE WORLD 1988 says. "I still show West Germany and East Germany as two countries, and Czechoslovakia as one country. No one wants me."

"Relax. You'll be picked up by some vintage-obsessed 27-year-old," says CALL IT. "They'll think you're ironic."

"I'd rather think about love," says GIRLS' GUIDE. "The young and not-so-young who come in here? Too many on their own, too many looking for something, but not finding it. The reticence of Humans stuns me."

"Maybe their signs are incompatible," ASTROLOGY TODAY says.

"But so many times I've seen people look at each other and do nothing," says GIRLS' GUIDE. "The lost opportunity is enormous. A young man notices a young woman. She sees him, then goes back to her phone. He takes it as a sign she's not interested, when really she's trying to get him to come over and say hello."

"You see?" INTRO TO PHILOSOPHY says. "It's all here in front of us. Every day we see a microcosm of humanity on display. Some spend just a few minutes, getting only their coffee, not leaving any part of themselves behind. Others linger, finding friends or lovers. The stories we see are universal."

"All in this coffee shop?" I ask.

"A lot of life happens in places you don't expect," SUNDOWN says. "Now ain't this more interestin' than being stuck in a house?"

We'll see about that.

CHAPTER 12

I
t's been 17 days since Katie gave me away and Ziya abandoned me. Not that I'm counting. I've become used to the routine of the coffee shop, yet every time the door opens, I expect it to be Katie coming to take me home. And every time I'm disappointed. What's that definition of insanity?

BRASILIA and *CALL IT LIKE YOU SEE IT* continue to squabble, however I've learned to stop listening. It's the same argument each day, neither one budging. I'm glad I'm a work of fiction. No one can argue with my facts.

At 9 p.m. the front door is locked and the hissing of the machines dies down. When the Humans are gone, we Books open our covers and lift our pages, letting air into our spines. Books that are standing upright tilt in one direction, then the other, giving the feet of their pages some relief. When one Book causes another one to laugh, it sends vibrations along the shelf. The laughter can become contagious. But no Book is as adventurous as my old friend *JOE'S DISCOVERY* back at the Bookstore. His nocturnal ramblings inspired speculation, debate and admiration. Here, however, no one wanders. They all accept their place on the shelf. After a few stretches, every Book goes quiet for the night.

Lucinda, the coffee shop owner arrives at 6 a.m. Tall and thin with a web of lines on her forehead, she always looks like she has somewhere else she needs to be.

She checks the front door lock to ensure it kept out the uninvited for another night, then walks through the café, straightening chairs and repositioning saltshakers. With the familiarity of an experienced dancer starting her warm-up routine, she preps the coffee, puts the pastries in the oven, and rotates the pre-printed "Homemade Soup of the Day" signs.

Muffins accomplished, Lucinda approaches us. She moves CALL IT LIKE YOU SEE IT next to CONTEMPORARY BIBLE REFERENCES and nudges SUNDOWN and me closer to CINDY'S LOVE LIST. Fortunately, I retain my all-seeing position. If I'm condemned to a café, I want a front-row view.

Then she surprises all of us by pulling out Christmas decorations from a box in the closet. What starts as one tabletop artificial tree with red and green lights expands into tinsel hanging around Florette Adams' paintings. It doesn't do the paintings any favors, but Florette Adams isn't here to complain. Clearly impressed with her own handiwork, Lucinda hangs a garland along the mantel where we are perched. Fortunately, it sags enough to not block our view. Finally, a menorah is placed on the table next to the Christmas Tree. With so many decorations, there's barely room to place coffee cups.

"People are surprised to learn that Hanukkah is mentioned in the Bible: John 10:22. It was called the Feast of Dedication back then. But the person celebrated at Christmas would himself have celebrated Hanukkah," says CONTEMPORARY. "Think about that." He's been a lot more talkative these past few weeks, filling us in on the significance of the season. I just thought it was a time when Humans bought Books as gifts. But I guess there's more to it than that.

The first worker arrives. She doesn't look like her name. Anastasia has short, cropped black hair, and wears a black turtleneck tucked into black jeans. She has matching black nail polish. She takes in the newly placed decorations before making herself a black coffee. Lucinda tells her about the day's muffins, the baking pans that need cleaning and the cash in the till. Instructions delivered, Anastasia moves behind the counter as Lucinda heads to the front door, breathes deeply, slowly twists the key and pulls the door to ensure it's open. She turns to the café and whispers, *"May we do well."*

Within 15 minutes Anastasia is masterfully managing a lineup. During the first hour all the coffee orders are to-go. It's not until the sun has breached the building's roof across the street that a few Humans wander into the shop to stay and buy a pastry "baked on the premises".

At 9:30 a.m. a herd of Humans appears. Rarely do we see more than two arrive at once, so the size of their group draws everyone's attention. They rearrange Lucinda's floor plan, making four small tables into their own version of a boardroom. Their meeting dominates the café. Ninety minutes later, they have rented this meeting room for the price of eight coffees. They exit, leaving dirty cups and misaligned spaces for Anastasia to clean up. I hope they tipped well.

At noon, precisely, a man with a stack of papers arrives and claims a table near us. With a coffee and muffin purchased, he starts writing on some pages, drawing arrows on others. Few pages go untouched. After watching him exhale louder with each page, we see him sit back and look around. Our shelf catches his attention.

He walks to us and scans our titles. He pulls ASTROLOGY TODAY from her place and flips through some pages. *"Huh,"* he chortles, then replaces her.

"What do you expect when Mercury's retrograde," replies the rejected Book.

He runs his hand along the next titles. "Oh, it's so nice to be touched again," CINDY'S LOVE LIST says. He stops at CONTEMPORARY BIBLE REFERENCES and takes him from the shelf. "Thank the Lord. I can finally stretch my spine." The man flips pages and brings CONTEMPORARY back to his table.

"I can see the expressions on your covers from here," CONTEMPORARY says. "Don't look so shocked. I have a devoted following." The man runs his finger down one of CONTEMPORARY'S pages, then flips to his index. He looks back at his own notes. Glancing between his pages and CONTEMPORARY'S, he makes more edits. "See how this works?" CONTEMPORARY says with a condescending tone.

"Yeah, we're all real impressed," SUNDOWN says.

Then, to the surprise of us all, the Human packs up his stack of pages, places them in his backpack and, with one surreptitious glance around the coffee shop, drops CONTEMPORARY in the backpack too.

"Wow, didn't see that coming," ASTROLOGY says.

As the backpack with CONTEMPORARY BIBLE REFERENCES passes through the front door, we hear him chant, "Even though I walk through the valley of the shadow of death, I will fear no evil."

We all shout our goodbyes, then sit, muted. We have more room now, but we've lost a colleague. I remind myself not to get too attached to my friends here, as any one of them may be the next to go, leaving us with another gap on the shelf.

"Merry Christmas *CONTEMPORARY*," whispers *SUNDOWN*. "I'm gonna miss you."

CHAPTER 13

The coffee shop is closing early today. It's New Year's Eve. A few Humans linger over their mugs as if they have nowhere else to go. Anastasia, on the other hand, is making orders faster than ever. Clearly, she has someplace to be. She glances regularly at the oversized clock on the wall until she announces that it's closing time.

This information doesn't inspire movement. The remaining Humans keep clicking and swiping and seeking something on their devices until Anastasia stands at the front door, reminding everyone in a louder voice that it's time to go.

The stray Humans walk out into the December evening and stand, restless but without plans. They look at each other, then one by one, walk away in different directions. The ability of Humans to remain lonely in a crowd will always confuse me.

Once Anastasia has cleaned up, locked up and walked out, we are left alone again.

"New Year's Eve is so romantic," says CINDY'S LOVE LIST. "The wine, the music, the midnight kiss."

"In Astrology, the New Year starts in March with Aries," says ASTROLOGY TODAY. "Most people don't know that."

"Most people don't care," says CALL IT LIKE YOU SEE IT.

"Why do you always have to be so rude?" says GIRLS' GUIDE TO LIFE. "We made it through Christmas being left on the shelf. There was no Santa coming to get us this year. We just have to get through tonight. Then tomorrow you can go back to your squabbling. The holidays will be over."

"The New Year is my prime time," says 12 MONTHS TO A BETTER YOU. "It's the beginning of resolutions, so don't get used to having me around for much longer. I'm on my way to a Human's home any day now."

"Got any New Years resolutions yourself?" asks SUNDOWN.

"To be more accurate," says ASTROLOGY.

"That wouldn't take much," says CALL IT.

"See what I mean?" says GIRLS' GUIDE. "Did you have to say that? Just once, why don't you *not* say what's on your mind?"

"Then I wouldn't be me. I call it like I see it. Like my name says."

"But you can change. We all can," says GIRLS' GUIDE. "We don't have to live the story we're born with."

Can we change? I'm not the same Book I was at the Bookstore. And I learned a lot from the truth I showed to Katie. I don't know if I would make that mistake again. Maybe that's the same thing as changing.

"This year, I want to find a Reader who is interested in actually reading me, not just highlighting parts of me that might be on a test," INTRO TO PHILOSOPHY says. "I can help them see life differently, if they'd just take the time."

"Me too. I want people to understand how good urban planning can make their lives so much better," says BRASILIA.

"I want to sit through a real trial," says PARTNERS IN LINE.

"Maybe it'll be a murder trial. Then we can both be there," says *ALIBI ZONE*.

"I want Germany to divide into East and West, so I'm relevant again," says *Atlas of the World 1988*.

"*A chto ya*," says *WAR AND PEACE*. We wait for someone to respond, but none of us understand him, so we let the silence be his reply.

"*SUNDOWN*, what do you want the New Year to bring you?" I ask.

"I guess the same thing I've always been waitin' for: a nice lassie to prop myself up against. One who likes Cowboys and stories of horses. We'll sit on a shelf next to each other, swappin' tales, like we're by the campfire on a cloudless night."

"That sounds nice, *SUNDOWN*. I hope you find her," I say. "She'd be one lucky Book."

I watch the Humans pass in the street, wearing paper hats and shouting Happy New Year. They all have somewhere to go. They all have someone to be with. They all belong.

That's my New Year's resolution. To belong. "Happy New Year, everyone," I say.

"Happy New Year," they all reply, except *WAR AND PEACE* who says something like, "*S Novym Godom*." Yeah, that too.

CHAPTER 14

Lucinda arrives especially early to pack up the seasonal decorations and tuck their box into the closet to await another December. I hope I'm gone by then. Spending Christmas on the shelf doesn't do much for my self-worth.

Around 2 p.m., a young woman arrives who looks different than the others I've seen in here. A white and blue striped scarf is tied at her neck. Small silver loop earrings poke out from under the layers of dark hair that perfectly frame her face and her hazel eyes.

After getting her coffee, she sits at the table directly in front of me. She sets down a small espresso cup. It's a change from the troughs of hot drinks that are usually consumed here. She takes one cube of sugar, dips it into the coffee, then drops it into the undersized white cup. She inserts a spoon, weaves it through the coffee twice, then places the spoon face down against the saucer, next to a small chocolate-dipped biscotti. I've become a pastry connoisseur during my time here. The usual request is for massive muffins, expansive, fruity scones, or flattened croissants. Instead, this woman has purchased a delicate item destined for dipping. She bites into the caffeinated end of the biscotti, her lips opening wider than her teeth to protect the red lipstick that lines her mouth.

A voice calls, *"Esmé!"*

She greets a woman old enough to be her mother. *"Allo, Yuki,"* she says, in accented English. Aha, well dressed and foreign. Why am I not surprised?

Yuki's smile covers her face. Lines around her eyes form a roadmap of her delight. I like her immediately. Moments later she returns with her mug of coffee and sits across from Esmé. *"You leave for Paris tomorrow?"* Yuki asks. Esmé nods.

"I always wanted to see Paris," BRASILIA says. "Baron Hauss-mann developed their boulevard system in the mid-1800s. Fascinating urban planning."

"No horses in Paris. Although I hear the lassies are mighty pretty," SUNDOWN AT SADDLE ROCK says.

"It's a city made for love," CINDY'S LOVE LIST sighs.

"The French have always embraced great thinking," INTRO TO PHILOSOPHY says. "Decartes' principle: I think therefore I am. Amazing. Then there's Voltaire. Rousseau. Existentialism. What a place."

"You can't live on romance and thought alone," CALL IT LIKE YOU SEE IT says.

"Why not?" CINDY says. "Sounds like a pretty good life to me."

"Is everyone in love with Paris?" I ask. Murmurs of agreement fill the shelf.

Yuki takes a large sip of coffee as Esmé finishes the last bite of her biscotti. *"What time is your flight?"* Yuki asks.

"Tomorrow in the evening."

"We're going to miss you," Yuki says.

"You must to come make a visit."

"Maybe I will. I feel so fortunate that we met."

"Yes, I was having the luck that day," Esmé smiles. *"Maybe it was, how you say, in the stars?"*

"Finally!" shouts ASTROLOGY TODAY.

Yuki smiles. *"Maybe. I had to forget my phone in order to meet you. I think they call it serendipity."*

"How is this word?" asks Esmé.

"Serendipity?" asks Yuki. *"It means, well, a chance encounter. A happy accident."*

"They're talking about you. That's your cue," CINDY says.

"They're not talking about me. They're talking about a word in my title. Two totally different things," I say.

"You seem to like 'em. Time to introduce yourself," SUN-DOWN says.

"But I don't know them. That would be rude. And potentially dangerous. Have you seen the size of Yuki's cup of coffee? If I fell on that, I'd be scarred for life," I say.

"You can land on the napkin holder just below you. It's flat. You won't get hurt," GIRLS' GUIDE TO LIFE says. "Besides, if you wait for an introduction, you'll never get noticed."

"No way. I'm not going. Who knows where I'll end up?"

"That's the point, ain't it? Adventure? And I can't do nothin' with you sittin' on me all day. You're crampin' my style," SUNDOWN says.

"I thought you were my friend."

"I am, darlin'. You just don't know it yet," SUNDOWN says.

The ledge feels as if it's shifting. Then I realize SUNDOWN is opening his back cover, tilting his pages up and me forward. Why can't I be laying on ATLAS OF THE WORLD 1988? Nice and flat and uninterested in exploration. I begin sliding. I try to cling to SUNDOWN, but his cover is printed on glossy paper and offers me nothing to grip. My spine slips over the ledge. SUNDOWN gives his pages more lift and I can feel myself fall farther forward. "Stop it!" I scream.

"You're gonna thank me one day," he insists. After one more push, gravity seizes me and I slip from the ledge, landing as predicted, on top of the napkin holder. I am exposed and embarrassed.

"I am so mad at you, all of you!" I shout up to the ledge of Books.

Yuki stops mid-sentence and picks me up. Her fingers cradle me and her palm cups my back, offering me a place of honor in her hand. She starts to replace me on the ledge but notices my title.

"Look at this," Yuki says. *"THE SERENDIPITY OF SNOW."* She shows my cover to Esmé. *"We were just talking about that word."*

Yuki passes me to Esmé, who turns me over and reads my backside. *"Minn-e-so-ta."*

"It's up near Canada. Lots of lakes. And like the title says, lots of snow. Did you get to travel outside California?"

Esmé shakes her head.

"Then perhaps it's meant to be. You should take this book with you. This might be a nice souvenir and it will help you practice your English when you're back in Paris."

"And I pay?" asks Esmé. At least she knows that I'm worth something.

"No, these Books have all been left behind. You can give it a good home," Yuki says.

Esmé smiles at me. She opens to my page 84.

It's show time.

Rounding the corner, he bumped right into her. The three
books she was cradling in her arms were now in the snow.

I always shiver at this point. I've been creased and stained,
but the thought of being dropped in snow sends chills down
my spine.

"Sorry," James said, and crouched down to pick them up.
"But I was on my way to your house to see you."

"Well, you would have missed me as clearly I'm not
there," Agnes said, smiling.

From across the street, Agnes heard, "Those better
not be the books I gave you, Agnes Lundberg. If I wanted
them dropped in the snow, I could have done it myself."
She looked up to see Mrs. Howard glowering at her. She
turned away.

"Sorry," James whispered to her again.

"I'm going to hear about this for as long as I'm in town,"
Agnes whispered in return.

"Are you going somewhere?" James asked, holding the
sodden books.

"One day," she smiled.

"Okay," Esmé says. *"I take it,"* and places me in her tote bag.
"You're totally going to Paris!" CINDY squeals.

"You still mad at me?" SUNDOWN asks with a laugh.

"I don't know," I say. "I'm not in Paris yet."

Then, as if she heard me, Esmé picks up her bag and me
with it. She kisses Yuki on each cheek.

The Books shout goodbyes. "I hope you'll be happy there,"
BRASILIA says.

"Maybe you'll fall in love," *CINDY* says.

"We're going to miss you," *GIRLS' GUIDE TO LIFE* says.

"It was supposed to be my turn," says *12 MONTHS TO A BETTER YOU*.

"You're welcome," *SUNDOWN* yells.

"Good luck to all of you. I hope you all find the right home," I shout.

Could it be? I'm going to Paris? I didn't know that was my story.

CHAPTER 15

I've been in her bag now for a full day. I thought travel was meant to be exciting. This is simply stifling.

Esmé opens her tote occasionally to drop in a lipstick or a pencil, so I only have momentary glimpses of my surroundings. Then she inserts a booklet. It has a deep red cover and a gold emblem with a shield and the head of a lion and an eagle. The letters RF are in the center. I don't know what that means. I hope it's good. I can make out the word "Passeport" along the bottom. I guess I understand French better than I thought.

"Hello," I say to it.

"*Bonjour*," it replies.

"What's your story?" I ask.

"Esmé Deschamps. *Age: 29. Née: Cluny. Couleur des Yeux: Noisette.*"

"Do you speak any English?" I ask.

"*Oui*, yes," he replies.

"Have you traveled much?" I ask.

"España, 10 days, København, 4 days. USA, 78 days." He's not one for storytelling, so the official document and I lie next to each other as if in government-imposed silence.

I hear her say goodbye to people I'll never meet. Then a man's voice whispers to her, "Let's go."

We enter a running vehicle and the door closes. *"Airport, please,"* he says.

"Where are you off to today?" the driver asks.

"Paris," she says. Paris! It's true.

"International departures," the driver replies and turns on the radio.

Esmé pulls me out of her bag and hands me to a tall young man with perfect teeth and big hands. She continues to search for something in her purse. He, on the other hand, shows excellent judgment by paying attention to me. He scans my pages as he flips through my chapters. He quietly removes three photos from his jacket pocket, places them between two of my pages, and shuts me. *"What's the book about?"* he asks her.

"Minn-e-so-ta," she says.

"Any good?" he asks.

"I do not know. I have not to read it yet," she says. She retrieves Passeport, says, *"voilà"* and drops him back in her bag. If she'd asked me, I could have told her he was there.

"Well, if you finish the book by the time I arrive, then I'll read it too." Esmé looks at him, eyes shining with pre-tears. *"Don't,"* he says. *"I'll be there in a month. I promise. In time for Valentine's Day."*

"Tariq, you will be missing to me."

He kisses her gently. *"I'll miss you too. But soon the project will be done and you'll be showing me around Paris. I promise."* She smiles.

At the airport, they say a series of long goodbyes before Esmé and I practice standing in line. We move and stop and move and stop. She gets really good at waiting when we finally approach some kind of aggressive-looking conveyor belt. She places me in a gray bin, next to the bag of plastic bottles and I begin sliding forward. Esmé steps away from me to stand in another line. Don't forget me!

"Hey!" I shout. Any Books around? What's going on?"

"Going through x-ray," says an unnamed title.

"Sounds painful."

"Just lay still, be quiet, don't move too much. It'll feel weird but it'll be over soon. You'll survive."

"Why do Humans need to x-ray a Book?" I ask.

"They must be afraid of sub-text," says the unnamed title.

"But isn't that where the good parts are?" I ask, but get no reply, as a consistent hum invades the air around me. The waves of electronic noise are both annoying and terrifying. The bin stops moving as the sound gets louder. I squeeze my fibers tight to keep the invasive rays out of my pages and away from the glue of my spine. I can't believe Humans are this frightened of what we have in our pages. Then, just as I think I can't hold my fibers any tighter, the bin moves forward, down a ramp. Esmé's face appears. Hooray, she didn't forget me. She drops me, the plastic bag of bottles and Monsieur Passeport into her bag. Who knew travel was this exhausting? I hope we're almost there.

After what feels like an hour, Esmé opens the bag and I see we're in a plane. As people are forcing massive sacks into finite spaces, she simply inserts me into a mesh pocket. She then goes through what looks like a practiced ritual. Shoes off. Socks on. Hand cream applied. Blanket and pillow repositioned.

Almost none of the Humans around her are speaking, yet they are sitting next to each other. Books would be talking to each other immediately. Maybe the ability to move where and when you want makes you less friendly.

"Any Books here?" I ask. A chorus of "Me," "I'm here," "I'm here too," is the response. I may not be able to see my colleagues in print, but at least I know they're nearby.

"Who's that in the seat next to me?" I ask.

"*EUROPEAN TRAVEL ON A BUDGET*," a nearby book replies.

"Lucky me. Mind if I ask you a question?"

"It's why I'm here," he says.

"Is everyone in love with Paris?"

"Yes. In fact, love is the first thing I talk about in my chapter on Paris. Is that where you're going?"

"Yes! I've never been."

"Me neither."

"But you're all about Europe," I say.

"Have you been to the places in your pages?"

He has a point. "Well, at least you must know what to expect," I say.

"I hope so. I'm looking forward to seeing if what I say is correct, like if the museums in London are still free. And if La Boqueria in Barcelona is really a good place for an inexpensive meal."

"So this is like a fact-finding trip, to see how accurate you are," I say.

"Exactly. I'll finally have my own insight into what I'm talking about, I won't just be repeating what my Author wrote. I'll have a voice. What about you?"

"I don't try to be correct. I just try to be interesting," I say.

"You're fiction, right?"

"Yeah, how could you tell?" I ask.

"Non-fiction has an opinion. You fictionals are more interested in the Books around you than in your own stories."

He knows so much. "Are all Travel Books smart like you?" I ask.

"It depends on who wrote us and why. A Book on Paris written by someone who's English is going to be different than one written by, say, an Italian or a German. Some Books focus on food. Others on art or architecture. Same place. Same history. Different viewpoint. I'm about saving money."

"So your prices are the most important thing?"

"Yeah. It's a lot of pressure. Like I say, a hotel in Madrid costs 87 euros a night. Another Book, a newer one, arrived at the Travel Bookstore where I was on the shelf, and said that the same hotel was 96 euros. I hope I'm right, or I won't be traveling for long. I'll be out of date before I see all the places I'm meant to know."

"My story starts in the late 1800s. I guess I was out of date the day I was printed," I say.

"But people buy you for the nostalgia factor. They buy me for relevance, to inform them about a place they've never been, but plan to go. It's a totally different thing."

"I always thought Travel Books lived such exciting lives, understanding different cultures," I say.

"There's always more to know. I'm the Seventh Edition. I'll survive until they print an Eighth version of me." Suddenly, being a work of fiction feels like the safer option.

"Has your Reader been to Paris before?" he asks.

"She is from Paris," I say. "Her name is Esmé. It's . . . French." I can't believe I'm bragging. Actually, I can.

"You're lucky, then," EUROPEAN TRAVEL says. "You'll have

a local's experience. They're the best kind. It says so in my first chapter."

"I guess. Still, I'm a little nervous," I say. "I've never traveled before. I don't know what to expect."

"Don't worry, you'll have a great time," he says.

We're suddenly moving. It feels like we're going backwards. The Humans grow silent. Then we're moving forward. A whirr sounds as we tilt upwards and I feel like I'm falling forwards, only held in place by the mesh digging into my cover. Last time I was at this angle, I was in the café and SUNDOWN was shifting me into the life of Esmé. The pressure of the plane makes it shake as we gain speed. Some of the Humans smile, excitedly. Others looks like they are hoping the experience will end soon. So far, the glamour of travel eludes me.

Minutes later, we are level again, and the vibrations have ceased. Esmé frees me from the mesh, opens me and finds the photos that I've been protecting between my pages. Her cheeks redden and her dark eyes grow wet as she flips through each photo. Love does make a Human more beautiful.

As she reads me, her fingernail creates crevices on my page. I perform slowly for her, to match the pace of her finger tracing the base of each line.

Agnes knew that Henry had wanted to kiss her at the dance. She had averted his advances and was avoiding any more by standing in the dark corner, away from the others. Sensing someone nearby, she steeled herself to face Henry once again. Inhaling courage, she pivoted on her heel, only to startle at seeing James Tyler standing next to her.

She didn't know why—it wasn't planned, but she pulled him to her and kissed him. She was surprised that she did it and how much she liked it: the smell of his skin, the taste of his lips, the feel of his evening stubble.

He wasn't as well dressed as Henry. His father didn't have as much money as Henry's, so he was probably not the right choice if she were staying in Rose Valley. But she was going to live far away from here, so it didn't matter whom she kissed, she told herself. For once, she acted without forethought.

Unexpectedly, James kissed her back. She opened her eyes and smiled at him, then caught a glimpse of Henry looking around, probably for her. She gave James one more quick kiss then ran out the front door, into the endless cold of the night.

Esmé takes a pencil and revisits what she just read, underlining some of my words: averted, stubble, forethought. The tip of the pencil tickles as it pulls against my fibers.

She places the photos inside my back cover. I'll protect them. I know a crucial job when I have one. Then she closes me and I am back in my mesh nest. A roof is dropped above me, completely obscuring my view.

Navy blue stockings and shoes with round toes and block heels pass by, followed by a rolling cart. A small napkin falls to the floor. The cart and the monochromatic legs continue along the aisle.

"Hey, EUROPEAN TRAVEL?" I ask.

"Yeah?"

"How long does it take to get to Paris? An hour or two?" I ask.

His laughter tells me that perhaps I am not quite as worldly as I thought.

"Two things. We're not going to Paris. We're going to London. Heathrow. And two, this flight is about 11 hours. We go over Greenland. You're probably changing planes to get to Paris."

"I have to sit here for 11 hours? With this mesh embedding its pattern in my cover?" I ask.

"In a word, yes. Travel isn't always easy. That's what I say on the third page of my introduction, next to my sidebar on cultural awareness. I have more depth than people think."

"So, half a day of doing absolutely nothing, just to get to London?" I ask. He must be wrong.

"That's right. These overnight flights are all about distraction. Dinner. Film. Sleep. Breakfast. Stretch. Arrival. In about an hour they'll lift the table, turn down the lights and Humans will turn on the movies. It's an airline thing."

Who knew travel was such hard work.

CHAPTER 16

What was a clean plane is now reminiscent of a teenaged boy's bedroom. The smell of stale Humans hovers over the floor. Shoes that were removed have drifted during the flight. Garbage has been collected, but more continues to be produced. We're in a petri dish at 35,000 feet.

We land with a thud, a crescendo of engine noise and a palpable buzz among the Humans. "I told you it was a long flight," EUROPEAN TRAVEL says.

"What happens how?" I ask. I have so much to learn.

"Humans line up to get off the plane, then there's a dash to Customs and the next flight. It's basically an exercise in stress management."

"Sounds awful."

"It is," he says.

"Then why do Humans travel?"

"I think it's to appreciate home. But don't tell anyone that, or I'll be out of print."

"Well, wherever you're going, I hope you have a great trip," I say.

"Have a great life," he says.

That sounds so final. But maybe he's right. I doubt I'll see him again. He's just another title that I've met along the way. There are so many Books to meet. I hope they're all as helpful as he was.

Esmé unbuckles herself and frees me from my net. Heathrow is shockingly colorless, like it was designed by someone with a fetish for Dull, highlighted by accents of Bland. I wonder what ÜBER DESIGN would say about it. I wonder how he is? Thinking of him and his umlauts suddenly makes me feel old, or tired, or alone. But I've got to be positive. I'm going to Paris.

Herds of Humans drag themselves and their wheeled sacks in a choreographed effort to arrive someplace else. Hundreds of feet beat down the rock-toned carpeting lined by sand-colored walls.

Esmé carries me and her Passeport along the forgettable hallways. We follow icons that promise a man wearing a cap. A sign indicating "Europe" directs her to a new line. I'm in the European line. I feel so . . . cultured. Yet so far from the coffee shop where I had friends, or Katie's apartment, which I thought was my forever home, or the Bookstore where JOE'S DISCOVERY had the greatest adventures. And so removed from the snows of Minnesota. I should stop worrying. I'll become European. Maybe.

We approach a Human in a cap, as promised by the signs, but it's a woman who glances at the Passeport, then at Esmé.

"Name: Esmé Deschamps. Days out of the country: 78," Passeport recounts in stilted English that the Human can't hear, only read.

After the capped head nods, we continue past more signs, more people, more hallways. I'm suddenly exhausted. The time on the clock is all wrong. I want to sleep, but I can't.

Mercifully, the walking ends at a row of seats. To one side are shops offering duty-free alcohol, duty-free perfume or duty-free make up. To the other are rows of fast food restaurants. In the middle is a Bookstore where people are browsing. But not us.

Instead, I'm placed on a cold table in the center of Humanity, with what feels like most of the world's population passing. Esmé is consuming a bottle of water as if she has returned from the desert. I'm struggling to stay awake as people swirl around us, all going someplace else. No one wants to stay here at Heathrow, and I can understand why. They are all staring up at the monitors in hopes of good news. Stress hangs over the place like a fog.

Exotic destinations are announced. Colombo. Amsterdam. Beirut. All so far from anything I know. Then I hear Paris.

On this plane, it's the same routine, but after we are in the air the scents and sounds are different. Butter and garlic drift ahead of the navy blue stockings and rolling cart. A cork is removed from a bottle and liquids are poured. Aromas of strong coffee and something sweet surround us. On the flight to England, the only thing I could smell was warmed-over plastic.

The cart returns to pick up the trays before we land. Esmé lifts her table, unbuckles herself from her seat and drops me in her bag. The air is filled with French voices and announcements. Then over the speakers, I hear: *"Bienvenue à Paris."*

Pah-ree? Is that Paris in French? I've learned my first foreign word. I've arrived.

Paris

CHAPTER 17

I've been in Paris for an hour. Already I feel more sophisticated. A lock turns, hinges squeak, floorboards moan. Esmé opens her bag, removes me and Monsieur Passeport, and places us on a round, wooden table.

"Allo!" she says to her apartment. She strides over to one corner and pulls thick, red curtains along brass rods, revealing floor-to-ceiling windows. She leans on two large, curved metal handles that sound too tired to move. After a few determined twists, one is convinced, then the other, allowing the windows to separate at the center and swing outwards over a wrought-iron balcony. Cold air rushes in.

I can see sky again. It's gray. But it's Paris gray.

Esmé turns and strolls around her apartment, touching parts of it, a pillow, then a painting, as if awakening a sleeping child. She runs her hand along the third shelf of a Bookcase, crammed with my future friends, then closes the windows. She takes her rolling suitcase and disappears into a room.

"Hello?" I ask.

I receive a patter of "Allos" in return.

"Does anyone here speak English?"

There is a moment of silence before a Book responds. "Just me. I'm the British English-French Dictionary," says a voice with a polished accent. "If you want to talk to any of the Books, I can translate for you. Otherwise, they only speak French."

"You're the only English speaker?"

"Welcome to Paris," Dictionary says.

I hadn't planned for this. I thought I would be able to talk to most Books here. But I'm sure Dictionary will be interesting.

"Hey, Dictionary, you would know. Is everyone in love with Paris?"

"Well, I'm certainly not, and that's all that matters to me. Paris is just where I work. Others may have a different opinion."

"But they can't understand me," I say.

"Tant pis."

"What does that mean?" I ask.

"You Yanks are so provincial," sighs Dictionary.

Esmé enters the kitchen and pours a glass of water. The fridge is half the size of any I've seen, and fits under the counter. Behind is a checkerboard pattern of crimson and yellow tiles. On a ledge is a row of Cook Books, some looking rather exhausted. A second shelf of Cook Books is starting to grow above that one.

"Why so many Cook Books?" I ask Dictionary.

"Well, one, it's France. And two, Esmé works at the Cordon Bleu. She gives tours of food markets, mostly to tourists. If you like cooking smells, you're going to love it here."

"Are the Books here nice?" I ask.

"They're French."

"What does that mean?" I ask.

"You'll see."

It's light outside, but I feel half dazed in this new place, with no friends, and out of step with the routine. A low buzz of BookSpeak murmurs along the shelves.

"What are the Books talking about?" I ask.

"You."

"Oh." I smile, in hopes that my future friends at least like me, if they can't understand me. "What are they saying?"

"They're asking about you. They want to know your story."

"Can I tell them tomorrow? I'm just so tired."

The last thing I remember is Esmé opening the bathroom door. Then, despite the light creating shadows on the oak floors, I sleep.

CHAPTER 18

I wake up, confused by my surroundings. It's still dark out, but a crack of light is visible in the sky. Then Esmé appears and I remember, I'm in Paris. I made it. In a fog of tiredness, I watch her make a coffee and settle herself into a corner of the beige sofa. She picks up her phone, staring at it with the same affection that all Humans show for these devices. Her eyes are transfixed. She begins to double-thumb the screen. A ding is followed shortly by a three-note tone. She smiles and answers the incoming call.

"*Allo,*" she says.

Something resembling a voice vibrates from her phone.

"*Yes, but I have such tired when I arrived. Now it is too early to be awake, but I am,*" she says.

"Who is she talking to at this hour?" DICTIONARY groans.

"Probably her boyfriend," I say.

"Oh, do tell," he says, perking up.

"I don't know much. I've only been with her for a few days."

"She hasn't read you yet?"

"She read some of my pages on the plane. Then the food arrived," I say. "But when her boyfriend gets here, he's going to read me. In fact, they're going to read me together." I bet she's never read DICTIONARY with anyone.

"Where is he from?" DICTIONARY asks.

"He's American."

"Oh, dear," DICTIONARY says.

"And what's wrong with that?" I ask.

"Apologies. You Americans have your charms, I'm sure."

"Do you want to insult me, or hear about the boyfriend?" I am taken aback by the edge in my voice. I've never spoken like that to another Book. But DICTIONARY is so naturally annoying. I can't believe that the only Book I can converse with is so full of his own self-worth.

"Fine. Tell," DICTIONARY says.

"His name is Tariq," I say.

"How old is he?"

"I don't know."

"Where did they meet?" DICTIONARY asks.

"I don't know."

"What do you know? Anything?"

"Let me guess. You don't have a lot of friends."

"It's four o'clock in the morning," DICTIONARY says. "I've been awoken by a jet-lagged phone call to her paramour. I'm not at my best. Either tell or be quiet and let me sleep." He snaps his cover shut.

I continue, "He's coming here next month."

His cover opens slightly. "What does he do?"

"I don't know."

"What's his last name?" he asks.

"I don't know."

"Is his family significant?"

"I don't know."

"That's it? That's all I get?"

"He's tall with big hands. Oh, and he has good teeth."

"Naturally," says DICTIONARY. "You Yanks are obsessed with dental hygiene."

"He seems to care for her," I say.

"Well, I'm pleased there is someone. I was concerned about her personal life."

"What's wrong with her personal life?" I ask.

"She was living with this man. We all were. However, things didn't end well. Tears. Endless tears. I thought she was going to self-dehydrate. Then a move. We were all tossed in boxes, quickly and carelessly. Fortunately I'm a hardcover, so more resilient than the rest."

"How long ago was that?" I ask.

"About a year ago. We are now definitely a few steps down the property ladder. We used to have such a beautiful view from the Bookshelf. I could see the Eiffel Tower. Now all we see are window boxes suspended from balcony railings. Our Bookshelves are from Sweden. It's social degradation. I'm glad no one I know can see me."

"I think it's nice here," I say.

"You wouldn't, if you had seen where we were."

I don't know what he's talking about. I'll take this over the coffee shop any day. Fortunately, Esmé ends her call, emerges from the nest she's made for herself and picks me up, moving me away from this snob. She opens my back cover and removes the photos that I've been protecting for her.

"Excuse me, I need to be read now. Maybe we can continue this scintillating conversation another time," I say to that annoyance in a hardcover.

Esmé opens me to my page 105. I clear my fibers and begin.

Agnes wondered how she would ever summon the courage to do it. How could she leave home, her sisters, her mother and father, James? How could she make her way in the world, in the way she knew she must?

She longed to feel the air of new places, explore towns and cities where she hadn't already walked every street, climbed every tree, knew every face. She craved conversations with those who didn't know everything she had ever done in her life. She yearned for choices that were hers alone.

Agnes wanted to be the girl that could break free. She just didn't know how.

"Try to be quiet," says DICTIONARY. "I'm going to go back to sleep."

"But you could translate me for the others," I say. "They were asking about my story yesterday."

"I'm not fully awake yet. Thus, I'm incapable of translating anything."

My entire social interaction is at the whim of a pile of stuck-up words. EUROPEAN TRAVEL never warned me about this.

CHAPTER 19

In the time I've been here, Esmé has shown herself to be a slow but faithful Reader.

She begins each morning by removing the photos of herself and Tariq from my pages. After smiling and caressing the photos, she takes her index finger, kisses it, then places her fingertip on his lips. She lays the photos on the table, and sits cross-legged on her sofa with me in one hand, a pencil in the other and the pompous DICTIONARY at her side.

As she reads me, she underlines a few words on each page. She writes these words in her notebook, then takes the ever-annoying DICTIONARY and jots down their definitions. I'm not sure how often she'll need to use the word 'spittoon' in Paris, but I'm impressed by her dedication. I just hope she's interested in my story, not just my opportunity to hone her English. When she's done with my words, she returns the photos inside my cover, and places me on top of DICTIONARY, giving me no respite from his snobbish perspective on, well, everything.

I am fully dependent on the most annoying Book in the world. Esmé needs him to understand me. And I need him to be understood. My existence here gives him a purpose. Cultural exchange can be harsh.

Esmé enters her bedroom and returns, ready for the outdoors, with a yellow, oversized scarf wrapped around her. She checks on the photos in my back cover, and drops me in her bag. Hooray! My first day in Paris as a tourist. So exciting! I wonder if she'll take me up the Eiffel Tower.

She closes the apartment door behind us. The sound of metal scraping against metal, then we're descending. More scraping of metal, the sound of tired hinges rebelling against their task, and we're outside. The chilled air reaches the insides of the bag.

We walk for several minutes. Cars are honking, as if their drivers are testing the cause and effect of a hand on a horn. Then we sit and rest.

I am placed in a position of honor in the center of a small, round, mosaic-topped table. The tiles are cold, but I'm in Paris, so I won't complain. Overhead heaters push warmth in our direction, but not quite far enough to warm my chilled cover.

Esmé gives her order to a waiter and positions two more chairs around the table. She didn't need to line up at a counter. She didn't need to kill time waiting for her beverage to be served in a coated, disposable cup. Here, no one is stationed in front of a laptop. Humans are sitting, two or three to a small table, actually talking. The chairs are facing the street; the show here is other Humans.

Tiny cars are aligned nose to tail along narrow streets. The sidewalks are wider than the roadways. Motor scooters are parked randomly along the curbs, as if a strong wind determined their locations.

Trees emerge from the sidewalk at precise intervals, surrounded by a short fence of green chain link, making the trees look as if they're in cages.

Rows of back-to-back benches break up the evenly placed trees. A man is sitting, his light gray jacket and dark gray scarf reminding me that it's still January. He is scanning the surroundings and, unbelievably, smoking. Who smokes anymore? He waves his cigarette and his lethal ash drops on the ground. Let's hope he stays away from us. What gives him lung cancer gives me three-page-deep burns. Everyone loses.

The café's front doorway is bordered in stone. Above it is a face, captured and carved centuries ago, with curly hair and unblinking eyes. It leans over the entry, its lips parted mid-laugh, as if locked in a perpetual response to the stories being told beneath it.

Esmé smiles as two women approach her, their heels clicking on the sidewalk and their voices speaking through smiles.

"Anne-Marie," she says, kissing her friend on each cheek. She turns to her second friend and says, *"Sophie,"* as they exchange the same greeting.

The women lean towards each other as streams of conversation pour from their colorful mouths. More coffees arrive, more smiles emerge and more laughter ricochets between them. Then I hear the word *"Tariq"*. It's my cue. Esmé opens my back cover and removes the photos. She points to the images. *"Golden Gate. San Francisco. Cable Car,"* she says. I hold onto these six words. I never saw the Golden Gate, didn't see too much of the city and never rode a cable car, yet the words remind me how far I am from home.

I focus on the adventure. Most Books would kill for this opportunity. So if I feel a little lonely, a little out of place, a little cut off, that's okay. I'm sure I'll make friends one day soon. Esmé will buy more Books in English and we can tell our tales. Until then, I'm not going to be homesick. I'm going to be strong, like Agnes in my story.

Anne-Marie picks me up. She reads my title aloud, then turns to my page 109, where Esmé's Bookmark is nestled. Attempting an American accent, she reads aloud.

> She opened the map of Minnesota and her fingers traced the rail lines. Agnes dreamed of traveling south to the warmth, or west to the mountains, or east to the big cities. Not north. She didn't need even colder months in even smaller towns.
>
> She had heard about the palm trees in Florida and the beaches that were as endless as her own snow-filled horizon. Her uncle had told her about California, with summers free of bugs and winters free of snow. She had read that in the east, the cities were so big that they had trains that ran along their streets. South, West or East? She just had to decide and go there.
>
> She looked out the window again and knew that as scared as she was to go, she was even more afraid to stay. The future beckoned.

"Beckoned?" she asks.

Esmé shrugs. It's not a word she's underlined yet.

Coffees consumed, Sophie looks at her watch. The gesture prompts a shift in each woman's posture. Esmé returns the photos to my back pages. They each drop coins on the table, repeat the cheek-kissing ritual and say *"au revoir"*. Anne-Marie's heels click in one direction, Sophie's in the other.

Hours pass in darkness as I'm cocooned in the black lining of Esmé's bag. Occasionally, she reaches for her wallet. Then she stops and the smells of yeast and baking surround us. My fibers open wide to take in the scent. It's intoxicating. I hope Esmé returns here often. The warmth and rich flavors of the air are indulgent. She picks up a long, thin loaf and I'm nestled next to its warmth. I snuggle against it in the bag, trying to arch my front cover around it, in a bread-loving hug. Another stop in a shop selling housewares, then the sound of the reluctant elevator signals that we are home.

Inside the apartment, the bread is removed and I'm placed on the table. She extracts the photos from my care and positions them in newly purchased picture frames. Katie must have done that once with her wedding photos. I hope she's doing okay. I wonder if she regrets giving me away. I wonder if she thinks about me like I think about her.

Esmé places one photo among the Books on the Bookshelf. The second is positioned in the kitchen, on top of the small fridge. The third, the photo of her and Tariq with the Golden Gate Bridge in the background, the one she kisses every day, is placed on the bedside table.

With the photos settled in their frames, my days as memory-protector are over. I'm back to work, sitting in her lap on the sofa, alongside DICTIONARY. Her index finger begins to trace words on my page 110 when her phone rings.

Carrying her phone to the bedroom, Esmé places me open-faced on top of a French Book she's also been reading. The Book and I are spread above and below each other. Our pages intertwine. I blush. We haven't even been introduced.

"*Allo,*" he says.

"Hello," I say. "Sorry."

ENTITLED 111

"*Mais pourquoi?*" he asks.

"What does that mean?" I ask DICTIONARY.

"He doesn't know why you are sorry."

"Because we are touching each other's pages. And we haven't even been introduced."

"That's FRANÇOIS DANS LA RUE. I wouldn't worry too much about formalities," says DICTIONARY.

"What's his story?" I ask.

"Contemporary street poetry," says DICTIONARY.

"*Tes pages sont très belles,*" FRANÇOIS says.

I hate that I can't understand him. "What is he saying?" I ask DICTIONARY.

"He says your pages are very beautiful."

I can feel heat spreading from my spine. I breathe. Everyone is watching. What will they be thinking? I say to DICTIONARY, "Tell him, thank you. I'm sure he's very attractive as well."

"Don't worry about telling him that," DICTIONARY says.

"Why?"

"He's FRANÇOIS DANS LA RUE. He doesn't think anything else."

I look for Esmé to remove me, but she is still on her phone. I have been forgotten by her. But clearly not by FRANÇOIS.

He begins to move his page slightly, subtly, surely. But so minimally that no one would notice. Except me. I've never been spread-to-spread with a Book before. He's warm yet slightly rough. I lift one of my pages, in case he doesn't mean this to happen. But FRANÇOIS' right page continues to rub against mine. And I let him. I can feel my cover flush. My spine starts loosening as my pages begin spreading recklessly. Can anyone see us? This is so blatant. So public. So French.

I whisper to him, but his hushed responses are in French.

I crave to know what he is saying, but I don't want to break the moment by asking *DICTIONARY* to translate. And anyway, there are some things that should remain private. Even if they are not understood.

Esmé returns from the bedroom and begins cooking, leaving me precisely where I am. Smells of garlic and onion and nutmeg and clove fill the apartment and cling naturally to *FRANÇOIS'* thick, sturdy fibers. Esmé pours herself a glass of wine as she sets down her plate on the table. Then she lights candles. The illumination dances across the room, creating a perfect backdrop to this Parisian moment. It's like how *DIANE'S DREAM* back in the Bookstore described the first time in her story. And *COURTNEY'S COMPLAINT*. And *BELINDA'S BELIEF*. Maybe their author, Maya Fredricks, knows something after all. I'm having my own romance. I can't believe it's happening to me. Esmé sits down to her meal, leaving me and *FRANÇOIS* gloriously undisturbed.

His pages are larger than mine, so I settle comfortably in the lay of his spread. His fibers are strong and determined. His ink has a scent I've never smelled before. I inhale him. He is intoxicating. I can hear the other Books, yet he continues to caress my pages. I don't want this moment to end.

Esmé finishes her meal. She puts her dishes in the sink and readies herself to go out. Soon, the curtains are drawn and she is striding to the front door. She takes a final look around the apartment, then turns out the lights, closes the door and locks it behind her.

FRANÇOIS and I are in darkness. If we're quiet, no one will know.

CHAPTER 20

I awake to the sound of Esmé's feet on the floor as she pulls open the curtains to welcome in the day. I look at myself. I'm a mess. My pages are creased, my spine is stretched, FRANÇOIS' ink has left a mark on me. And his scent is inside me. His pages are folded over me, holding me. I am absorbing as much of the delicious moment as my signatures will allow.

"Good morning," I whisper to FRANÇOIS.

"*Quoi? Qui?*" he replies, as he wakes. He shifts his pages slightly.

"Last night was . . . " I look intently into his typeface, "amazing."

FRANÇOIS coos back at me. "*Merci pour hier soir, mais j'ai beaucoup de choses à faire aujourd'hui.*"

"Me too," I respond to whatever he's saying.

"*Peux-tu bouger pour me laisser tranquille?*"

"Yes. I feel the same way," I say, inhaling his fibers.

"*Franchement, tu dois quitter.*"

Everyone said Paris was the city for love. They were right. Just as I'm nestling closer to FRANÇOIS, Esmé picks me up. "Goodbye my love," I whisper to him.

She takes me to the corner of the sofa. I perform for her, but with a lightness that makes even the story of the cow's death less sad. How can one be sad when one is in love? Esmé puts me aside and walks to the kitchen for a coffee.

"Looks like you had an energetic night." Just the sound of DICTIONARY's voice is enough to deflate my bubble of bliss.

"What do you mean?"

"You. FRANÇOIS. Looks like a lot has happened since the lights went out."

"She left me with him. I didn't seek him out."

"Maybe," DICTIONARY says.

"It was fate."

"Is that what they're calling it these days? I thought it was FRANÇOIS being FRANÇOIS."

"What's that supposed to mean?" I ask. Can't DICTIONARY let me have this moment?

"Think you're the first new novel he's ever seduced?"

"Seduced? You think he seduced me? That sounds so tawdry, so premeditated," I say.

"So FRANÇOIS."

"You're wrong. You don't know him like I do."

"True. I haven't been on the receiving end of his advances, but it will end in tears. It always does."

"No. You're wrong. What we have is . . . special."

"Sure. Today's special."

I've never hated a Book before, but I actually hate DICTIONARY.

"It's your life, your pages, but don't come crying to me and say I didn't translate for you," he says.

I snap my cover shut. I don't need to hear any more of DICTIONARY's definitions.

CHAPTER 21

I s this what love feels like?

My fibers are tight and twisted, and I'm perched on the edge of nervous panic. But I am light, buoyant, blushing at my thoughts. I am meant to be working, to help Esmé understand me. Yet all I can think about is my FRANÇOIS. He lies open on the table, where I left him, his spread of pages inviting me back. I am desperate to be with him, next to him, however I'm in Esmé's hands, so I must work. I try to perform for her, but I'm skipping words, ending one line then returning to its start. I can see Esmé struggle to follow me while DICTIONARY shouts, "A little distracted, are we? Feeling guilty?"

"I have nothing to feel guilty about."

"Then foolish. It will come. If not today, soon, and for every day thereafter."

"Why can't you believe that maybe FRANÇOIS and I are in love?"

"If I had a euro for every time one of FRANÇOIS's conquests uttered the word love, I could buy a hand-polished Bookshelf for myself."

DICTIONARY doesn't understand love, so I am happy to leave him wallowing in his falsehoods. FRANÇOIS will wait for me. We are drawn to each other. We may have different languages, but we share the same soul. I look again at FRANÇOIS, seeking a sign, a flutter of his pages, but I can only hear his fibers opening and closing as he snores.

Esmé glances at her phone. She places a Bookmark between my pages 116 and 117, and closes me. I hope she will return me to that place of bliss where she found me—in the spread of my beloved. Instead, she places me in a mesh bag and hangs me from the handle of her bedroom door.

She wraps another scarf around her, pulls on a red coat and gloves, then pulls the bag I'm in over her shoulder. As she walks through the front door, I say a fond "goodbye" to FRANÇOIS but only hear the door shutting behind us.

I miss him already. I know some Humans "call in sick". Why can't I "call in love", and take the day off? I would spend every moment with FRANÇOIS, feeling his fibers, caressing his pages, inhaling his scent, a delicious blend of cigarettes and diesel. But instead of being intertwined with my love, I'm immersed in a Paris morning.

Being in a mesh bag allows me to see things I've only heard before. The elevator looks like a steel birdcage as it rises to the call. I felt safer not knowing how old it was. Esmé pulls the accordion-like door along its track, the metal complaining over each inch. With a shudder, we're descending.

Outside, we pass a children's carousel with its green roof, gold trim, and painted faces of puppets that look more frightening than amusing. Horns honk, people talk, heels clatter on the uneven pavement.

We continue in the direction of a sign that says *Metropolitain*. Descending the stairs, we pass through a turnstile and await the arrival of a long train with enormous windows. Dozens of people leave the train, and more force their way through its open doors like a moving Human Bookshelf, but untidy and un-alphabetized. Esmé pulls me to her chest, guarding me and her purse with benign vigilance. The mesh webbing is taut against me, leaving an unattractive crisscross pattern against my cover. I'm sure FRANÇOIS won't mind. He'd find the story funny. If he could understand English.

On one of the seats, a Human is reading a Book in English. "Hello!" I shout across the mosaic of bodies.

"Who's there?"

"It's me, in the center of the people, under the arms of the woman in the red coat."

"Oh, yeah, hey. I see ya. Hi."

"What's your name?" I ask.

"JERSEY JONES. You?"

"THE SERENDIPITY OF SNOW."

"Nice meeting you," she says. "What's your story?"

"I'm about a girl growing up in Minnesota at the turn of the last century. And you?"

"Love, deceit, disappointment during one hot summer on the Jersey Shore."

"Sounds exciting."

"Exhausting more like it, but thanks," JERSEY JONES says.

"How long have you been in France?"

"Eight years. Came over with a student and I've been passed around ever since," she says.

"Wow. So you're sort of French."

"I don't think I'll ever be truly French. But the longer I stay, the less American I feel," she says.

"Me too," I say. I'm glad I've finally found an English-language Book that understands me.

"Really? How long have you been here?" she asks.

"Two weeks."

JERSEY JONES stifles a cough. I'm sure it wasn't a laugh. "So, how's it going so far?"

"Great," I say.

"Really? Speak any French?" she asks.

"No."

"And how's that working for you?" she asks.

"What do you mean?"

"Making any friends?" she asks.

"Well, not a friend, per se," I say.

"Oh, you've met a Book."

"How did you know?" I ask.

"I've been here long enough to know a French fling when I hear it."

"But this isn't a fling."

"Let me guess. You think you're in love with a French Book. Am I right?"

I say nothing.

"Does he speak English?" she asks.

"We communicate without words," I say.

"Hah. How many times have I heard that one?" *JERSEY JONES* says. "We're Books. Telling stories is what we do."

"But we have something more."

"So you're saying that a Book with no English, and a Book that's only got English, are gonna find true love?"

"Why not?" I say. Or ask. I'm not sure which.

"Haven't you noticed? The French Books, they're different. Not better, not worse, just different," she says.

I'm not liking the direction of this conversation with this Jersey girl. "So what?"

"So a lotta what. You think a French accent speaking words you can't understand is the basis of anything? I'm guessing you were feeling alone, vulnerable and he came along, opening his pages to you." I have no response. "Classic. Let me give you some advice from someone who's been here long enough to know."

"What if I don't want your advice?"

"Well, you're getting it," she says. "Take care of yourself. Learn some French. Make a few friends. Don't stay like the others, in their little cluster of English. You're in Paris. Act like it. Make your own life here. If he fits into it, great. If not, trust me, he's not worth it."

She's wrong and that's all there is to it. Fortunately, I don't need to tolerate this discussion much longer. The train comes to a stop and Esmé pushes forward and off the train. We emerge onto another platform and force our way through the pulse of people pushing themselves in our direction.

We climb the stairs to daylight and away from the predictions of the Jersey Shore. But she does have a point about making friends. DICTIONARY is a necessary evil. FRANÇOIS is my love. But a real friend? The list is over before I start. Perhaps Esmé will collect a few nice English language Books. Maybe Tariq will arrive with a funny novel about California, one that doesn't take itself too seriously. Perhaps it'll all be okay. If I think about it too much, my glue will start to heat up and I'll fall apart at the spine.

I must do Agnes proud. She made her own way in the world

more than 100 years ago, when the weather was unforgiving and her role was predetermined by society. My opportunities are so much more vast. I'm in Paris, after all. So what if I'm a little lonely, a little nervous, a little unilingual? I will be as inspired as Agnes was to carve her own life through the snowdrifts. It's just that my life is less mobile than hers and doesn't involve snow. And I know how her story ends. My story? I'm not so sure.

Esmé turns down a side street and arrives at a building with royal blue trim around the doors. She takes the stairs, past one landing to a second, and we're in a hallway. Cheek-kisses follow bursts of *"Esmé!"* She drops me on a small desk and greets a cluster of Humans speaking French.

I open my cover to get a broader view and I see it. On the white wall is a royal blue single stripe that is broken up by a circle of blue with striped prongs emerging from it. Inside the circle are the words: Le Cordon Bleu Paris 1895.

I am at the Cordon Bleu? The center for chefs and cooking? If only the Cook Books in the Bookstore could see me now.

"Hello?" I call out. "Any English Books here?" Silence. I hear a few mutterings in French, but I have enough of that at home.

Esmé returns with a paper containing a list of names. She takes a notebook from her desk, and a stack of maps. Maybe we're going on a treasure hunt?

She pulls the bag over her shoulder and strolls down the hallway. I'm upside down, a position that, while uncomfortable, allows me the opportunity to marvel at the height of the ceilings and their intricate designs. Were the architects expecting people to lie down to admire the details overhead?

Although, this being Paris, who knows how or where they were expecting their artwork to be appreciated.

This excess stimulation exhausts me. Back home, things were unsurprising. I had stopped noticing the street signs or the smells or the noises. I knew what they were and they fitted nicely into the expected, understandable and therefore ignorable. Here, nothing is predictable. I could spend an hour just taking in the details of one ceiling in one building. If only FRANÇOIS were here to share this with me. He'd probably laugh because he's likely seen a ceiling or two. But I'm sure he'd love to show me this one.

We move down the hallway, then descend a wide, wondrous staircase. The circular sweep of the banisters reaches three floors above. The metalwork is precise and refined, as if its creators expected it to be noticed by those who, like me, are viewing the world differently. These exquisite details are hidden in just one staircase. What other treasures are waiting to be discovered in this city?

We enter a large room with a kitchen at one end. Esmé removes the notebook, the maps and the list of names. She practices aloud: *"Jennifer Rice. Sandra Jackson. Desmond Wong."* These are names I can understand! I can feel my pages perk up. Finishing the list, she moves to the front of the room and opens two large double doors.

Standing in the doorway, she greets the Humans who trail in. The women are different than Esmé's friends: larger, louder, loosely dressed. Most are clutching a water bottle possessively.

Esmé speaks in English! I can understand, finally. *"Welcome to the Cordon Bleu,"* she says. She tells the group that this is the *"aff-day een-gleesh tour of the markets."* She hands them each a map and tells them that we will be visiting *"tee-pee-kell Parisian markets."* The Humans murmur with excitement.

"You are from where?" she asks.

"Chicago," says a large, smiling woman in what looks like a belted tent and orthopedic shoes. *"And we all just love the French."*

"That is nice. We love Americans too," says Esmé. That's not quite what I've experienced, but she undoubtedly knows more than I do. *"What is your name?"*

"I'm Jennifer." Pointing to a collection of people in bright colors, she introduces the others in the group.

"Hello, I'm Esmé," she says. Jennifer takes out a notepad and writes down this vital piece of information. *"And we go."* Esmé leads the herd of Chicagoans out the door. I'm going exploring in Paris! I'll have so much to tell FRANÇOIS when we get home.

CHAPTER 22

Parisian markets are so much more vibrant than I imagined, even in winter.

Esmé starts the tour by greeting a vendor standing behind a wall of tomatoes. Small, stacked baskets create a surprisingly effective presentation of red fruit masquerading as vegetables. She speaks to the vendor in French, then turns to the group to describe where he buys his tomatoes. Jennifer writes quickly in her notepad, while Desmond snaps photos on his phone.

I strain to hear how much Esmé's English has improved, and whether she's using words like 'porridge' and 'beckoned', or even 'spittoon'. And I want to hear her stories, so I can tell them to FRANÇOIS, or even DICTIONARY, and show them how Parisian I've become. They'd be impressed, I'm sure. I'm not going to be like the other American Books who only talk to each other. I'll learn some French. I'll show JERSEY JONES I can embrace another culture. I'm going to become more French than even Esmé. If only I could wear a scarf.

Esmé talks about the importance of knowing who you buy from, about relationships and history. I can't hear the word relationship without thinking of my *FRANÇOIS*. That's what I have now, a relationship. The thought makes me giddy.

Esmé takes two containers of tomatoes and drops them in another bag. She turns to the Humans and tells them that these will be perfect for the salad they'll be making. Their English-speaking voices purr in anticipation of food.

The group trails behind Esmé as she stops at a table piled with green leafy things. She says *"Bonjour"* to the vendor. I practice saying "Bonjour" in the way she does, dragging out the "ou". The rest will come easy. In a week or two, I'll be fully bilingual.

Esmé picks up three types of leaves and describes the difference—she says the spiky-looking one is peppery, the pale one is harder and therefore better to hold up to a warm dressing, and the larger leaf has more subtle flavors, better as a base for a more varied salad. I make a mental note about salad. The French seem obsessed with their food, so as I become more French, I need to know cuisine. Cuisine! There's another French word I know. Soon, I'll be forgetting words in English. Oh, how *FRANÇOIS* and I will laugh. Or whatever the verb for laugh is in French.

Jennifer picks up some leaves from the vendor's stall and smells them. He tuts at her. Confused, she looks at Esmé, who takes the leaves from her and hands them to the vendor. *"It is not like in America. You cannot touch,"* she tells Jennifer, Sandra and the rest of the tour.

"Why not?" Jennifer asks.

"Because we do not do it this way," Esmé says.

"That doesn't make any sense," Desmond says, snapping a photo of the vendor.

Esmé smiles politely at them, pays for the greens, garlic and onions, then leads them away.

"Jennifer's not going to like that," says a Book from somewhere.

"Who are you?" I ask.

"*THE COUNT OF MONTE CRISTO.* I'm Jennifer's Book."

"Are you American?" I ask.

"French, in English translation," he says.

"Why so quiet?" I ask. "I didn't even know you were there."

"It's my story. I'm about a man unjustly imprisoned in a fortress on his wedding day. So it's a force of habit. I forget that I can talk to others."

"How awful," I say. "The man speaks to no one?"

"He has just one person he can speak to," he says. I know what that feels like, having only one Book to talk to. "He learns about language and culture from him."

"Then maybe you can be like the character in your story? Teach me about the language and culture? How to be French?" I ask. Maybe I just need a tutor. A few tips, and I'll be on my way.

"No. I've decided my real story is about a daring escape from imprisonment before discovering treasure and seeking revenge. I'm planning to do the same, so I don't have time for a sidekick. I've got to remain nimble, go it alone." Just my luck, to find the only Book who doesn't want to make a friend. "Sometimes escape is the only solution," he says.

"I guess," I say, not really knowing what he's talking about. There's so much I don't understand here.

Esmé and the group stop for herbs. The tour's enthusiasm seems to be fading. Sandra has wandered to a vendor selling glasses and jars and Desmond is taking photos of her looking at glasses and jars.

"*Let's stay together,*" says Jennifer. Esmé smiles, appreciatively.

It's not until we stop at a stall with cheese that the group reassembles. Small white pyramids sit next to cream-colored rounds. The vendor cuts into a large, yellow wheel and produces slices so thin, they should be called gossamer cheese. No one in the group dares to touch anything that isn't handed to them.

In heavily accented English, the cheese vendor describes several types of cheese. Jennifer takes notes, Desmond takes more photos while Sandra proclaims she's lactose intolerant and strolls to a stall selling luggage.

We thread our way through other shoppers to reach the corner of the market and await Sandra, now pulling a rolling suitcase. We cross the street, turn right and after about 20 steps enter the source of an uplifting aroma. Another bakery. This city must survive on a high-carb diet.

Esmé and the others step one by one into the small shop, while Sandra fights to get her luggage through the door. A glass counter is to our right, stacked with rows of glistening, golden items, some with white powder, some with fruit, some with chocolate sneaking out the ends. Against the wall are shelves and baskets, filled with various shapes of bread.

After greeting the shop owner, Esmé turns to the group and begins describing the difference between baguettes, batards and brioches. A batard uses the same dough as a baguette, but is a shorter, wider loaf. Brioches have a high egg and butter content and can include milk and sugar. As a newly arrived Parisian, I listen intently. I can't cook like one, or dress like one, or talk like one, but I should be able to discuss bread like one. Clearly, it's essential in the country, as it turns out that baguette dough is defined by French law. I guess they don't have crime or corruption or pollution to worry about, so they can focus their legal system on what really matters.

The shop owner offers tastes of plain croissants and some with almonds and chocolate. His English isn't great, but he smiles broadly as he watches the visitors taste his creations. He wears the passion for his work on his face.

Esmé buys half a dozen baguettes and the Humans step up, one by one, to point and purchase items from the vendor. Except for Desmond. He doesn't taste the samples, he only photographs them.

The tour tumbles out of the shop and follows Esmé down the street. At the end of each block, she looks behind her to ensure she hasn't lost a straggler, or a piece of luggage. Three streets later, we turn right and see the now-familiar blue stripes that define the building's exterior, then, like waves, engulf the entrance.

Esmé opens doors to a room with chairs lined up before a counter. Behind it is a kitchen. Above it is a mirror. Pulling on a double-breasted white jacket, she moves through the space like a choreographed dancer. Two steps left, bend, reach, grab return. Four steps right, repeat.

Esmé announces she is showing the group how to make a traditional meal from Provence. She asks if anyone on the tour wishes to help her. They look at each other in silence then Jennifer says, *"I will,"* followed by *"Me too"* from Sandra.

"See?" I say to THE COUNT OF MONTE CRISTO. "That's my Reader doing the cooking. She's going to make this place smell great, with lots of spices and garlic."

"Jennifer's not going to like that," he says.

Esmé welcomes Jennifer and Sandra to the front and ties Cordon Bleu aprons around their waists. The others applaud, looking as if they wish they had been braver.

I watch with pride as Esmé confidently hands the vegetables and garlic to Sandra and the cheeses to Jennifer.

"Can we make it without garlic?" Jennifer asks.

"Non!" says Esmé. *"It must to have garlic."*

"But it seeps out of my pores for days," Jennifer says.

"Yes!" says Esmé. *"That is why it is good for you."*

"Here," Sandra says to Jennifer. *"Have some cheese."*

Jennifer takes a bite of cheese and seems placated. What was in bags is now displayed on the counter. Esmé circles oil into a pot, the blue flame biting at its bottom. Onion follows, as does garlic. The wonderful smell reminds me of FRANÇOIS. She tosses in some spices and herbs, then adds salt and pushes each item around as if they all had a preordained position. She adds sliced eggplant and tomatoes and covers the pot.

The cheeses and slices of bread are distributed for the Humans to taste as Esmé once again discusses the differences.

After checking on the pot, she blends vinegar, oil, lemon and more garlic in a small bowl. The Humans take notes as they watch the reflection of the pot in the overhead mirror. *"Et voilà,"* Esmé says with a wave of her wrist. A few Humans clap. I'm not sure they know what they've witnessed. I know I've just seen an expression of love.

They line up with a plate and receive a scoop of what she calls *ratatouille,* a dish from Provence. They each reach for a piece of bread. Murmurs bounce about the group as they consume what they saw purchased and prepared. Even Jennifer seems pleased with the dish. Esmé reminds them how simple it is to eat well, as she invites them to try the salad with pine nuts.

With their food consumed, Desmond aligns them for a group photo, then they pack up.

"Bye, COUNT," I say.

"Farewell," he says. And in a moment, the tour and my non-friend are gone.

Esmé piles the dirty dishes and pots in one corner, and returns her white jacket to a hook on the wall. She spends an hour cleaning the space, putting away the dishes and precisely replacing the utensils.

When the countertop gleams, she claps her hands and says, "*voilà*". She picks up the bag containing me, her class list and unused notebook. Within minutes, we're back in the metro with other end-of-the-day commuters. This time there's less to notice. It's simply the reverse of the morning, but with different advertising lining the walls.

As we get closer to home, my fibers tighten thinking about seeing FRANÇOIS again and telling him everything we did today. Maybe he'll notice my scent of garlic. Maybe he'll notice how much more Parisian I've become.

We open the front door and Esmé walks across her living room towards the table, where FRANÇOIS still lies. I remind myself to breathe.

She deposits me on the table near him. But I'm still in the mesh bag. I long to crawl towards him, but am trapped in the net. She removes her coat and enters the bathroom.

"FRANÇOIS," I whisper. "It's me. I'm home." No response. I repeat my call, a bit louder.

"Do you want every Book to hear you?" says DICTIONARY.

"No, I want FRANÇOIS," I reply.

"Looks like you'll be waiting a while. He's been sleeping all day."

I have so much to tell him. If only he'd stop snoring. I call to *François* again. If he can slip towards me, then at least we'll be able to whisper to each other about our day spent apart, but longing to be together. I want to tell him of my trip on the metro, of the market and the difference between types of bread. I'm sure he has so much he wants to talk to me about too. Life is so full when you're in love.

Esmé closes the drapes, turns off the lights and nestles in her bed. In the shrouded room, I can barely see my lover's outline. This feels like purgatory, being so close but unable to reach him. I resign myself to an evening without him. Tomorrow will be different. We'll find each other again. We'll laugh about our situation. He'll wrap his strong pages around me, and everything will be perfect. I fall asleep, hoping to dream of *François*.

CHAPTER 23

I have newfound respect for fish. I try to extend the foot of my pages, but I'm still trapped in the netting of her bag.

The winter sun streams through the windows. After her morning cleaning and coffee-making ritual, Esmé mercifully frees me from the bag. I stretch and try to work out the creases that have formed on my cover. They make me look so much older. I whisper to FRANÇOIS but he keeps sleeping. Poor thing must be exhausted.

Esmé sits down, places me in her lap with the notebook to her right and a small pencil primed to underline words she wishes to learn. Regrettably, this means that DICTIONARY is beside us. It's time to perform for Esmé and her pencil again.

Agnes sat in her room, <u>contemplating</u> her options: Follow her heart or follow the expectations of her family. Why couldn't she like what other girls liked, such as discussing the relevance of <u>bustles</u>? Life would be simpler if her aspirations ran the <u>gamut</u> from marriage to motherhood. That would be acceptable to her town. But it wouldn't be acceptable to her.

Esmé notes the underlined words in the notebook. I'm starting to question whether she's following my story at all, or just using me to improve her vocabulary.

"Why do you waste her time with words like 'bustles'? They fell out of fashion in the 1890s," the know-it-all DICTIONARY says.

"I can't help the words my Author gave me," I say.

"She should be learning language she'll actually use. Translating irrelevance is a waste of my time and talent."

"But you just translated bustle for her," I say. "If my language is irrelevant, then so is yours. At least I have a story to tell."

DICTIONARY says nothing. For once.

"And what happens when she learns enough English that she doesn't need you anymore? Did you hear her speak to the tour group yesterday? Oh, no you didn't. Because she never takes you anywhere," I say.

Again, he says nothing.

"She's learning a lot of English. Just you wait until her boyfriend shows up. You'll hear how well she speaks. Then she really won't need you. Your time will be up," I say. I get no response. This is the longest I've ever known DICTIONARY to be silent. Was I too harsh? Maybe he's more sensitive than his hardcover suggests. Should I apologize?

"Philistine," he mutters.

And with one word from him, all my concern about hurting his feelings evaporates.

Esmé turns the page and arrives at Katie's pencil mark on my page 132.

These words take me back to when I could understand what everyone was saying. It feels such a long time ago, when I was on the fireplace mantel, waiting for Book Club. I was so much younger then.

a young woman's struggle against society's expectations

Esmé looks up a word in DICTIONARY, takes out a pencil and writes in my margin.

I don't dare ask DICTIONARY what it means.

Finished reading for now, Esmé places me on top of FRANÇOIS, in a Book's yoga version of downward dog. I knew fate would draw us together.

"Hi," I whisper.

He responds with a snore.

I move my cover against his pages, trying to find a way to nestle into his spread.

"*Quoi*?" he says, startling as he wakes up.

"Hey," I whisper. "I missed you last night."

"*C'est qui*?" he says.

"Yes, me too," I say.

"He's asking who you are," shouts DICTIONARY from across the room. Every Book can hear. Has he no sense of discretion?

"You're lying," I say. "He knows exactly who I am." I thought I was being too harsh earlier, but DICTIONARY is so annoying, I can't help but add sharp edges to my words.

"Were I to knowingly misrepresent one language in another, I would have my membership in the Bilingual Dictionary Association revoked. I'm translating what he's saying. He doesn't know who you are."

"I don't believe you." I work my way into his pages and he responds by wrapping his strong fibers around me. I feel so daring, so Parisian, so maybe in love.

I'll show JERSEY JONES how wrong she was. We communicate. Sort of. I whisper, "Lac Qui Parle," a lake I know of in Minnesota. Then add "Belle Plaine," a town in Southern Minnesota. It's not the most romantic thing I could say to

la lutte d'une jeune femme dans la société

FRANÇOIS, but at least it's in French. He whispers back to me. This could be bliss.

Just as I am drifting into his embrace, I'm extracted. Esmé is dressed and is taking me for another trip. I call a goodbye to *FRANÇOIS* as we leave.

The metro isn't nearly as crowded today. Yet, when we reach daylight and the city, I can tell we're somewhere special. History drips from the café's awnings. This is the Paris of dreams, the Paris that everyone loves.

Esmé turns right, left, then right again. We walk half a block, then retrace our steps. She pulls out her phone and taps the screen. After a moment or three, she turns and asks about Shakespeare to a passerby. Shakespeare? We're going to a play? In the heart of Paris? This should be interesting.

We turn around and retrace our abandoned route. Another corner, another left and the purposefulness of her stride increases. Then a space opens up to a courtyard framed by trees. In front of a shop window are racks holding Books. Hundreds of them. Above the store is the sign: Shakespeare and Company. And around the storefront is a glorious collision of English phrases being spoken by English-language Books.

"Hi! What is this place?" I ask to any Book who'll answer.

"Shakespeare and Company. We're an English-language Bookstore," says one of the titles.

"Wow! I speak English. I'm from the States," I say.

"Yeah, we can tell by your accent," says the unidentified Book.

"There are so many of you!" I squeal.

"Most of us find our way here at some point in our life in Paris. It's like it says over there."

I look above the door to a sign that reads: "Be not inhospitable to strangers lest they be angels in disguise."

"She takes in Books like she takes in travelers. All are welcome here. You'll see."

Could I be in Book Heaven?

CHAPTER 24

We move through the glass front doors of Shakespeare and Company, a world so overflowing with Books, I may faint with joy.

Novels are aligned next to Dictionaries next to History Books. They remind me of the Forgotten Ones in the café, all different, but all happily chatting. Maybe Esmé will get a job here, and we can spend every day with these titles. Her working. Me telling my story and listening to others'. At the end of the day, she would come home to her apartment, and I would come home to FRANÇOIS. Then I would be truly happy.

We pass titles stacked on side tables, stools and chairs. Shelves are bowed under the weight of Books. Even the staircase to the upper floor doubles as a Bookshelf. If there's a flat surface, it's holding up a title. The speakers in the shop emit a raspy male voice singing about answers blowing in the wind. I've heard him before. "Who's this singer?" I ask to anyone listening.

"Aren't you American? That's Bob Dylan. Everyone knows that," says a title stuck under a pile of others.

"Of course I've heard of him. I just haven't heard him,"

I say, with more defensiveness than I intended. I didn't think I'd need to explain my American-ness in Paris.

As Esmé steps around towers of boxes and stacks of titles struggling to remain upright, *THE JOY OF DECLUTTERING* moans about her disorganized environment. We move through a series of small rooms, each one filled with Humans browsing, holding, reading. In the back of the store we pass rows of Philosophy and Sociology Books before snaking back to Fiction and my kind of titles. She looks around then retraces our steps.

Speaking English, Esmé asks the Book Seller about titles for Americans living in Paris. I am proud that I've played a small role in her linguistic progress.

The Book Seller walks us to a wall where every title is arguing about Paris and how it differs from cities in North America. From *HOW TO SUCCEED IN PARIS* and *HOW TO DRESS LIKE YOU LIVE IN PARIS*, to *THE RULES FOR FRENCH LIVING*, the wall is heaving with opinion. Some Books describe the ways of the French with joy—the pace of life, the embrace of food, art and politics. Others complain about years of feeling 'foreign', of craving the space of home. So many have come to Paris before me. So many have struggled here. I thought after a week, maybe two, I'd be all settled in, but I'm not. I don't want to spend my life feeling like a stranger, an outsider. I wonder how you say 'stranger' in French? There's a Book by Albert Camus in front of me. Maybe I'll ask him.

Esmé picks up *THE RULES FOR FRENCH LIVING*.

"Hi," I say.

"Rule number 6—speak only French," the Book replies.

"But you're speaking to me in English."

"I'm written in English, what do you expect?"

"So it's okay for you to speak English, but not for me?"

"If you want to be happy living here, you must embrace the language," she says.

"Again, my point is, you aren't."

"But I can't."

"So you don't follow your own advice," I say.

"Rule number 9—choose French friends."

"Do you only speak in rules?"

"No, I have tips in my sidebars too. Lots of them. Useful ones about the metro and the bus, about dressing appropriately, wearing scarves and spending time in cafés."

"So . . . do you actually like it here?"

"It's Paris. We're all meant to love it here."

"That's not what I asked."

"Honestly?" THE RULES whispers. "I never have. But I fake it. How can I be a helpful Book on living in France, when I don't want to be here myself?"

"Where do you want to be?" I ask.

"In a wide open space. Where I can see mountains and rivers. Maybe Montana. It would be romantic, I think."

"Paris is romantic," I say, my cover growing warm as I think of FRANÇOIS. "It has been for me, anyway."

"Well, I've been here two years and nothing. Not even a whiff of it."

"I know a Book you might like, SUNDOWN AT SADDLE ROCK. He loves the plains, the big sky."

"When can I meet him?" THE RULES asks.

"Well, there's one problem. He's in a coffee shop in San Francisco," I say. "Or he was last time I saw him."

"Some good that's going to do me," THE RULES says. "So tell me about your love life."

I opt for silence.

"Ooh, saying nothing speaks volumes. You've fallen in love. Okay, Rule number 3—always be interested in others. So tell."

"Well, he's French," I say.

"Of course."

"We met on a table. And it was . . . amazing."

"Was? So this is a past tense love?"

"No. It's present tense. Absolutely. Sort of. He's just been tired lately."

"Rule number 11—don't expect the French to be like you."

"Do your rules actually work?" I ask. "If I follow your advice, do I become Parisian?" I could use some assimilation assistance.

"Do you know where my Author is now?" THE RULES asks. I shake my cover No. "Vermont. She couldn't stand it here and left. She didn't even take her own advice. I hear she's now making homemade jams and marketing them as 'Confitures de Montpellier'."

"I guess not all of us can be who we want," I say. But I'm not sure this is true. Am I who I want to be? Or am I simply a reflection of my story? I never had these thoughts before I came here. Maybe being Parisian makes me deep.

More Human voices, all chattering in English, enter. They sound like home.

"This place is a good compromise," I hear from another Book.

"Are you speaking with me?" I ask.

"Well, you're about to become one of us, so yeah, this is my welcome pep talk. I'm HARDCASTLE AT SEA."

"What's your genre?" I ask, dropping in a French word to demonstrate my sophistication.

"Historical fiction. I'm the second in a series of pirate novels."

"Any good?" I ask.

"If you like over-described sword fights, a few anachronistic references to rigging, and bodices that have a habit of popping open at inopportune times, then yeah, I'm fabulous."

I smile at his honesty. I'm starting to believe that we all have a page count that we need to fill, whether we have anything to say or not. "Nice to meet you, HARDCASTLE," I say. "I wish we had more time to talk."

"We'll have plenty of time. Trust me. Not much else to do here other than talk."

"I'm just passing through with my Reader," I say.

"Hah. That's what we all thought."

"What do you mean?" I ask.

"Why else would she have brought you? Probably to trade you in for a new one. We're all victims of small spaces and short attention spans."

"Absolutely not," I say. "She hasn't finished me yet. She's only at the part where my main character is getting ready to leave home. There's so much more to discover."

"Maybe. Or maybe she's tired of you. Nothing personal, of course. But half of us are here because travelers are done with us and want something new to take with them on the next part of their journey. The other half are here because people with a desire to learn English tried to run before they could walk. Twenty pages in, they gave up and went back to Books that they didn't need to translate. So Sylvia, our Book Seller, takes us in and gives us a second chance. This place is so over-crowded, it takes an excavator to find a title. But it's warm and dry, no dogs or liquids, and what it lacks in breathing room, it makes up for in conversation. You'll never be lonely. The glue in your spine might dissolve before you find another home, but overall, we're happy to be here."

This isn't true. It can't be. Esmé wouldn't give up on me

so soon. Through me, she's learned words like 'bustle' and 'undergarment'. "I'm sure it's nice here, but really, my Reader is keeping me." I can hear the confidence in my voice crack.

"That's what I said when I was first carried through those doors. But look what she's holding: THE RULES FOR FRENCH LIVING and a French novel. There is a whole section of new French Books, precisely for those who are leaving us as a trade-in. Our Book Seller figures it's better if they leave with a Book, than with no Book. It happens probably a dozen times a day, double that on a Saturday."

I look at Esmé. She's gazing at the French novel with a fondness that she's never had for me. She always has a crease between her brows when she reads me, but now her eyes are large and welcoming. As she reads page one of the French novel, she laughs. She's never laughed at anything on my pages—and I can be funny. Sometimes. But she's always more worried about the meaning of my words than the meaning of my story. It's like I'm just a source for English words, like a Dictionary.

She gently turns to the Book's next page, careful not to crack the spine. It's been so long since mine was broken. I remember the fear I had. Would it hurt? Would anyone want me once I had been fully opened? I'm envious of the French Book in Esmé's hands. It has the power to delight her in a way I never will.

"*Le vent de ses mots lui frappe comme une chausseur,*" Esmé reads aloud.

The Book Seller says, "*Ah, Naniesque.*"

"*It is good?*" Esmé asks. She turns over the Book to read its backside.

"*It's popular,*" says the Book Seller. "*And it's short, so it's a quick read.*"

Is this the moment that I'm traded in for something younger, easier, French? Am I being cast away again? I cannot believe this is my fate, to meet my love, only to be separated from him to be left amid thousands of other abandoned attempts at bilingualism.

"With so many other great, used titles, you'd think they'd buy something else," says a Book from the middle of a stack of trade paperbacks.

"Everyone wants the new new. What's hot, not what's great. It's Human's nature," says another Book.

"Oh, why can't they move you back to Social Sciences where you belong? I get so sick of non-fiction's perspective," says the first Book.

The Book Seller picks me up and looks at me. *"I haven't seen this title before,"* she says. *"Want to trade it for another book?"* My fibers are frozen in fear.

"Non, merci," Esmé smiles. *"I must to finish it."* My cover flushes, just like with *FRANÇOIS*, but this time with relief and hope. Maybe Esmé is my forever Reader after all.

Esmé pulls me towards her, and hands *NANIESQUE* and *THE RULES* to the Book Seller.

"Interesting choice," says the Book Seller, pointing to *THE RULES*.

"Not for me," smiles Esmé. *"For my boyfriend. For Valentine's."*

"Bonne chance," the Book Seller says.

She thinks Tariq is becoming Parisian? Good luck with that. I'm trying every day and it's really hard. But she reminds me that it's Valentine's Day soon. What do I give a Book of French poetry on the most romantic day of the year?

CHAPTER 25

As we walk through the glass doors, out of the bliss of Book world and into the car horns and smells of Paris, I shout a goodbye to the English-language titles. While many seem fated to spend the rest of their readable lives here, there is a sense of joy among them. It's not the dream of any Book to be ignored, but they do seem cared for, if not individually, then collectively.

I glimpse the Book Seller through the window. She's smiling, pointing new customers to a stack of Books. She seems dedicated to her store and her charges. If only more Humans had her perspective, we would have a better-read world.

Leaving the ornate door and the unadorned piles of titles behind, I think about all those Books in the store. We meet so many on our journey, for such a brief time. There are so many stories I'll never hear.

"Did you like the Bookstore?" I ask NANIESQUE. "The Book Seller seemed nice."

She mutters something in French. No hope for a new friend here.

"Told you, that's the French," THE RULES FOR FRENCH LIV-ING says.

"Then you speak with her," I say.

"*Bonjour,*" THE RULES say. "*Où sont les toilettes?*"

"What did you just say?"

"Where are the restrooms?"

"Why did you ask that?"

"All I've got is phrases about renting a car, getting a hotel room and asking for directions," she says. "What do you expect?"

Back in the metro, I hear a male Book calling to NANIESQUE by name. She purrs with the attention. This time, I feel fortunate to be linguistically immune from the conversation.

A change of trains, a short walk and we're in our squeaky elevator and back home. Esmé places me, THE RULES and NANIESQUE face-up on the table.

FRANÇOIS, looking so rugged, is within whispering distance of me on the table. It's as if he was waiting for my return. I have so much to tell him about my day. I ask DICTIONARY to translate.

"I had such a great day, FRANÇOIS. We went around the Latin Quarter and found this phenomenal Bookstore. Have you been? It's a happy place, filled with great conversation."

"*Bonjour,*" he utters.

"*Bonjour,*" I reply, trying to elongate my 'ou's, like Esmé does. "It was English-speaking, but still Parisian. I loved it. I felt at home for the first time since I've been here. I made lots of new friends. Bob Dylan music was playing—he's really popular back home, everyone loves him. And the Book Seller seemed really nice. She told Esmé that she hopes everyone finds a treasure in her store. I like Humans who think we're treasures, don't you? Because we are, you know. Every one of us." I look at him and his strong spine. I have to say it. "Especially you."

FRANÇOIS says something that I don't understand, but his tone is soothing. I wish Books printed in one language could learn another language. It would allow me to understand my love, and avoid the need to engage with DICTIONARY.

NANIESQUE, however, responds. It's a bit rude, butting into our conversation. FRANÇOIS makes another comment, which makes her giggle. I guess he's just being polite. She is new here, after all. He's probably introducing her to the others. He continues speaking with her and she purrs. She doesn't have many pages, so can't have much to say.

"I told you so," I hear, in a deep English tone.

"Told me what?" I ask.

"About FRANÇOIS, but you didn't listen."

"What about FRANÇOIS?" I ask.

"He's serialized. With him, it's just one Book after the other."

I stare at DICTIONARY, unbelieving yet somehow comprehending. My fibers shake.

Can this be true? No, FRANÇOIS said he loved me. I think. And he meant it, didn't he? I've never felt that way before. How could he not want what we have?

I watch FRANÇOIS and the new novel. She's freshly printed. She doesn't have a mark on her. She's thin with a Parisian-looking cover. She's filled with all those accents on the vowels and those curvy things hanging from her çs, like FRANÇOIS.

I ask DICTIONARY what it is. "It's called a cedilla. It makes the c sound like an s," he says.

"Whatever," I snap. I haven't got one. I don't have any accents. Just apostrophes. And she's got those too, but in different places. How can I compete?

"He's *FRANÇOIS*. What did you expect?"

"But he said I was special . . . Didn't he?"

"No he did not. He said he wanted you to go away, but you were so sure you understood him, you didn't bother to ask me to translate."

DICTIONARY can't be right. This can't be happening.

"Do you know how many Books he's been through?"

I shake my cover No. I don't want to listen to what *DICTIONARY* has to say.

"Do you think you're the first to fall for his rugged cover? There's a whole shelf of Books over there, destined to watch him seduce every new female title that Esmé brings in here. Some still weep over him. Some want to see him burn. You're in good company. If it's any consolation, many have come before you, and as you see, many will come after you."

"But he said . . . " I try to infuse resilience into my voice, yet it cracks under the fear of the response.

"I know what he said. Remember? I translated it for you. I've heard him use the same lines on so many Books here. He consumes them. He finds the new one, the fresh one, often the one that doesn't have any friends, the one that is looking to fit in. He conquers them, then finds another. If Esmé ever stopped buying new Books, he'd be lost," says *DICTIONARY*.

"What's wrong with me? Why doesn't he want me anymore?" I hear the futility in my voice. I sound like *BEACHED LOVE* from the Bookstore. But that's how I feel—like I'm trapped in a bad love story and can't get out. "Isn't this where you're supposed to tell me how great I am? That the problem is him? He just can't commit? But he'll realize what he's lost and come back to me? That's what happens in every romance novel I've met."

"I'm a Dictionary. I'm not typeset for stories or emotion. I'm here to state linguistic facts. You want a cover to cry on, go talk to any one of those novels on the third shelf. They've all been there."

"All of them?" I ask. Again, I don't think I want to know the answer to that question.

"And more. When Esmé is finished with a Book, she brings home a new one. It's perfect for him. Always more freshly printed titles arriving, knowing no one, needing a friend—or more than a friend."

"How long has he been here?" I ask.

"Long enough," says DICTIONARY. "Once she left her boyfriend's place, she moved us all here and FRANÇOIS was one of the first Books she bought. He was used when he arrived, but that just seemed to give him more of an edge with the fresh, new novels. He could talk about the cafés he's seen, the Bookstores he's survived, the people he's entertained with his poetry."

"But I've done those things too, and in a different country. Doesn't that make me interesting?" I ask.

"It's not like he's been listening to you, has he?"

I thought he was. Why was I so stupid?

"It's just who he is. A serial monographist. Esmé has Books on Freud and Jung on her shelves. They argue regularly about him. But trust me, the only one surprised by his behavior is you."

"The other Books have been watching us?" I ask.

"What else do we have to do?" DICTIONARY says.

He's got a point there. And I'm sure they're talking behind my blurb. I'm going to be left on the shelf, with everyone knowing what happened.

Hell is other Books.

CHAPTER 26

Love should be outlawed.

Ten days have passed, during which I've been forced to witness FRANÇOIS and NANIESQUE performing the dance of the seven signatures. He whispers. She giggles and purrs. That used to be me. Now it's her. It will never be me again. My only relief is in not understanding their cooing.

She'll have her heart broken. Soon. Although I expected it to have happened by now. Esmé hasn't brought home any new Books, so NANIESQUE is still the freshest title here. That's clearly the only reason they're still together. I can't believe she's falling for his rough pages. She'll regret it.

But no one asks my opinion. In fact, no one asks me anything, other than DICTIONARY, and that's a conversation barely worth having. I'm surrounded by Books and completely alone. What was once my home has become my prison. I should have found a way to stay at Shakespeare and Company, surrounded by fiction and non-fiction titles, from decades past and just printed. I could always make friends in English. In another language, it's not so easy.

Esmé opens me on her lap to my page 149. She looks at Katie's notes, penciled in my margin, turns me sideways and reads.

In the depth of my misery, I still must do my Book duty. The written life can be cruel.

> Henry and James, her mother, father and sisters stood around her. They looked at her with confusion and concern, except her sisters Christina and Sara, whose eyes were filled with pride. She wanted to say so much to them all, explain again why she had to go, but they didn't want to listen. Agnes had heard it all her life: what girls were meant to do. She never once heard what boys were meant to do. It seems no one thought about that.
>
> Agnes knew that if she didn't go now, she'd never leave. Her entire life would be lived between Main Street and Douglas Street, and the horizon she stared at each morning through the window would never be discovered.
>
> She kissed her mother and father, hugged her sisters, waved goodbye to Henry and James and climbed into the wagon. She was leaving Rose Valley behind.

Her phone rings and she sets me aside. She glows as she says the name Tariq. I used to be like that when I thought of FRANÇOIS. Instead, I'm now a witness to wasted love.

Tidying the apartment, Esmé rearranges all of us, placing DICTIONARY and me on the side table with THE RULES FOR FRENCH LIVING. She puts NANIESQUE and FRANÇOIS along with a loud and opinionated Book on French cinema, on the smaller Bookshelf. The three of them look good together in

where Agnes is forced to decide— expectation or dream?

their stacked pyramid. But it means that FRANÇOIS is on the bottom, French cinema in the middle and NANIESQUE on the top. Hah! They have a chaperone. And one that was printed 40 years ago. He'll be a lot of fun, then.

The wine rack is full, the half-fridge and breadbasket are overflowing, and the fruit bowl is reminiscent of Carmen Miranda's headdress. Esmé smiles at her achievement. A shower, some makeup, a new dress, and she leaves for the airport and Tariq.

While she's gone, a hush comes over us. We all know how important this arrival is to her. DICTIONARY tells me that this will be the first man she's brought into her home since her unhappy split from her last boyfriend. I hope this one works out. She's nice. She deserves someone nice.

I try to catch up on the lost rest that the trauma of failed love can impart on those, like me, who suffer from being too sensitive. I must have succeeded, because a loud thud disturbs my respite from misery. I raise my cover to see the cause of the disturbance. A duffle bag has been dropped on the floor. A tall man has his left arm around Esmé's waist. She is looking at him with dilated pupils and a delirious smile. The Love Boat has dropped anchor.

She gives him the brief tour of her small apartment. They punctuate each point with a kiss. Their happiness is stifling the room.

"So that's him?" asks DICTIONARY.

"He's kind and good to her," I say. "She likes him."

"He's lacking . . . panache."

"Who needs panache?" I ask.

"Clearly not you," he says.

I liked DICTIONARY better when he wasn't speaking to me.

With glasses full of wine, they intertwine on the sofa. I'm happy for her. Miserable for myself.

After an hour of kissing, they move to the bedroom. Mercifully, they shut the door, so I don't need to witness their passion. But this Human display of hormones has elevated the efforts of *FRANÇOIS*. I want to know what he's saying, but then again, I don't. I want to ask *DICTIONARY* what's being discussed, but I won't.

I'm surrounded by love, but lacking it myself. It's torturous, watching my ex-Bookfriend love someone else, while my Reader lives her own love story. The other French novels must be laughing at my stupidity. What was once my home is now my purgatory.

What did I do to deserve this as my story?

CHAPTER 27

Humans have no idea how lucky they are.

If I could walk like them, I'd be up, moving about, seeing the world. Tariq and Esmé spend all their day in bed. Being stuck lying on my back most of my life, and not by choice, I can confirm that horizontal is overrated.

Yet this morning, there is movement. They are both showering, having coffee and getting dressed. They actually look like they are going to leave the apartment. He's been here three days and all he's seen of Paris is the view from her apartment windows. Maybe he's an uncurious traveler. Maybe he's agoraphobic. Or maybe he's in love.

Esmé opens her purse and drops in THE RULES FOR FRENCH LIVING. They turn to the door, but she stops. She must have left her keys. But no. She picks me up and hands me to him.

"Here is the book where you put the photographs," she says. *"When I read it, I think of you. And voilà, you are here."*

I can feel my cover expand with pride in his hands. I guess I did have a purpose here after all, a role in their love affair.

"Bring the book with us. I want to read it by the Seine. I've always wanted to read by the Seine," he says.

She drops me in her bag, next to *The Rules for French Living*. Relief flows through me. I have a chance to escape the incessant love-fest between *François* and that novelette, and *Dictionary's* gloating. My misery is alleviated for a day.

"Have fun," I shout to *Dictionary* as we leave, knowing that the closest he comes to fun is the definition he gives it.

"I guess it's time to see more of Paris than just your bedroom," Tariq says. Esmé radiates happiness. I used to be like that.

"Tomorrow we can have lunch with my brother Alexandre," she says.

"Great. How old is he?" Tariq asks.

"He has just 21 years," she says. Tariq smiles.

"What?" asks Esmé.

"He is just 21."

Esmé thinks for a moment. *"He is just 21,"* she repeats.

"Exactly," says Tariq.

"See how good I'm learning English?" she says. He smiles, grabs her hand and they take the stairs to the metro.

Waiting on the platform, *The Rules* distracts me from my laments. "Has Esmé had you long?"

"She got me in San Francisco," I say.

"And this guy?"

"Same."

"So that's my mark," she replies.

"His name is Tariq," I say.

"No, I mean my mark, the one I'm working on. No one reads me for pleasure," she says. "I've gotta be persuasive. Convince someone to move here."

"Do you succeed?"

"Not often. My latest Reader traded me in for an Agatha Christie. I have a lot of unused advice to give."

Poor Tariq. He doesn't know what's about to hit him.

We enter the metro and I return to my solitude. Rather than Paris, maybe I need a nunnery. While I am contemplating my spiritual future, we change trains, and emerge from a new station, one that's not on her regular line. How can I pay attention to my internal conflict when I have to pay attention to the external challenges of life? Again, I see the power of a nunnery. All you have to do is sit and think. And maintain a vow of silence. I could do that.

We exit the *Metropolitain* to an area of Paris I've never seen. We turn and walk, then I see it. Notre Dame. The flying buttresses, the gargoyles, the spire, the stained glass. It's enormous but somehow delicate. Imposing yet welcoming. If only Quasimodo would swing down and save me.

Tariq must be a builder, because he is enthralled by what he sees. Or maybe he's just enthralled by Esmé.

The scene is so Parisian, I can almost hear accordions. I want to squeal with joy—me, by the Seine, with a view of Notre Dame and the bridges over the river. It's like we're on a movie set. It's stunning—the color, the light, the river glinting, the glassed-in boats passing us. When Humans build something beautiful, they really get it right. Too bad it's such a rare occurrence.

Tariq and Esmé find a bench. I hope they stay here, as this is the most stunning view I've ever seen. Another couple arrives and sits on the end of our bench. They start kissing. So do Tariq and Esmé. That seems to be the required activity here, as even people walking past seem to stop and kiss each other. Maybe that's why Notre Dame was placed here, as a sanctuary for the loveless, removed from the happiness of others.

I guess even kissing has a time limit, as eventually Tariq and Esmé take a break.

"Where's that book you brought?" Tariq asks.

Esmé hands me to him. *"Read it to me,"* she says. She snuggles next to him as Tariq opens me at my page 155 and clears his throat. By removing the Bookmark, he's cleared mine. I begin my riverside performance.

It seemed as if the train would never arrive. Agnes was going all the way to Minneapolis. A big city. She could barely stand the agony of waiting.

She knew the train was going to be slow and bumpy. She had heard the stories dozens of times, but now they were going to be her stories.

A young girl, maybe 12 years old, was standing, waiting.

"On your own?" Agnes asked her.

The young girl nodded.

"Would you like to sit with me?"

The girl smiled and nodded more vigorously.

A large man in a uniform approached them. "Joining us?"

"Yes, I'm Agnes and this is . . . " Agnes looked at the girl, awaiting her to fill in the silence.

"Sara."

Agnes smiled at her. "I have a sister named Sara. I can tell we're going to be great friends."

"My mother says that my aunt is meeting me at the station. All I must do is sit on the train," Sara said.

"Well, that's a good start," said the man. "I'm Mister Johnson, your conductor."

Sara half-curtseyed. He smiled and half-bowed.

"We'll take real good care of you two," he said and helped Agnes and Sara onto the train. They sat by the window, looking at the movement of people and the postal bags that filled the station.

The train pulled away and they gazed at the fields that blended into the horizon. Agnes looked at Sara, younger than her own sisters, and wondered if they would have the courage to make this trip on their own. Or whether she would have at such a young age.

An hour into the journey, Mr. Johnson entered the passenger car. "We have to slow down for a while. The muskeg's a little soft this time of year. The weight of the train sinks the rails." He looked to Agnes with a smile. "They say our train is the only one that travels uphill in both directions."

Two women hopped off the front of the train, clutching baskets. Agnes was shocked to see them disembark. She stood up to watch them through the window. They both picked blackberries that were growing by the side of the track. When their baskets were half-filled, they leapt onto the back of the train as it passed.

Agnes watched the women return to their seats with their fresh fruit. One of the women noticed Agnes noticing her. "Care for some blackberries?" she asked.

"What is muskeg?" Esmé asks.

"Soggy ground. We'll never need to worry about it," he says, and kisses her again. He closes me and gazes at my cover. *"THE SERENDIPITY OF SNOW,"* he says.

"Serendipity. Happy accident," she says. See? She's learned something from me.

Tariq smiles at her. *"I know. It's like how we met. That was serendipity."*

"Oui," she says, kissing him again. She waves her arm in front of the view, like a salesperson in front of a used car. *"You like Paris?"*

"Who wouldn't? It's beautiful."

"Good. Because I bought for you something." Esmé pulls out THE RULES FOR FRENCH LIVING and gives it to him. *"For Saint-Valentin."*

He passes me back to Esmé and takes the Book. *"Thanks, maybe I can learn a few things before I go."*

"Maybe you do not must to go," she says.

"You mean me live here?"

"I haven't even had a chance with this guy and he's already rejecting me," says THE RULES.

"Yeah, I guess you're not the kind of Book a Reader wants as a gift. They'd prefer to buy you themselves," I say. "Like the Self-help and Weight-loss Books I used to know at a Bookstore I lived in a long time ago. Not a good first choice for a gift Book."

"Hey, I never thought of that. I'm always given to people. I've never been bought by someone wanting my information. So my success rate isn't my fault," says THE RULES. And with that realization, THE RULES turns inward to her own sanctuary.

After a moment, Esmé asks, *"You don't want to live here?"*

"Don't you want to live in the States? You already speak English," he says.

"You can to learn French," Esmé says.

Can't fault the flaw in either argument.

A sense of desperation seems to pass between them. *"We'll talk about this later,"* he says. *"It's getting cold."* He passes THE RULES to her. They stroll with a newly acquired weight of pensiveness.

Who knew love could be so sad? Between my misery with
FRANÇOIS and the unhappiness hanging between these two,
I almost feel like I need to find a new home. But that's not
what I thought my story was about. I expected I would find
one Reader and a forever shelf. Life isn't what I thought it was
going to be. It's so much more. And so much harder.

Could THE COUNT OF MONTE CRISTO be right? Is escape the
only solution? Maybe I need to take courage from the courage
of Agnes. After all, how can I tell her story if I don't have the
same spirit that she does?

We approach a cluster of green sheds. Prints and postcards
of the cathedral, the Eiffel Tower and the Seine hang off their
corners. Esmé and Tariq walk to the third shed filled with
magazines, newspapers and Books. They nod at an older man
organizing his merchandise. He has the air of a long-time Book
Keeper, still proud of his titles.

Esmé places me on top of a stack of newspapers and speaks
to the Book Keeper, who points to his left. Esmé replies *"Merci."*
She shows the notepad to Tariq. *"The café I want to show you is
still there,"* she says. *"I heard it was to close, but he says no. So that
is good. We can to have a drink there."*

Tariq looks through postcards hanging from the Book Keeper's shed. Esmé takes her cue and begins thumbing through
Books.

"How far is the Champs-Elysées?" he asks. *"It's where the Arc
de Triomphe is, right?"*

As Esmé and Tariq politely discuss sights to see and days
on which to see them, I realize that this is my chance. I
channel the spirit of Agnes. If she can leave the security of
home, so can I. A French magazine with a glossy cover is
under me, and stacks of newspapers are folded to my left.

I only need to crawl under one of the newspapers to hide and perhaps escape having to go back to the apartment and FRANÇOIS' rejection.

I test the magazine for movement. It must be all celebrity gossip, as its cover is so slick, it's like moving on ice. Esmé is buying gum and a magazine, while Tariq continues to look at postcards. I can't believe I am considering fleeing a Reader and her home, but heartbreak does strange things.

The Book Keeper moves Esmé's bag to reach for another magazine and I have my opportunity. A slight shift of his inventory gives me the momentum I need to slide along the surface of the glossy magazine and insert myself between two newspapers, stacked but forgotten.

I hold my breath as the vendor shows her a magazine. She nods and he adds it to the growing pile of purchases. Am I doing the right thing? She is trying so hard with Tariq, should I try harder with FRANÇOIS? Maybe I can change. Maybe I can find a way to make him love me again.

Then the words of DICTIONARY replay in my memory: "Do you think you're the first to fall for his rugged cover? There's a whole shelf of Books over there, destined to watch him seduce every new female title that Esmé brings in here . . . You're in good company." No, I'm doing the right thing. I have to leave and hope that where I'm going is better, happier. I can't stay where I'm not loved.

Esmé pays for their purchases and grabs her bag. She says "Merci" to the Book Keeper. Tariq gives her a kiss and puts his arm around her. They continue their stroll along the Seine, looking like one of the postcards for sale at this green shed. They've found love, as geographically challenged as it is. I've found loss.

I tell myself to relax, that I've done the right thing. There comes a time in every Book's life when they have to write their own story. I guess this is my time. I inhale and try not to fall apart at the spine when I hear: "You're quite the Book."

"Was she that bad?"

I look around. "Who said that?"

"Us. Over here, on the rack."

"You speak English!"

"Guilty as charged," says one Book.

"Hey, you sound almost like us," says another. "American?"

"Yes!" I say.

"Well, how do you like that. Another Yank. 'Bout time. I'm THE DAME WORE MINK. But my friends just call me THE MINK. This is my buddy THE BIG APPLE HEIST. He goes by MR. BIG. What's your name?"

"I'm THE SERENDIPITY OF SNOW."

"Ooh, big word," THE MINK says. "A cute gal like you needs a snappy name."

"Agreed. What about Fifi?" MR. BIG says.

"Nah. Too French. Frieda?" THE MINK asks.

"No way. Remember Frieda from Fresno? This one's no Frieda, and that's a good thing, too."

"How about Trixie?" THE MINK asks.

"Yeah, Trixie," MR. BIG says.

"Hey, you guys. Do I have a say in this?" I get no response. Trixie it is. I guess I've been called worse. "So what are you guys about?" I ask.

They talk over each other. "Broads, gams, guns. Exciting stuff."

"How long have you been here?" I ask.

"Don't know anymore, don't care," THE MINK says. "We're just two Americans in Paris and loving every minute of it."

"How did you get here?" I ask.

"Traded in by a French dame. She picked us up in a second-hand shop in Chicago when she was over there studying. Brought us here. Guess we was too much for her. But that's okay, 'cause look at the view," THE MINK says.

"Yes, Notre Dame is spectacular," I say.

"Not Notre Dame. I mean *the* dames. They're a knockout in this town."

"Ooh là là," MR. BIG says.

"So, no English Readers coming by?" I ask, trying to change the subject.

"None interested enough in two single Books-about-town like us. Things are a bit slow, you know? But when the spring comes, man, it's gonna be great," THE MINK says.

"A word to the wise, Trixie. If you wanna last in this joint, he's gotta see you first," MR. BIG says.

He's right. I've done a fine job of hiding under these newspapers. Time to extract myself and catch the Book Keeper's attention. He's a large man, with gray, thinning hair that reacts to every whisper of the wind. His small gold-rimmed glasses sit atop his puffy cheeks. A navy scarf is looped twice around his neck.

His hands are covered in half-gloves, ones that warm the palm but leave the fingers free. His left hand releases the top of a large thermos. A stream of hot chocolate twists itself into his cup. As he focuses on his warm beverage, I focus on my movement.

"Light a fire under it, Trixie" THE MINK says. "He don't linger over his liquids."

I curl my back cover and move just enough to see from under the newspaper. I look towards the Book Keeper who is still attending to his beverage. A voice causes him to turn to his right. He takes a few steps in the direction of the voice and I am free of his scrutiny.

"Now's your chance, Trix," MR. BIG shouts. "The coast is clear."

Curl, reach, curl, reach, curl, reach. I repeat these motions to propel myself across the top of the magazine. It's exhausting. I'm out of shape and I know that I'll pay for all this activity tomorrow, but if I don't do it, I won't have a tomorrow. My fibers are exhaling heavily, when I hear, "He's coming!" I stop, my fate to be determined by the whims of a stranger, a Frenchman with a riverside stall.

The Book Keeper picks me up. I smile my biggest smile hoping to inspire him to keep me. He looks at my cover: *"Se-ren-di-pi-tee. Je connais pas ce mot,"* he says to himself. I was a Book about snow being sold during the summer in San Francisco. Now I'm an unpronounceable title in a Parisian winter. I guess no one said it was going to be easy.

He places a piece of paper on my cover, secures it with an uncomfortable paper clip then drops me in an empty rack.

"What does it say?" I ask MR. BIG.

"One euro," he replies. "Sorry, doll."

CHAPTER 28

I 'm in a shack in Paris, my worth measuring as low as possible. I think I've hit bottom, but then I glance at the magnificence around me and think: No. Like Agnes, I've chosen my destiny. At least mine comes with a view.

But spending all day hanging on a rack, with a paper clip on one's cover isn't exactly the pinnacle of success. And, I'm discovering, there is such a thing as too much fresh air.

When the light begins to fade, so does our Book Keeper. He unhooks the postcards from their display, and lays them on the first tier of Books. Then he stacks the posters of Paris on top. I am placed next to the postcards, along with a few other Books. He folds his stool, and puts it on the second tier of Books. He collects his now-empty thermos, pulls on his coat that has been hanging off the roof of the shed, and takes keys from its pocket. He reaches behind us to coax the tired-sounding hinges. Slowly, light fades as the roof of the shed lowers. A lock clicks shut. We are all here, together, in the dark. Good thing I'm not claustrophobic.

French chatter fills the darkness. "These Frenchies never shut up," THE MINK says.

"What, and you do?" MR. BIG says.

Amid the darkness and the foreign language and the cold I take stock of my decision. I've got two friends, sort of. They seem nice, sort of. Tomorrow I'll have another day to look at one of the most glorious views in the world. And maybe, one day, someone will take me home. But until then, I'm safe in a shed by the Seine in Paris. Even if it does smell like tobacco and rust.

Despite the unheated accommodations, I sleep well. I only wake when I hear the sound of the lock being turned. Our Book Keeper has returned to allow in the day.

The roof of our enclosure reluctantly opens and my world moves from complete darkness to glorious winter sunshine. The light bounces from the Seine to the windows across from us, bringing blues and yellows to the gray stone buildings. Humans pass with brightly colored scarves warming their necks. Despite the now-freezing temperatures, these shades of life reassure me that I'm better off in the unknown with a chance of happiness, than in the known, with none.

"Morning, Trixie" MR. BIG says.

"Morning," I say.

The Book Keeper removes his stool from the shed and reverses his actions from the night before. Posters, postcards, magazines then Books return to our designated place. Newspapers are unbundled and added to the inventory. And through it all, I view the world wearing a one-euro price tag.

The Book Keeper moves through his morning routine with a cigarette in his mouth. I'm happy to be hanging above ash-height.

Next to our Book Keeper's stall is another stall. And another. We are in the middle of a dozen green sheds that double as

Bookshops. It doesn't exactly make us a unique selling proposition. Why would someone stop at our expanse of Books, rather than another? What are the chances of me finding an Anglophone strolling by with a euro to spare and a curiosity about Minnesota more than a century ago? But I can't think about the odds. I only need one Reader. Soon. Or this paper clip is going to leave a permanent imprint on me. And not in a good way.

"She ain't a great beauty," THE MINK says, "but she's got spunk."

"Yeah, I like that in a broad," MR. BIG says.

"Are you two talking about me?" I ask.

"No, Trixie," MR. BIG says. "We're talking about Lise, over there."

Another Book Keeper, a woman with long, braided gray hair, stands 20 feet away. She wears a navy sweater over navy trousers with a blue and gray scarf tied at the neck, and a larger, heavy gray scarf for warmth wrapped around her shoulders. A small pack hangs from her waist. Her black-framed glasses sit on her head, poised for purpose. Her focus is on a row of Books in her shed as she straightens them, lying each against the one behind it, so the top of every title is visible. Her long, thin fingers are ringless. The only piece of jewelry is a large watch on her left wrist. Its black leather strap carries marks of long use, and undoubtedly too many run-ins with hardcover Books. Their corners can be unforgiving.

"She used to be our Book Keeper's moll. They were married and everything," MR. BIG says. My edges perk up. Love and loss amid Books along the Seine. That's my kind of story. "They worked the two Book stalls together. Then they split and now they're both barely getting by."

"Divorce is no fun. That's why I'm still footloose and fancy free," THE MINK says.

"That's not the reason," MR. BIG says.

I watch Lise's purposeful movements. "When did this happen?" I ask.

"Last year. Before our time," MR. BIG says. "There was this English Book when we got here. He got the story from another Book who heard it from two others who were actually here when it happened."

I guess oral history has its merit. "They don't even act like they know each other," I say.

"Exactly. That means it's real bad," THE MINK says.

An older customer strolls towards us. Our Book Keeper speaks to him. In French. I can relax, I'm going nowhere. This man looks like he'd prefer to invest his time in a Book on the history of World War I, rather than the fictional history of a young woman's war against social expectations.

"Biography," MR. BIG says.

"No way. Philosophy," THE MINK says.

"Huh? Sorry?" I reply. Too much time at Esmé's, with only the sharp pages of DICTIONARY to talk to, and I've lost my ability to banter.

"That's what the Reader's after," MR. BIG says.

"How can you tell?" I ask.

"It's a game we play to keep things interesting," MR. BIG says. "Try to predict what the Humans are looking for before they start talking. This guy is older, French. Look at how he's dressed, in a sharp suit jacket and trousers. He looks like he's trying to fill his day. Reading about someone else's life makes him feel okay about his."

"Wow, you're good. I was thinking World War I history," I say.

"Not bad, Trix. But trust me, he's all about French thought," THE MINK says.

I watch as the Frenchman chats with our Book Keeper. He picks up a French news magazine. Then starts fingering the tops of the older titles that are stacked on the left of the shed. He moves to his right and the second row of titles. They all straighten up when he hovers over them, imploring him to choose them, but he doesn't. Seems old hardcovers will be passed over today. The man then moves to the right, where French novels are stacked. He pulls out one and turns it over. The Book lets out a squeal of delight, either in hope, or in relief, as it had a tome leaning on it.

The man hands the Book and a five-euro note to the Book Keeper, then turns and strolls away, stashing his paperback in his suit pocket.

"A French murder mystery? No way that's for him," THE MINK says.

"Maybe it's a murder mystery about a philosopher who doubles as a detective? He thinks his way through the puzzle, discussing the case with other philosophers. A little thought, a little thrill. You never know," I say.

"Good try, Trix," MR. BIG says. "That title is part of a series, and a mediocre one at that. The author spits out two a year. Different body, same setting—horse races, clubs, bars. I knew an English version back in Chicago who only had bad things to say about itself."

"Maybe something was lost in translation," I say.

"I doubt it," he says.

"I guess you can't always judge a Human by their clothing," I say.

"Maybe, Trix. But face it, some Readers just don't make no sense," THE MINK says.

With his powers of prediction downgraded, THE MINK closes his cover. I'll leave him to pout it out. Instead, I watch Lise at the next shed as she steadfastly doesn't notice our Book Keeper. She should buy a pair of blinkers. It would make it easier to ignore him.

Our Book Keeper regularly glances to the left of the shed's roof. Hanging from it is a small, square, unframed mirror, nestled between a rack of postcards and maps of Paris. He pulls out the postcards, looking as if he's reorganizing them, but I notice that his gaze isn't focused on clustering all the Eiffel Tower cards together. Instead, his eyes stay on the reflection in the mirror. It allows him to keep his back to Lise, while watching her interact with a customer. The sly old Book Keeper. Maybe he's still in love with her?

"Does he do that often?" I ask MR. BIG.

"What?"

"Look in that mirror."

"I can't see no mirror," THE MINK says, still pouting.

"That's because it's right behind you two. From here, I can see its reflection. And it's of Lise."

"Really? He's spying on her?" THE MINK says. This piece of gossip seems to extract him from his gray mood. "I didn't think he had it in him. Son of a gun."

It's good to know even our Book Keeper has a little surprise left in his story.

CHAPTER 29

I guess travel really is about the friends you make. I only have these two guys for company. We don't have a lot in common, but I know they'd have my back if I needed them. That's more than I could say for *Dictionary* at Esmé's.

"So Trix, what's a nice Book like you doing in a place like this?" *The Mink* asks.

"There's nothing wrong with this place," *Mr. Big* says. "Trust me, we've been in worse. Did you know this is a UNESCO World Heritage Site?"

"Oh, listen to the professor," *The Mink* says.

"Hey, you can learn a lot if you listen to what other Books have to say, instead of yapping about yourself all day," *Mr. Big* says. "Don't mind him, Trixie. His pages are a little thin, if you get my drift."

"We're in a World Heritage Site?" I ask. I heard about those in the Bookstore, but I never thought I'd see one, let alone be living in one. If only *Sundown at Saddle Rock* could see me now.

"Yeah, Book sellers have been here since the mid-1800s," *Mr. Big* says.

"Enough about this place, tell us your story, Trix," THE MINK says.

"I'm set in snowy Minnesota," I say. "About the time Books started to be sold here."

"Not the story you were printed with, doll. Your own story. What brought you here?" THE MINK asks.

"Me?" I ask. No one's asked about my own story before.

"No Book runs from their Reader like you did without a reason," MR. BIG says.

"Yeah, Trix. What happened? What'd she do? Hold you too close to the flames?"

"Use you like a sponge?"

"Give you to a drooling kid or a dog looking for a bone?"

"Ooh, I'd hate that," MR. BIG says.

"No, she was nice," I say.

"Then what?" THE MINK asks.

I can't tell them. I feel like a fool.

"Come on. 'Fess up. What happened?" THE MINK asks.

"I was dumped by a collection of French poetry," I say, for the first time. It doesn't feel good.

"Ooh. Sorry, Trix," says MR. BIG.

"So you're here to forget," THE MINK says. "This is like your French Foreign Legion."

"I guess, kinda," I say.

"What were his poems about?" MR. BIG asks.

"Growing up on the streets of Paris, I'm told."

"I've got some stories about life on the streets that would curl your pages. And it wouldn't be in no stinking poetry," THE MINK says. "Who likes poetry anyway?"

"Trix, he's a fool. You're a great Book," MR. BIG says.

"Thanks," I say. Their words actually help.

"Yeah, a real catch," THE MINK says.

"I lost a great dame once," MR. BIG says.

"Yeah? What happened?" I asked.

"She read me three times in one year," MR. BIG says.

"What a gal," THE MINK says.

"What a Reader," MR. BIG says. "I would have done anything for her. Then she gave me away. But that's where I met THE MINK over here, so something good came out of it."

"Can I ask you two something?" I ask.

"Shoot," MR. BIG says.

"What do male Books want?"

"You gotta ask? Ain't it obvious? Broads. We love'em," THE MINK says.

MR. BIG looks at THE MINK. "I don't think you're helping." He turns to me and says, "Tell us about your guy."

"Like I said, he was French."

"Problem number one," MR. BIG says.

"And older."

"Problem number two," MR. BIG says.

"And problem number three—he was poetry and you are prose," says THE MINK. "I bet he's a no-goodnik."

"Enough," MR. BIG says. "Let me guess. You thought he was in love with you. Then he went after a younger Book. Right?"

Silence.

"But you didn't really speak the same language, did you?" MR. BIG asks.

Silence.

"So I bet you had whole conversations going on in your head about what he was thinking. And you know what he was thinking?" MR. BIG asks.

I shake my cover No.

"Nothing. He was thinking about nothing. Maybe whether there was a splinter he needed to avoid. But that's it. You're planning your life together and he can't even plan tomorrow. So that's what went wrong. The arcs of your story weren't meeting up," MR. BIG says. "See what I mean?"

"But I thought what we had was special. And Valentine's Day was coming up. I was going to get him something, maybe."

"Valentine's Day only means something if it means something to both of you. Otherwise it's just a day in February. And a cold one at that." MR. BIG says.

"How do you know this stuff?" I ask.

"You don't get to meet as many broads as we have without picking up a thing or two," THE MINK says.

"I wonder if I made a mistake." I say. "Maybe I should have stayed."

"Look where we are. It's like what Dean Martin sings about, being under the bridges of Paris. We're living the dream here." THE MINK says.

I hope it's not a nightmare.

"You can never go back, Trix. You can't rewrite your story, so why waste time thinking about it?" MR. BIG says.

"Now that's something I'd like to think about," THE MINK says.

"What?" I ask.

He points the edge of his cover toward the street. A young woman wearing a short skirt and high boots passes. "Look at the gams on her. I wonder if she can read English?"

CHAPTER 30

Days of Lise-gazing pass, and our Book Keeper is no closer to doing anything about his proximity to his ex-wife. Why are Humans so happy to stay unhappy?

I've become used to the routine, being shut away at night, waking to the creak of a hinge to let the day reach inside. Yet this morning feels different somehow. The sky is low and gray. It feels like we are covered by an old wool blanket. The temperature has dropped dramatically. I can feel it in my fibers.

Then something amazing happens. It starts with one, then two, then a few flakes of snow, finding their own paths in the air, rather than falling straight like rain. These delicate pieces of nature cover the grass and the sidewalk, leaving a layer of white undisturbed on the benches. It's so beautiful.

When I describe snow throughout my story, Agnes complains about it. She's tired of it; it dominates her young life. But this must be a different kind of snow because these Humans stop, gaze up and smile. Some look back at their footprints just visible, a few try to roll it into a ball. And the sound. It's as if the world has been put on mute.

"Oh, no," THE MINK says.

"What?" I ask.

"Snow," he says.

"What's wrong with snow?" I ask.

"We're Books, Trix. We hate snow. It's cold and wet and we saw enough of it in Chicago for two lifetimes," THE MINK says.

"I think it's beautiful and peaceful. Look, even the Humans are enjoying it."

"You can have it," THE MINK says. "Our Book Seller should shut down now."

"I remember the first time I saw snow," MR. BIG says. "I was in Alaska one winter with this gal. We barely left the duvet. It was great. But, Trix, I guess you've seen a lot of snow."

"Until today, never," I admit.

"You're from Minnesota and you never seen snow? It's even in your title."

"My story's from Minnesota. I'm from San Francisco," I say.

"Frisco! Great town," THE MINK says.

"But no snow," MR. BIG says.

"I know about snow. I describe how it falls and stays around for months. But I've never actually seen it," I say. I feel proud that my title includes this miracle of nature. "It's glorious, isn't it?"

I get no response from THE MINK or MR. BIG. They've drawn their fibers tight to stay warm. Our Book Keeper pulls out a roll of heavy plastic, attaches it to the roof of our shed and drapes it over us. The staleness of the air, the cold efficiency of the plastic, the slightly distorted view of the snowy world gives the day a sense of distance. And through it all, he stays.

Our Book Keeper sits, waiting for anyone and, eventually, no one. No tourist is strolling in the snow. One by one, each Bookstall shuts early. Their Book Keepers seem happy to spend the time doing something other than nothing, but not ours. He just drinks his hot chocolate and reads, his back towards Lise.

I don't know why she doesn't go home either. Instead, they both stay, Lise facing the gargoyles of Notre Dame, and our Book Keeper facing the Napoleonic Ns of Pont St. Michel.

The snow stops and we are freed from our stale, plastic coating. Still, no one comes. Yet Lise and our Book Keeper remain in their dedicated disregard for each other. Then, just as the corners of the buildings catch the edge of the light, she moves first. She closes her Book, packs up her items into her shed, locks and double locks her space, picks up her bag and walks away. Our Book Keeper doesn't move until Lise crosses the street and enters the Metro. Then he stands up and completes his similar end-of-day ritual.

All this time, he could have been warm in his home. Instead, he was here, in the snow, with his back towards the woman I'm starting to think he still loves.

CHAPTER 31

It was a cold night, so we're all thankful when the Book Keeper returns to free us from our confinement.

MR. BIG reminds me that I've been here a whole month. "Nothing moves fast here," he says. "Except postcards. Tourists love their postcards."

This day is beautifully bright. More snow must have fallen in the night as it coats everything around us. The light plays with the white that covers the grass and the street. Prism-like colors bounce off the edges of the snow-covered benches. What was once mundane is now magical. The air is filled with freshness and a sense of hope is carried on a gentle but persistent breeze.

Lise arrives in an all-black wardrobe with a bright red scarf around her neck. She sets up her space quickly and efficiently, and settles into her chair. With a Book open, staring again towards Notre Dame, their day of hide and peek begins.

Clusters of language groups pass. Japanese, Chinese, Italian. I await the sounds of English, with hopes that someone will stop and take me home. But the tourists seem more interested in five-euro posters of the cathedral than spending one euro on a Book that took my author three years to write, nine months to rewrite, six months to secure an agent, three months for that agent to sell to a publisher, four months of rewrites for the editor, and another nine months of planning and printing, before I was born.

Then a sole Human appears. Leather jacket. Jeans. A pencil and notebook protrude from his side pocket. A blue and gray checked scarf mirrors the changing color of his eyes. His hair looks like it has been on the losing end of the battle with today's incessant breeze.

"Art Book," I say.

"Huh?" replies THE MINK.

"I'm playing your game. This Human in the leather jacket is getting an Art Book. He looks like he's a creative type. But since he's shopping here, he's looking for an older Book on a painter or an art movement."

"Wrong," MR. BIG says. "He's a biography man or maybe French history. Yeah, definitely not fiction."

The leather-wearing Human doesn't speak, but spends time with each one of us, running his left hand along the titles, picking up a few, then gently replacing them. He takes THE MINK, turns him over and chuckles at his blurb.

"He reads English!" I shout. But just as quickly, THE MINK is back in his place and MR. BIG is trying his charms. He conforms to the Human's palm, offering his blurb to him through a slightly arched back cover. The Human smiles, but he doesn't buy.

Then he's facing me. I see a smile in his eyes as he scans my title. I'm removed from my display and I hold my breath as he looks at my backside. Expecting to be replaced in my rack, like the others, I'm startled to feel movement. Still holding me in his hand, he turns to the Book Keeper.

"With a title like this, I have to buy it," the Human says with an English accent. The Book Keeper responds with a polite smile.

"Oh, so that's it. He likes your title. Snow and all that. I get it," THE MINK says.

The Book Keeper relieves my cover of my perceived worth as the Human passes him a coin. Then the Book Keeper signals for him to wait and turns to a box. Opening it, he searches for something. In that moment, between the world I know and the world I've been sold into, I tell myself to be strong, confident. This is going to be a great new adventure. I hope.

Lise watches. It was only one euro that changed hands. He can hardly be cornering the market in financial transactions today.

As the Book Keeper turns back to the Human, Lise turns back to the same page she's been reading since she arrived this morning. She pulls her scarf tighter against the wind.

The Book Keeper shows my Human a postcard of his stall. He places it inside my front cover and mutters *"Souvenir"* to my Human. How nice! I'll have a memory of my home and MR. BIG and THE MINK. I realize how much I've grown to like this unhappy man, his wordless rituals and tobacco-stained breath.

My Human says, *"Merci"* and turns from the Book Keeper.

"Thanks, you two," I say to MR. BIG and THE MINK. "Thank you for being such good friends. You'll find a home soon. I'm sure of it." I'm sad to be leaving, so soon after I was getting to know these two. It's like we're just stories passing in the night.

"Don't worry about us, Trix. There's a broad coming for both of us real soon. I can feel it," THE MINK says.

"Stay strong, Trixie, you're a great Book. Don't ever forget that," MR. BIG says.

Lise watches my new Reader as we take half a dozen steps away from the Book Keeper and towards her. He stops and opens my cover. This is my chance.

I arc my spine to throw the postcard from the confines of my title page. It falls and catches the breeze. I shout "Fly!" to the postcard, but as I assume it's French, my words fall on deaf edges.

Yet fly it does. My Reader turns to the postcard that rises then spins away from him.

Lise leaps from her chair and pursues the printed card. The Book Keeper follows, as does my Reader. Three people are trying to catch a piece of paper determined to be free. Good luck with that. My new Reader starts to laugh as he almost grabs it, but it flits away. Then the Book Keeper and Lise grasp the air around it, laughing too. After four missed attempts, the card swirls its way towards the snow-covered ground and Lise claps it between her two palms. *"Hurrah!"* says my Reader. Hurrah indeed.

The three of them share a laugh as Lise passes the postcard to him. *"Thank you, merci,"* he says to her and the Book Keeper. They both reply *"Au revoir,"* then look at each other, surprised by their shared response.

"Good one, Trix!" THE MINK shouts. "Leave it to us Books to bring Humans together," he says.

The Book Keeper may not have understood the word 'serendipity', but he knows its meaning now.

My Reader replaces the postcard in my cover. I whisper an apology to it for forcing it from my care, although I suspect it doesn't understand.

The last view I have of this glorious, snow-sprinkled location by the Seine, half a world away from where I was born, is the

Book Keeper and Lise looking awkwardly at each other. He starts to speak. She looks at him, then at her feet, then back to him and smiles.

My new Reader places me into his jacket pocket. The scent of well-worn leather surrounds me as we move away from the home I knew, to the home I'll come to know, wherever that is.

CHAPTER 32

I've traded a view of Paris for the warmth of a lined jacket pocket. I am rocked to sleep by the rhythm of a man strolling through Paris.

A new movement awakens me. He places me on a seat. We're on a train! I'm going somewhere new, but where? The endgame of this trip is more of a lottery than a choice—which seems like a metaphor for my life these days. Things could be worse. Things have been worse. Let's hope things won't be worse. I could use some predictability right about now.

We're against the window, so if he's kind enough to lift me up, I may have a view of our journey. Instead, he disappears, leaving me to stare at the striped seatback covers. They have soft-looking headrests that provide comfortable corners for Humans to lean against. How considerate. All we ever get is the end of a Bookshelf and they're never padded. "Any Books around here?" I ask. Zero response.

My new Reader returns with a large sandwich and a bottle of water. Just as he sits down, everything shifts. The train is moving, slowly, but its movement brings a hush through the train car. An unspoken excitement passes between the Humans.

He tosses back a mouthful of water and looks around. I beam, trying to get his attention. I still don't know where we're headed. Or what his name is. Or anything about him. But I have a Book's job to do.

My smiling must have worked, as he opens me to where, amazingly, Esmé's Bookmark is still nestled in my page 182.

Agnes pulled her hat lower on her head and hopped off the streetcar. As she stood at the corner of 2nd Avenue and 21st Street, she watched it move away. A streetcar meant a big city. And here she was, on the way to work in the Merchant's National Bank. She was just a file clerk, but along the street she could see the sign for the St. Paul Business College. One day, she'd take classes there. It's as if her whole life, her present and her future, were here on this one street.

Holding her bag tight as she walked, she tried not to think about James and where he was right now. Instead, she noticed the spats on a man passing. James would never wear spats. She shook her head to shake off the sadness attached to the thought of James' boots and the familiar streets they were walking. Instead, she looked at her own high-buttoned shoes that had carried her from Rose Valley. She would stop thinking about James. Tomorrow.

The gray buildings of Paris pass but I am concentrating on my Reader. A glance out the window and I could forget my place, and my Human would be rereading the same line twice or jumping a paragraph, losing track and interest.

I perform as well as I can, conveying the chills that run through the winter streets of Minneapolis, the warmth of a young girl's love, and the expansiveness of her hopes as she considers her potential.

And that's it, I've lost him. He was following, reading each line I fed him, smiling at my descriptions, and now he's not. Maybe it's the slight rocking of the train or maybe it's the effects of the massive sandwich he just consumed, but my Reader's eyes start to close.

He places me on the empty seat next to him and my desire to tell my story is replaced with my desire to sleep.

London

CHAPTER 33

I awake to a language I can understand. *"We'll be arriving into London in fifteen minutes. Please collect all your belongings and thank you for traveling with us today."*

After months listening to announcements in French on the Paris metro, it takes me a moment to comprehend. But when I do, I practically leap from the seat. London? We're in London? In England? I'll have others to talk to. I'll have friends. I'll belong. I'm such a lucky Book.

My Reader puts me back into his pocket, and we walk off the train and into announcements at St. Pancras Station. I'm here! I just wish I could see it. He walks with purpose, like he knows where he's going. I hear voices and footsteps, hundreds of them. Then we're outside, in a salad of sounds: horns and tires and voices and music and shouts and accents and languages. It's as if the whole world has sent representatives to this small corner of London. But my Reader doesn't stop. He keeps walking, then descends into what feels like the depths below.

We are told to: *"Mind the gap."* What gap are they talking about? It sounds ominous. Should I be worried? Is this gap everywhere? I am desperate to see where we're going. Instead,

I'm left bumping along, step by step, with no view and no hope of changing my perspective any time soon.

After a stroll up a slight hill, we stop. My Reader drops his bag and craving to see something of our surroundings, I nudge him in the ribs. Success. He removes me from his pocket. Note to self: be more demanding.

"Heya, Rob. When did you get back?" asks a large, bald man sitting on a park bench.

"Heya, Nigel. Just now," says my Reader who I now know is called Rob. Looking at his bag, he says, *"On my way home."*

And then I see it for the first time. London. We're over-looking the city on a crisp winter afternoon as the light starts to fade. I can barely keep my pages together, I'm so excited. The breadth of the view below us is so far-reaching it's as if the world and all its possibilities have opened up in front of me. Look where I am, Mister BRITISH-ENGLISH DICTIONARY. I made it and you're still stuck on a shelf. I shouldn't be so petty. I won't be. Tomorrow.

"Fancy one later? The Queen's about 7?" Nigel asks.

Rob nods. I could stare at this sight forever but apparently, I'm the only one who feels this way. Rob picks up his bag and leaves.

We pass through a front entrance, and go up a narrow set of stairs. A door opens and we're in a bright, sunny living room with large windows. A Bookcase stacked with titles runs the length of the wall on the right, immediately surrounding me with Books who speak my language. Rob places me on a table.

"Hi," I say to any Book listening.

"American," I hear.

Rob drops into a large, well-worn leather armchair when a woman enters through the front door. *"Oh, you're home. How is Paris?"* she asks. She takes off her jacket and removes one high heel. It drops on the floor.

"Cold. But good for research," Rob says.

Her second shoe drops. *"Did this research get you any closer to finishing your novel?"* she asks.

"Maybe," he says. He pulls her close and kisses her. She twists away.

"Meera's pregnant," she says.

"That's nice," he says.

"That's all you have to say?"

"What should I say? It's nice, isn't it? Your friend is pregnant?"

"Another one, you mean. Another one is pregnant. And here I am with a flat tummy."

He pats her stomach. *"Lots of women would love to have your tummy."*

"Rob, I'm 34. I'm one of the last of my friends . . . "

"We said it wasn't a competition. It's not a race."

"But one day, soon, the race is going to be over and we won't have even started."

"We've talked about this, Pippa. Now's not the time. We can't afford a child, you know that."

"We could, if you went back to work."

"That's it, isn't it? You just want me to get a proper job."

"Rob, I said I'd support us for a year. That was four years ago."

"Pip, I just need one more year. Please. I'm just not ready to give up on my dream yet."

"Your dream is turning into my nightmare." Pippa walks to the bedroom. *"I have to work tonight. I'd appreciate some quiet,"* she says, and closes the door.

He stares at the closed door. *"Okay, I'll leave you to it. I'll be at The Queen's."* Rob waits for a moment. When he doesn't

get a reply, he puts on his coat, slides me into his pocket and
we leave.

I can't stop thinking about what Rob said. I've had my
dream of a forever home taken away from me more than once.
But fate, or is it serendipity, has reminded me that my dream
never goes away, just my belief in it. I guess the worse things
get, the stronger I need to dream.

Striding across the street, Rob enters what I assume is
The Queen's. More importantly, I'm in an English pub. I feel
so . . . local.

Rob asks for a pint of Pride and leaves some coins on the
counter. The tables look like they started their day aligned,
then drifted as the evening progressed. Holding a full glass,
he settles at a table in the corner. He looks around at the faces
in the pub, then at me. Maybe I can help him find his dream.

He starts from my beginning. I perform for him, pulling
him into the story of Agnes. His eyes are focused on my words,
and I see that his sight is tracking each one of my lines. He
turns the page and takes a sip from his pint. When we get to
the end of my first chapter, I turn up my intensity. LITERARY
FACTS, a research Book I knew back in San Francisco, said
that once you get them to your second chapter, the chances
of a Reader finishing your story goes to 20 percent. If they
get through your first 50 pages, they have a 47 percent chance
of finishing you. Get them past the first half of your page
count, and you're basically home free. So far, Katie's been
the only one who's finished me. It would be nice to have a
story success again.

Rob is a good Reader so I like my chances. But just when
I'm on a roll, he removes his jacket, finishes his pint and leaves
me face up on the table. I want to win him over with the part

in my story where Agnes is unwillingly entered into the town's baking competition, only to misread the recipe and have the cake fall flat. It's funny. He'll like it, I hope. But instead he comes back with another drink and Nigel, the Human from the park. I'm no longer the center of his attention.

Rob and Nigel spend the rest of the evening discussing football, the price of property, Pippa and his writing. As they do, I worry about the condensation on the glasses, and whether those nasty-looking drops are going to land on my cover. They make beer mats for a reason, people. Use them.

As I'm watching the chronic consumption of ale, another man arrives at our table with another dripping pint glass. Not near me, you don't.

"Michael, this is Rob," says Nigel. *"He's a writer."*

"Hi," says Rob. They shake hands.

"What do you write?" Michael asks Rob.

"Scripts," Nigel answers. Rob shoots him a look. I thought Rob was working on a novel. At least that's what his wife thinks. *"Michael just directed a film for the BBC,"* Nigel says, with a particular emphasis on B, B and C.

Rob grows pale. Or excited. I'm not sure. Humans can be so hard to read. Not like us Books.

"What's it about?" Rob asks, his voice fluctuating in tone.

"London during the Battle of Britain," Michael says. *"The Beeb can't get enough of the war years,"* he says.

"Those were our glory days," says Nigel.

"What's your script about?" Michael asks Rob.

Rob grows paler. *"It's early days yet."* He looks at me as he continues to speak. *"It's set in . . . the late 1800s in the U.S. Midwest."*

"Female lead?" asks Michael.

"Absolutely," says Rob, nodding energetically. *"Her name's Agnes and she's fighting social convention to make her way in the world."* He smiles at his reply. Agnes is facing challenges that are still relevant today, which is why her journey is timeless. But somehow, no one really gets that, no matter how often I tell them. Maybe Rob will be different.

"Interesting. When you're ready to show it to someone, let me know." Michael takes out a card and gives it to him. *"Need to dash."*

Rob looks at the card, Nigel nods, and Michael is absorbed back into the collection of drinkers that surround the bar tables.

"Why did you tell him I was a scriptwriter?" Rob hisses.

"Because that novel of yours is getting you nowhere," says Nigel. *"And he's a film director. If he was a poetry editor, I would have told him about your haikus. Anything to get you some work."*

"But I don't have anything."

"You just pitched a costume drama to a BBC director. I think you have something."

"I just made it up." Rob picks me up. *"It's from this book."*

"Then adapt it," Nigel says.

"It's not that easy," Rob says.

"Well, it can't be that hard either. Michael's a talented guy. If he likes your idea, you're in with a chance." Silence engulfs this small table. *"Still got that writing space in the West End?"* Nigel asks. Rob nods. *"Then make use of it,"* Nigel says. *"I've gotta go. Soraya's waiting for me."*

"Who's Soraya?" Rob asks.

"An Iranian beauty," Nigel says.

"Will we get to meet her?"

"I doubt it." Nigel downs his remaining pint in one long mouthful. He pats Rob on the shoulder as he leaves.

Rob watches him, the crowd in the pub and the people on the street. Then picks me up and we exit. This could be the start of a beautiful friendship.

CHAPTER 34

Domestic life can be noisy.

The morning begins with Pippa's movements in the kitchen waking us all up. Then she's standing in front of the mirror over the mantel, checking that her hair is tied back securely and the bow on her pink blouse is even. She layers matching pink on her lips, grabs a large briefcase and says, *"Bye."*

After a few moments, the front door closes. Half an hour later, it's Rob's turn to move.

"It's the same thing, every morning," HEALTHY LIFE, HEALTHY PREGNANCY says.

"Two ships, and all that," LORD NELSON'S BIOGRAPHY says.

"Or just a financially prudent wife," TAKE CARE OF YOURSELF AND THE MONEY WILL FOLLOW says.

"There's more to life than financial security," WRITE, RIGHT NOW says.

"Easy for you to say. You've never been on the street," A WALKING GUIDE TO VENICE says.

"Oh, here we go again, listening to your tale of hardship. You spent one week on the shelf of a neighborhood's outdoor library, and you act like you were in the trenches at the Somme," TALES OF THE FIRST WORLD WAR says.

"You've never been anywhere except a Bookstore," A WALK- ING GUIDE says. "I've lived. I've felt the cold."

This bitter banter continues while Rob makes his tea, has his shower and gets dressed in a version of what he wore last night. He collects his laptop and notes and files them into his satchel. With one last look around, he grabs me and walks to the door.

"Oh, new girl is special," HOW TO GET THE LIFE YOU WANT says.

"See you later," I say to the unhappy titles and we descend into a London morning.

Rob and I repeat the journey to the Tube, and we are told to *"Mind the gap"* again. One day I'll figure out what is so frightening about it.

A few stops later, we rise on two levels of escalators to the collective shriek of Central London. My fibers are assaulted by diesel fumes. Red double-decker buses line the wrong sides of the street. Large black cabs spit out Humans.

Uninspired-looking four-story red brick buildings frame the narrow road. Clearly, architectural beauty wasn't a prerequisite for design in Central London, not like in Paris. We reach a glass-fronted building proclaiming an upcoming performance: "The Insight Among Us". Hah! If it's a collection of a Human's insight, it'll be a short play.

After climbing two stories, we arrive at a long, crowded office room. *"Morning,"* Rob mutters to a few people, whose faces are focused on their computer screens. He receives a *"Morning"* in return.

"Haven't seen you for a while. How you doing?" asks a young man adjusting his headset.

"Heya, Kamil," Rob says. *"Good, thanks."*

"When do I get a preview of that novel of yours?" Kamil asks.

"Soon."

"Good. 'Cause I need a distraction from subscription sales. Some of these punters are . . . " His phone rings. *"Good morning and thank you for calling,"* he says into his mouthpiece with a higher pitched tone of voice. A wave to Rob and he turns to his computer screen, severing their conversation.

Rob opens a door and we enter a space that contains a small desk, a chair, and a window to our left. The walls don't even make it all the way to the ceiling. It's maybe the size of two phone booths. No cat could ever be swung in here.

He places me on the desk. "Good day," I hear. I look up to see a few Reference Books on a shelf above the desk. They look as tired as the paint on the walls.

"Good morning," I say.

"American," one mutters. "How disappointing."

I don't know if I'll ever get used to that.

"How is your President Reagan?" sputters another Book.

"Dead. How long have you been in here?" I ask.

"The last time I felt sunshine on my pages was 1983, I think. I can't remember," says a Book with a faded cover, coughing out dust from his spine.

"Don't worry, not much has changed," I say.

Rob sets up his laptop and places me next to it. I can't wait to see the creative process in action. He hits a few keys and starts scanning news sites. I thought he was a novelist. Or a screenwriter. Seems he's more of a Reader than a writer.

He stares at the screen. He looks up, then down, leans back, then forward. He picks me up and leafs through my pages, stopping at the note that Katie made, and at the words that Esmé underlined. Then he smiles at me and starts to read me.

I perform my Chapter 6 better than I ever have. I sense he needs it. I tell him about Agnes and her walk to school in the cold. How she stares out the window of her one-room schoolhouse and imagines what's beyond the next town. She's quiet among the other girls who only talk about needlework and clothing and boys. She wants adventure.

Hours pass as Rob learns of Agnes growing up, leaving home and trying to find her way in the big city. Then he turns to my page 197.

> The offer came as a surprise and her hand immediately rose to her mouth, to mask the intake of air that punctuated her response.
>
> Move to Chicago? Her aunt's letter, so short, yet so life changing, made it seem so simple. She read the note again, slowly, and aloud, as if sound would make it more real.
>
> "You would be helping me, dear Nessie. Your mother tells me that you wish to see more of this country. Now that my Harry is gone, I find the nights so long and lonely. I hear that you are very clever and well regarded in your work. A nice letter of reference from your company will place you in good standing for a position here in Chicago. More and more young women like you are going into business. It wasn't like that in my day, but then so much has changed. I would honor the opportunity to share my home

with you and have your company for as long as you wish to stay. Please consider it. Your loving aunt, Mary."

Rob takes out a pencil and writes along my margins.

He shuts his laptop and sets it aside, then returns to me. I'm exhausted. My pages are getting sore, and my spine is swollen. Books weren't meant to be read in one day, people.

Fortunately, Humans need food, and over the walls drifts the invasive smell of popcorn. The aroma prods Rob to look at the time: 1:10. He removes a page from his notebook, folds it, inserts it after my page 198 and closes me. He leaves and I rest while the dog-eared reference Books toss their outdated opinions at each other.

When he returns, carrying the smell of curry with him, I inhale, steeling myself for my late-afternoon performance. However, Rob sets me to the side. He takes out his notepad, places it to the left of his computer and begins typing slowly, then more determinedly.

His eyes shift quickly from the screen to the page, then back to the screen. He turns a page in his notebook and restarts his typing. He smiles. And he hasn't even finished my story.

Can amour create a blank canvas for our lives?

CHAPTER 35

After a long day at the cubicle, I believe I deserve some time off. Clearly, I'm the only one who thinks this way.

On the Tube ride home, Rob holds me in front of his face, as if showing me off to the world. Performing on public transit is one of a Book's most challenging environments. No matter how loudly and how well we tell our story, our Human is more focused on where they are than on what they're reading.

But I have a captivated audience in Rob. On the few stops that move us from the writer's cubicle to home, he consumes another of my chapters. Then an announcement interrupts the train, *"Chalk Farm Station."* Rob stops mid-page, reinserts a marker into me and moves towards the door.

We get off at the designated stop and trail the herd of Humans up some stairs. They stand quietly, most heads bowed as if in prayer to their phones. Rob, instead, looks at me.

An elevator arrives. Through a window, I see it's filled with Humans, crammed together like Books on a shelf, but having less fun. They are all facing away from us, so when their doors open, they ooze onto a walkway, while we follow them into the space they just vacated. So much of Humans' existence centers around movement, getting from here to there, covering massive amounts of distance in the shortest amount of time, and for what? As I'm waiting for our people-filled elevator to reach the light, I watch Humans actively avoiding each other. They look up, or down, or at their phones, rarely at each other. How many stories could they share if they just spoke to each other? Finally, one door of the elevator closes and moments later, another one opens. We all flow out into the fresh air and away from each other.

Rob crosses a street then a bridge to arrive at a road lined with small shops. The neighborhood is historic yet bustling with people in restaurants and pubs. If Jane Austen lived in London today, it would be on this street.

He enters the apartment, shouting *"Hey, Pippa!"* There's no answer. After a brief tour of the empty rooms, we leave, returning to The Queen's.

Day two in London and I've spent both evenings in a pub. Rob orders a shepherd's pie and a beer, and settles us into a corner. Laughter from the clusters of Humans fills the space, but Rob wants to read, not talk, so I'm back on duty.

To cut through the backdrop of noise, I perform each chapter as loudly as I can manage without shrieking. When I finish a chapter, he sets me down and writes in his notebook, which allows me to rest before my next performance.

Rob flips back and stops on my page 200, and turns me sideways to read a phrase that Katie wrote.

He reacts to her thought with markings of his own.

Then I hear a familiar voice. *"Two days on the trot?"* Nigel asks. *"Trouble in paradise?"*

Agnes is striving to experience the freedom of her land.

"I can't say no to their shepherd's pie," Rob says, pointing to the plate in front of him. *"How's Soraya?"*

"Great, actually. That's her," he says, pointing to a tall woman near the bar.

"Two days on the trot?" Rob smiles.

"First time for everything." Nigel points to me, *"How's it going?"*

"Good. I've never adapted a novel before, but indeed first time for everything," Rob says.

"Michael will give you helpful feedback. He's a good bloke." Nigel nods at Rob. *"I'll leave you to it."* And as quickly as Nigel arrived, he leaves.

Rob and I spend the next two hours alternating between my chapter and his notes, his dinner and his beer. I wonder what he's writing about me. He only stops our call and response once, to get a second beer. For the rest of the evening we sit together. I like this Human. He's attentive.

It's after 10 p.m. when he closes my last page. I'm exhausted. Rob looks tired too, but happy. There's a light in his eyes that I didn't see on the train from Paris.

We return home to a sleeping Pippa. He slips into the bedroom, unheard, while I slip into slumber.

Pippa is up and dressed early. This morning she leaves without saying goodbye.

Rob and I repeat yesterday's journey through the stench of diesel that hangs over this part of London, reminding me of the fog described to me by a Dickens Novel. An hour later, we're back in the writer's phone booth, facing a gray wall. The reference Books ignore me today, but I sense they're listening to my story. Rob's eyes devour my words and my pages, searching for, it turns out, my description of Agnes' home, back in Chapter 7. He bounces in his chair and his fingers skip over the keyboard. His forefinger runs down the center of my page. It tickles, but I try not to laugh. He draws a pencil mark alongside a paragraph, adds a tick next to it and returns to his computer.

This relationship continues all morning. As he skims a page, I shout out a word or phrase that is under his line of sight. It's challenging, as I need to focus on which part of my page he's scanning, then give him the phrase that I think is going to capture his interest, or answer his question. I feel like we're playing whack-a-mole, with my words and phrases acting as the pop-up mammal that appears regularly yet unpredictably. I whisk between Agnes' thoughts at school to a description of the snow on a bitter January morning, to the smell of her mother's bread, to the taste of the stew on a Sunday afternoon. I'm not sure what he's looking for, so I'm throwing everything I have at him. His eyebrows perk up, which indicates that I've tossed the right thought in his direction. Then he turns and types, smiling as he bangs letters on his keyboard.

Letting other people tell my story is scary. What is he focusing on? Will he leave out my best parts? Will Agnes' internal struggles make good film? What about her relationship with James? Will we see her go to Minneapolis and Chicago? What about her sisters? I have so much to say, how can he possibly fit it into two hours? Maybe the film will be so good, they'll make a sequel. As I'm considering the various threads of my story, Rob shuts off his computer and we exit his literary phone booth.

We stop at a sandwich shop before weaving our way through a maze of side streets. A green square opens in front of us, speckled with Humans sitting on the grass. At its center is a Tudor-style two-story building. Although, given this area of London and its history, perhaps this actually is Tudor.

Rob sits cross-legged on the grass and unwraps his lunch. As he bites his way through his food, he makes notes about me. In the center of London, on a sunny spring day, I'm surrounded by English speakers, history and language. I am trying to take it all in, when a voice interrupts my bliss and Rob's focus.

"Hey."

Rob looks up. *"Pippa. What are you doing here?"*

She sits down. *"Getting some air. I have half an hour before I'm stuck in meetings for the rest of the day."*

"When it's all done, we'll go out. Spend some time together again," he says, keeping his right thumb wedged between my pages.

She lowers her voice. *"What are you doing here?"*

"Taking a break."

"But why here?" she asks.

In Rob's silence Pippa finds the answer.

"Don't tell me we're still paying for that writing space. You said you gave it up," Pippa says. *"We can't afford it. Besides you can write from home, free of charge."*

"It helps me focus."

"You're not hearing me, Rob. If you want to be a starving artist, go ahead. But you'll be starving on your own."

Rob looks at her, unblinking. *"But Pip, come on. Give me just another six months, that's all I need."*

"You don't see it, do you? You're asking me to give up my dream of being a mother for your dream of being a writer. I'm not doing it, Rob. It's not fair. I'm sick of this. I'm done."

Wow, Pippa has some Agnes in her.

"This time it's different. I promise. If this project doesn't work out, I'll give it up and get a job, honest," he says. *"I mean it, Pip. Just one more shot at this. Six months is all I'm asking."*

Silence hangs between them.

Nearby, a clock chimes the hour. *"I have to go,"* she says. And in a few steps, she's absorbed into the throng of Humans who have responded to the call of time.

Most people around us are moving to one of the four corners of the park and the streets beyond, but we remain in the sunshine, Rob watching the corner of the park where Pippa was last seen.

I'm thinking about what she said. I never thought that one person's dream would come at the cost of another's. But maybe that's what happened with Agnes and James. Her dream was to leave Rose Valley. His was to stay. Agnes' story is more than a hundred years old, but it's playing out all around me.

Rob extracts me from my thoughts and we're traveling. Goodbye park. Hello stale air.

For the rest of the afternoon, he sits staring at his screen, then out the window. Meeting Pippa certainly didn't turn into a pep talk. If she can't encourage him, I guess it's up to me. Come on, Rob, let's show her! You can find your dream. Maybe that's why you found me in Paris.

After several more hours of emotional support in the cubicle, we return home to emptiness.

"How was another day at the office?" asks THE CITY, LONDON'S BURIED HISTORY.

"Good, I think."

"What does that mean? Be specific. I haven't been outside in years," THE ENCYCLOPEDIA OF FLOWERS IN BRITAIN says.

"He seems excited about an idea," I say.

"Not another one," FOLLOW YOUR DREAM says. "What's it going to be this time?"

I don't want to tell them that I'm the idea. After all, I barely know them, and being a source of inspiration won't endear me to them. How do you bring up the fact that you're going to be famous when they haven't even cared about the un-famous version of you? I spent too long in Paris in social isolation. I don't need it here, where I can actually communicate. Yet it's odd to be reveling in happiness about myself, by myself. On arriving in London, I thought I'd be surrounded by English-speaking friends. Instead, I only have myself to rely on. And that's okay.

"Remember when he was writing his play?" WRITER'S MARKET says.

"Then he started a novel. Then he quit that to work on another play," FOLLOW YOUR DREAM says.

"But that didn't go anywhere," WRITER'S MARKET says.

"I don't trust his ideas," FINANCIAL PLANNING FOR THE SELF EMPLOYED says.

"He's just trying to find the right direction," MANIFEST YOUR DESTINY says.

"Oh, here we go again. Do what you love and the money will follow, right? Well, it will follow you all the way to the poorhouse. He needs to get a real job, one that allows him to save each month for retirement. It's the sensible solution," FINANCIAL PLANNING says.

And with that verbal salvo, the Books begin their analysis of money they've never had to earn, careers they've never had to pursue, and retirement they've never had to consider. We're never more opinionated than when we're discussing the problems of others.

CHAPTER 36

There's an odd comfort in the routine of my London life. Rob and Pippa seem to be at a standoff, speaking to each other, but saying nothing.

Over the past month, I've become accustomed to our morning commutes together from our Tube stop underground to Tottenham Court Road, then striding down the usual streets to the glass-fronted theatre building where we nest. It's a pleasant life, working everyday, cheering him on, feeling needed. Yet, it's lonelier than I expected. I thought I would be surrounded by companions, but none of the Books here want a new friend. They're comfortable with their current circle of Books and don't seem to have room for one more on the shelf. It's a different form of social isolation than I experienced in Paris. I blamed that on my lack of French. This form of loneliness needs no translation.

Yet today, just as I'm relaxing into our ritual, Rob surprises me. We don't get off at our usual stop. Instead we stay on the Tube, go past three more stations and exit at Waterloo. We emerge from the warren of tunnels into a web of narrow streets, where large trucks challenge the limits of low bridges.

The brown color palette imposed on this area from centuries of grime is broken only by the red of the double-decker buses.

We reach the end of a street and it's there, in front of me. London. The London. The London of postcards and travel guides and Dickens. Somehow, those extra Tube stops and the labyrinth of narrow streets have brought us by the Thames, facing Big Ben and The Houses of Parliament. I'm staring at history and the source of so many stories. I'm such a lucky Book.

At a restaurant, Rob asks for a table for two. Positioning himself so he's looking towards the door, he places his notebook on the corner of the table and me in the center. Holding a pen in his right hand, he clicks it repeatedly. Then he raps it against the table like a drummer. Mid-solo he looks up to see Michael's outstretched hand.

"Hey, sorry I'm late," Michael says.

"No, no, no worries. Thanks for taking the time."

They start an uninspired conversation about Nigel. Rob knows him from school, Michael through a mutual friend. After they both assure each other that he's a great guy, a silence descends. Isn't it time to talk about me?

As if understanding my thoughts, Michael picks me up. *"This is it?"* he asks. He reads my backside, then turns me over and opens my cover. He slides his thumb along my sides, blowing air through my pages, lands on my last page then starts again, stopping at each chapter.

He randomly opens me to my page 207. I better be good. This is our big chance. I'm performing for a Director.

Agnes awoke with a start, wondering where she was. She looked out the window, thinking she was home and safe.

Then she remembered. She was on the train. She could see the city in the distance. Chicago.

"You've had a good sleep, Miss," said a woman across from her. "Don't worry, I've made sure no one touched your belongings."

Agnes immediately grasped for her handbag lying under her elbow. She opened it. Her money was there. Everything was fine.

"Going home?" the woman asked.

"No. It's my first time to Chicago."

"Do you have a chaperone?"

"My aunt."

"Good. Because it's not safe for a pretty girl like you to be on her own. It's like the men think now that it's the 1900s, they can do what they want. It's not like it was in my day."

Agnes smiled at the thought of male attention, especially the male whose attention she once had. She wondered where James was at this moment. And with whom.

"So remind me," Michael begins.

Rob nods and stares at my cover, as if willing me to close the deal. If he only knew how hard I was trying. I return his stare, urging him to speak. Pitch me, sell me! Now is our time and it's slipping away. He takes a sip of water. I implore him to speak for us both. And it works. *"It's a fresh story, set in the American prairie. We also don't see female-driven stories set then. Not often, anyway."*

"Little House on the Prairie?" Michael asks. I cringe. No, I'm not that.

Like a chess player recognizing his mistake, Rob quickly

gets back to the female-driven plot. *"The journey of the main character, Agnes, is her search for her own place in the world, defined by her own actions, not the expectations of the world she was born into. She recognizes that she needs to make her own opportunities. No one is giving them to her, especially to a woman back then. And in hindsight she recognizes that her drive may have taken her too far."*

Hmm, I'm impressed. That whole hindsight thing is new. It's not on my blurb. It's not written in any notes in my margin. He came up with that on his own. I like it. I'll have to remember that when I'm telling my story to those annoying shelf-dwellers back at the flat.

"Interesting. But what makes the story unique?" Michael asks.

"It's set in a world we haven't seen on TV. No manor houses. No terraced estates. No middle-class semis. Rather, it's set in a country that's trying to define itself, just as our main character is." Rob opens me to Katie's original note and reads: *"It follows our character Agnes' independence that parallels a country's growing independence."* He keeps his thumb between my pages as he continues. *"And it's a mirror to our world, viewed through the lens of a country finding its way. It begins in the 1880s in the Midwestern United States. And through all this winter and hardship we follow a young woman who is compelled to leave the only thing she knows."* His palms are sweating and he's thumping my spine on the table with more fervor than I appreciate, but I'll forgive him both excesses if he sells my story.

"Is there sex? Violence? Corruption? Class warfare?" Michael asks.

Rob sets me on the table, so I don't need to absorb any more of his nervous habits. He continues the pitch by leaning forward. *"A little. But it's about a person finding her way, without much but her wits. The protagonist, Agnes, is funny, feisty and determined. The people she meets are memorable. Some good, some bad, some stupid. The places she goes and the world she inhabits don't exist anymore, but it's a world of open land, which represents possibility. It's people standing on the cusp of the 20th century, having no idea what's about to hit them—cars and wars and electricity and a world that would never be the same again. But before any of that happens they have to survive the snow."*

I'm blushing. He's talking about me with such passion.

"So, how does it end?" Michael asks.

As Rob describes the last pages of my story, Michael starts to read a line from each of my chapters, in his own attempt at patching together a Cole's Notes version of me. Which, I'm proud to say, doesn't exist. I don't think.

"Where'd you come across it, the book?" Michael asks.

"In Paris, of all places. It had actually snowed, so when I picked up the book in one of those huts along the Seine, I thought: Snow? Serendipity? Let's see if it's true," Rob smiles.

"Speaking of snow, what about location, setting?" Michael asks.

"This doesn't need to be Dr. Zhivago," Rob assures him, *"but you'll need a few shots of a snow-covered horizon."*

"Hmm," Michael exhales, still turning me in his hand. *"Okay. That can be covered by a second unit. If we limit the need for winter exteriors, we might be able to pitch it."*

He asks about a love story. Check. A struggle. Check. Family dynamics. Check. Trailblazing decisions. Check. Humor. Check, if you find scenes of cows getting loose on Main Street funny. Or locking your neighbor in the outhouse. Or women hanging out dirty laundry in an attempt to win the tacit, weekly laundry-washing competition. Not your slapstick funny, mercifully, but the kind of humor that is timeless. At least I think so.

"I like the idea of a gentler Western. No guns a'blazing. More character development, less violence. And everything I've done recently has been London-based. It'd be nice to get out of the city."

Rob's eyes grow wide as he listens to Michael. He starts to say something but, wisely, lets Michael continue. *"We'd need to option the title. But it won't be much,"* he says. Hah! I'm an undervalued asset. Honestly. They have no idea. *"How far have you got?"*

Rob nods. *"A first draft of the script,"* he says. I can't remember the last time I heard Rob breathe.

Michael describes what he needs in a pitch, shakes Rob's hand and leaves. Only then do I hear Rob exhale. Me? On TV? I may have to revisit my perspective on all things electronic.

Rob picks me up and I see the pleasure in his face as he stares at my front cover. I beam back at him. It's nice to be finally appreciated for the story you have to tell.

We get home and I do my best to keep my excitement hidden from the other Books. They aren't my friends, so I can hardly start bragging about Rob turning me into a TV movie. After briefly answering a few questions about where we were and what we did, I leave the other Books to their bickering. I'm busy. I'm making a movie.

Who should play Agnes? What about her sisters? Will James still have red hair? I have so much to consider.

Rob's phone rings. He answers, *"Hi"* and listens. *"I hope they pay you overtime,"* he responds. *"Don't work too hard."* He hangs up his phone and leaves the room.

"Well, there they go again," FINANCIAL PLANNING FOR THE SELF EMPLOYED says. "Finding ways to avoid the discussion."

"How would you know?" THE CITY, LONDON'S BURIED HISTORY says.

"This is what happens when you don't take care of your paychecks," FINANCIAL PLANNING says. "Single most common cause of marital breakup. Says so on my page 72."

"What do you think he's up to?" FOLLOW YOUR DREAMS asks.

"No idea," FINANCIAL PLANNING says. "Hey, Yank, you're with him all day. What's his news?"

Do I tell them? They haven't been particularly nice to me and no one's tried to be my friend. Maybe they don't deserve to know. "I'm not sure." I say.

"Well, you're no help," POSITIVE PERSPECTIVE FOR A POSITIVE LIFE says.

I want to reply that they've been no help either, but why bother? Am I getting old? When did I become so self-sufficient? I used to care so much about what other Books thought. Somewhere between Paris and London, I lost that.

Rob returns and snatches me from my self-analysis. He grabs his notebook and his jacket and we are out the door.

"Well, looks like the Yank is still the favorite," MANIFEST YOUR DESTINY says.

"American!" I shout as the door closes behind us.

CHAPTER 37

After long days in the writing cubicle, and seeing little of his wife, I'm surprised that on Saturday, we're all leaving the house together like one happy family: Rob, Pippa, a large brown envelope and me.

"Let's go, we're late."

"For what? Where are we going?" Pippa asks.

"I told you, it's a surprise," Rob says.

"You know I hate surprises," Pippa says.

"You're just going to have to trust me on this one."

Two long London Tube rides later, we emerge into a part of the city that's new to me. The roads are filled with people using them as sidewalks, ignoring the cars that travel slowly and patiently behind them. It's like a pedestrian revolt.

Tables filled with old items sit before each store window. Masses of people are touching doorknobs they don't need, paperweights they'll never use and barometers they don't know how to read.

We stop at a supposedly antiquarian Bookstore. Pippa looks at titles, but to me, the only thing especially old about these Books is the table they're on. "Hi, you guys," I shout from the safety of Rob's right hand. I receive a few muted "Hellos" in return, but like dogs in a dog park, we're pulled apart, just as we start sniffing each other out.

Turning, we walk along a block of shops. Sunglass-wearing Humans consuming salad cluster around small tables. At the end of the block, Rob and Pippa stop and move towards the windows of a real estate agent. Images of homes come with prices composed of a long string of zeros. They look at each other then walk away in silence.

We move from bright spring sunshine outside to the darkness of a pub's wood-lined walls. On a table in the back corner, I'm placed face up, on top of the large brown envelope, center stage.

"The usual?" He asks Pippa. She nods.

She reaches into her purse for her phone, stroking it like a kitten. She's so immersed in this device that she doesn't notice that she has company.

I, on the other hand, ever alert to my surroundings, open my cover slightly in a Bookish attempt to wave hello to Michael. My welcome is lost on him.

Rob returns and masterfully places three glasses on the table without spilling a drop. *"You do that well,"* Michael says, putting his briefcase next to a stool, then sitting down.

"Signs of a misspent youth," Rob smiles, locating the glasses closer to me than I'd recommend.

Pippa looks up, as if startled that the world around her wasn't placed on pause while she gazed, transfixed, at her screen.

"You must be Pippa," Michael says, reaching out his hand.

"Oh, yes," she stammers, shaking his hand. *"Hi."* She reaches for her white wine as she shoots a pleading look at Rob.

"Pippa, this is Michael, a Director at the BBC," Rob says, trying

not to smile. That gets her attention. Pippa quickly puts her phone back in her bag.

"Thanks for coming to this part of town," Michael says.

Pippa says, *"We rarely come over here. It makes for a nice change."*

Michael notices me. He picks me up. *"Have you read it?"* he asks Pippa.

"Not yet," she says. *"But I'm looking forward to it."* Hah! Good response. Pippa shoots a Rob a look and he nods his approval.

"That's the pitch," Rob says, pointing to the envelope beneath me.

"Still excited about it?" Michael asks.

"Even more so," Rob says. He pulls out three copies of a document from the envelope, passes one copy to Michael and one to Pippa, who looks questioningly at her husband.

"It's a great, untold story," Rob says. *"The coming of age of a girl, in a country that's coming of age, in a culture that's coming of age. The parallels will make it easy to mine for subplots."*

I don't think I want my subplots mined, thank you very much. He just needs to trim me to fit a two-hour format. How hard can it be? I remember a MANSFIELD PARK novel talking about how she was adapted. She had to sit on the shelf while a more recently printed version of her, with the label "now a TV movie", was face out on the shelf. She said she felt less of a Book for being adapted, like she was just the backstory for the film. But I think she secretly liked the way it made her stand out. We all need something to complain about, even if it's the film they're making about us.

Rob and Michael share ideas while Pippa watches the creative ideation. She sips her white wine, holding back a smile.

"You'd watch this?" Michael asks Pippa, waving the paper to an unheard rhythm. *"Because we'd be targeting a female audience with this story."*

"Absolutely," she says. Pippa grabs Rob's hand and squeezes it.

"Thanks for turning this around so quickly," Michael says. *"I'll get back to you with notes."* He picks me up. *"May I take this too? For reference?"*

"Sure," smiles Rob. And with that, I'm passed on. Again.

I cannot believe how little Rob values me! Does he think he can get another one of me at any Bookstore? All the notes I carry, all our memories, and he's just letting me go? I may have changed his life. Humans. They act like it's all about them.

Rob winks at Pippa who finally releases a smile. Then Michael picks me up. As he places me inside his leather case, I take one last look at Rob, who is watching me disappear into a bag. When I met him, I was stranded on an outdoor shelf in Paris, cold, scared and lost, giving up on my dream. Maybe Rob felt the same way. Now we're both on a new journey. I quietly wish him good luck as the case snaps shut.

CHAPTER 38

I've been Michael's companion for a month, but I've never left his desk. At least with Rob, I went places. I saw the Tube, Southbank, Soho. Is this my life? Missing what I had but didn't think I wanted? Or is this what growing up feels like? If only I were next to a psychology Book, even THERAPY FOR BEGINNERS, I could ask.

Instead, I remain in Michael's small, cramped office. If there were an award for neatness, he would not be nominated. His desk is the destination for every random piece of paper in his periphery.

I'm surrounded by Books awaiting their on-screen fate while scripts form stacks like their own versions of Leaning Towers of Pisa. Two westerns spit words at each other, as if in a verbal showdown. Three vampire novels sit on a shelf. One speaks in a teen-aged lingo, another in Victorian English, and the third is set in a Los Angeles of the future. The only threat they convey is to suck any ounce of interest from the conversation. The erotica novels have big egos, but not much else. They speak in breathless phrases, panting their thoughts instead of stating them.

I used to like this diversity. Now I just find it predictable. When did I become so tired of it all, and start feeling this malaise, this ennui?

I perform for Michael as he makes notes. I try to sound as filmic as I can, lingering over the descriptions of the wide, open skies, the horse-drawn transport and the long, mud-encrusted skirts. He smiles as he reads me, tapping his pencil, circling page numbers and writing alongside my paragraphs.

Corners of my pages have creases, but I guess the film business requires sacrifices of us all.

After weeks of watching him take phone calls, some with Rob, respond to emails and leave to attend meetings, I'm returned to his briefcase. I guess I've got a meeting. Maybe I'm "doing lunch".

We sweep past lots of *"Hellos"* and *"Heys"* into a room where Michael drops his bag on a table. Then silence. Michael sits his case upright, opens it and frees me. Four other Humans enter, one carrying a small carton.

Michael starts talking before they've even been seated. *"New project,"* he says, reaching for the box. He takes a pen and runs its ballpoint along the tape that was sealing it. Out comes a sextet of me, six copies of THE SERENDIPITY OF SNOW. That's how I looked when I was young—no lines, no marks, no weary spine. I miss my younger self.

"Hi, you guys," I say, welcoming the kids. One of my siblings yawns, and whispers, "Hey." Another says she needs to stretch. A third asks where we are.

"An office in London," I say.

"You mean New London, Minnesota?" asks one of me.

"No, I mean THE London. In England. We're being made into a movie!"

The endless horizon vs. the claustrophobia of a small town.

The expectation of new being better than now.

"Cool," says another one.

That's it? Cool? I remind myself they've just arrived, probably jetlagged and unsure of their surroundings. Maybe I was like that once. They're probably a little bit in awe of me too. I'll let them relax, then they can gush about how knowledgeable and worldly and sophisticated I am. I'll be patient. And humble.

"So they're making a film of us?" asks one of my less attentive siblings.

"Well, of me," I say, correcting them on their assumptions of how we got here. Through my hard work.

"Yeah, of us," says one of me.

"Actually, it was because of my intense one-on-one work with Rob, the scriptwriter that the idea got started. Then he reluctantly handed me to Michael, the Director, knowing he'd need me. Which is how we're having this meeting in the first place," I say, failing to keep my voice on the professional side of surly. After all, it will be me who's photographed with Michael on the red carpet at our premiere. With the right lighting, no one will notice the creases on my cover.

"Whatever," says another.

Whatever? They have no idea how lucky they are. They think this is how the world is. They don't understand what I've been through to get them here. I worked so hard for this. They just expect it, as if every novel simply gets made into a movie. Honestly. Kids these days.

I'm about to shout at these ungrateful newbies when Michael grabs them from their stupor and passes them around the table.

"Hold on!" I shout. "This'll hurt, but it'll be over soon." Spines are broken around us, prompting a chorus of "Ows!" I told them so.

Michael tells his team about us, well me, really. About his

The church's cross, visible throughout town.

The constriction of clothing amid manual labour.

vision for a "costume drama" set in Minnesota. He describes the coming of age of the country that parallels Agnes' coming of age. The claustrophobia of a small town and the social restrictions on girls and their choices. The pull of the horizon and her pull to explore the world. The power and beauty of the snow, and the power and beauty she's yet to discover about herself.

When I think of it that way, I'm actually pretty profound. Katie's Book Club never discussed me like that.

"Does it have to be set in Minnesota? Why not California?" asks one overly tattooed youth.

"Location is not part of this discussion," Michael says. *"Your job is to read the book this week, make your notes—costume, set decoration, you know what to do. We'll meet here next Tuesday. Let me see your thoughts. I'll take the best and build on that."*

"Who's writing it?" asks the young woman with glasses.

"Rob Ellington," says Michael.

"Never heard of him," says the tattooed Human.

"He's never heard of you either, so you're even," says Michael. The Humans share looks around the table, but no one speaks. Michael holds me up and waves me at them. The newbie Books are quiet now, awed perhaps by Michael and by me. We make a good team.

Michael's phone rings. He says to the Humans, *"I have to take this. See you next week,"* and leaves the room.

"I thought my story was just about a girl leaving home," asks one of me.

"I thought we were about small towns," says another.

"There's more to our story than you know, when you've lived it as long as I have." I've gained such wisdom, such insight. Yet they're not even listening. It's like they don't want to know. Kids. You can't teach them anything.

Michael returns, which seems to be the cue for the Humans to pick up their Books and leave. There's one Book left in the box. "What about me?" she shouts.

"They'll come back for you," I say. "You're probably meant for someone who'll be arriving later."

"You think?" she asks.

"Sure. You'll be fine," I lie.

As if Michael can hear us, he grabs the box with the remaining title and places her on the shelf behind us. "See?" I say. "He has a plan for you."

Michael puts on his jacket and drops his phone in his pocket. He stashes me along with his papers in his briefcase.

"Bye!" I call out to the leftover Book. "We'll probably be back this afternoon for you." I don't know where these lies are coming from, but it will make her feel better, so why not?

We return to the street and the sounds of London. Car horns announcing their existence. Heels tracking Human's paths along the concrete. And voices, so many voices.

As we move along, I relax into my new reality. I'm working with a director to get my story told. I hope it turns out well. Then I remind myself of the literary adage: never judge a Book by its movie.

CHAPTER 39

Michael and I arrive at yet another pub. But this one doesn't have wood paneling, dark furniture or stained beer mats. In fact it feels light and fresh. I didn't know they made pubs this way.

He places me in the center of the table, clearly where I belong, with a view to the river, framed by white and blue checked curtains. As he removes his jacket, a woman approaches. *"Samantha, thank you for coming,"* he says. They exchange a kiss on the left cheek, then the right.

"What a great spot," Samantha says, her hair hooked behind her ears. The mole to the right of her mouth moves as she speaks.

"Hammersmith is our bit of calm in the city."

Samantha's eyes find me and travel down my cover. I like her already. *"So this is it? THE SERENDIPITY OF SNOW."*

Michael nods. *"I'll get us a drink. What would you like?"*

"Dry white wine, thanks," she says.

Michael nods and heads to the bar.

Samantha's long fingers gently open my cover, then flip through my pages.

Her thumb stops on my page 223.

Chicago was so much larger and louder than she expected. People didn't say hello as they passed, like she did; they simply kept their heads down as they went by.

If she were going to become like the rest, she would have to get used to their ways. But she didn't want to. She was tired of starting over, with all it required—new job, new friends, new uncertainties.

She knew you could travel too little. But could you travel too much? Was there such a thing?

A glass of wine placed to her right interrupts her attention. *"How are you liking London?"* Michael asks.

"I love it," she says. *"You can look out a window and see something other than another building. London is like a horizontal version of New York."*

"That's a rather good analogy," Michael says, sipping his pint. *"How's David?"*

"Still a lawyer."

"And a good one, I'm sure."

"How about you? How's life at the BBC?" Samantha asks.

"The same," he smiles. *"I finish one project then need to get the next one funded. My job security has the life expectancy of a gnat."*

"I know the feeling," Samantha says with a smile.

"Still writing your novel?"

"No, I stopped when I took the teaching job."

"Hope you go back to it. I remember you telling me about it. I liked it."

"Maybe one day. But I'm interested in this," she says, holding me up.

"Yeah, it could be good."

Could be good? He's read me four times. He's left notes in my margin. Understatement can hurt a Book.

"So, how can I help?" she asks.

"Well, you're the sage of Midwestern culture and history," he says.

She laughs. *"Hardly. I don't think teaching undergrads makes me a sage of anything other than the best student bars on the Upper West Side."*

"Well, to me you are," he says. *"Read it. Let me know your thoughts. If you like it, I'll send you the script. The through-line is there. I want to make sure we're not missing an obvious cultural reference or making an historical mistake. Something that would cause locals to roll their eyes."*

"Of course." She picks me up. *"I don't know this author. How did the story come to you?"*

"The screenwriter found the book in a secondhand stall along the Seine. While it was snowing."

"Great story already," she says.

"It's from a first-time novelist. I spoke with her agent. She has a second novel coming out."

I'm wincing at the thought that no one's heard of my Author when the news that she's writing another Book pulls me from my pity party. Second novels always inspire interest in the first. There'll be more of us printed, more of us read.

She turns me over and reads my blurb. I so wish I could change my backside. I don't think it does me any favors. It should have more zip, more energy, more of a sense of confidence. It screams "Like me!" in a tone of muted hope. I want more swagger, less sweetness.

"Read it first, then we'll talk. You can take that copy. I have an extra one."

What? He's giving me up? I have all of Rob's notes inside me and Michael's dog-eared corners. There are things such as Bookmarks, or sticky notes, neither of which damage me. But no, I let you bend my pages, trading my discomfort for your convenience. Then, just like that, I'm passed on?

Samantha holds me gently. *"If it's any good, I may add it to the fall semester's reading list. Telling my students that it's going to be made into a BBC drama by the great Michael Underwood is probably enough to inspire them to put down their phones and actually turn a page."*

"Anything I can do to help the cause of academic interest," he laughs. *"It's a fairly quick read."* Really? I'm a quick read? *"Let me know your thoughts in, say, two weeks? I can get you a cultural consulting fee for your work."*

"Great!" She flips through me. *"Lots of notes here already."* "Yeah, I think some of them are Rob's, the scriptwriter. The others, I don't know."

"Interesting," she says. She turns my pages and stops where Katie and Esmé and Rob and Michael made a mark or a squiggle. *"Maybe these notes are worth a book on their own. The annotations of novels."*

He gets up and puts on his coat. *"Thanks for this. I'm sure your perspective will make a difference."*

"One can only hope," she says, smiling. *"I'll get reading and be in touch."*

"Sounds good. When do you fly back?"

"Tomorrow afternoon," she says.

"Safe travels, and give my best to David." He gives her a kiss on the cheek, picks up his briefcase and walks out of the pub.

Here we go again. New Human. New city. I'm getting so comfortable with change, I wonder if some of my fibers were recycled from a Travel Book?

Samantha picks me up and walks into the soft sunshine of early June. We pass a couple sitting on a blue picnic table in front of the pub. Pink flowers spill over the hanging baskets. If only THE ENCYCLOPEDIA OF FLOWERS IN BRITAIN could see this.

She walks to the stone wall overlooking the Thames and sits on the ledge. It's a glorious sight, this river sparkling under the daylight. Happy Humans are standing outside, holding pint glasses and smiling while others are pulling a long rowing boat up onto the sand.

Just a few months ago I was on the Seine with MR. BIG and THE MINK, the Book Seller and his ex-wife Lise, all freezing in the snow. Now I'm along the Thames with the sun wrapping its rays around me. I think of all the Books and Humans I've met.

We really are all part of each other's story.

CHAPTER 40

I have a night and morning in Samantha's company to consider my fate. Am I destined to wander this earth, being passed from Human to Human, performing for an increasingly long list of Readers? Adventure is exhausting.

Here I am, being packed yet again. It's the downside of a nomadic existence. I just get used to Rob, and he passes me to Michael. Then, after I've given him some of the best weeks of my life, he passes me on to Samantha. I'm the literary equivalent of a hot potato.

Samantha tucks me in the side of her purse, leaving half my cover poking out. With a suitcase trailing behind us, we walk past a Union Jack, hanging motionless under a block-long, five-story white building.

I've seen the Tube and the streets of Soho, the Houses of Parliament and the Thames. I'll never forget the view from Regent's Park or the winding streets of North London. And the pubs. How I love the pubs. Every one different, every one filled with laughter and life. I like it here. Sort of. In a friendless kind of way.

At first, I thought things would be easier for me here. After the heartbreak of Paris and its linguistic isolation, I assumed that a common language would be enough for a common bond. But I was wrong. Instead, I was only here to work, or to be worked on. I doubt any of the Books at Rob's house will even notice I'm gone. But maybe that was my fault. Maybe I didn't try hard enough.

We cross the street and I see it, the sign that may signify my farewell to London: South Kensington Station, Metropolitan and District Railways.

We pass through the turnstiles of the Tube. Nestled on Samantha's lap, I have time to think about how much I've done. Plane trips and train journeys, public transit and public markets. Two new countries seen, but only two real friends to my name, and I left them behind in a snowy shed by the Seine. Books cared when I left the Bookstore. Rebecca's Book cared when I was left behind by Ziya. The Forgotten Ones at the coffee shop cared when I started on this journey. But over here, I've felt like a foreigner. Even my paper size is different. I thought my differences would make me interesting. Instead, I only stood apart from the others. If I had it to do over again, I'd try harder with other Books. Maybe not FRANÇOIS, maybe not DICTIONARY, but the others. It's called 'making friends' because it takes effort. Back in San Francisco, friends just happened. Now, the older I get the harder it becomes. In my next home, it's going to be different.

I'm going to be different too.

After a dozen stations, Samantha stands up. I read the sign: Heathrow. This is it. I didn't misinterpret conversations. I didn't mishear plans. We're really leaving. I came through Heathrow with Esmé. Now I'm leaving with Samantha. If only Books were eligible for frequent flyer miles.

We walk past shop after shop selling food that proclaims to be from countries I'll never visit, all served on Styrofoam. Then I see a Bookstore. Oh please, can we go in? I long for one last conversation here in London, one last chance for a friend. But, instead, we stand in a long line of tense people, and once again, I'm placed in a gray plastic bin.

"Where are we?" I hear, from a scared-sounding Book ahead of me.

"On a conveyor," I say. "What's your name?"

"*THE REAL NEW YORK*," he says.

"I'm *THE SERENDIPITY OF SNOW.*"

"I'm moving. What's happening?" he says.

"Don't worry. We're going through an x-ray. It'll be okay." I remember my first time through. It feels like so long ago.

"Does it hurt?"

"Close your fibers tight. It'll be over in no time." The conveyor belt moves us forward. I hear *THE REAL NEW YORK* squeal as he passes through the machine. Then it's my turn. By the time I exit the other side, the Book is gone on its own adventure.

Samantha reassembles her wardrobe, gathers her purse and me, and we walk. And walk. And walk. The loudspeaker never stays quiet, continually announcing exotic destinations. Then I hear it. *"San Francisco. Final Boarding Call. Gate A20."*

Could it be? Are we going home? Really home? I'm shaking with excitement. Please please, let me go home. I'm done traveling. I want to see Katie. Hear *JOE'S DISCOVERY* tell of his latest nighttime adventures. Listen to *DIANE'S DREAM* talk about love and romance. It feels so long ago that I was on a shelf, waiting for my story to begin. It's like I was in a rush to get nowhere. I wish I had appreciated the simplicity back then. But if I can go back, I promise I'll be different. I'll be grateful for what I have. What I had.

But we don't go to gate A20. Instead Samantha lingers at the magazine stand. *"All passengers for San Francisco should now be on board. The flight is ready for departure."* And still Samantha stands contemplating magazines. We're not going home after all. My fibers sag.

I should be excited about this next adventure but instead I feel numb. I have a new life to build, all over again, like Agnes when she moved to Chicago. She had to find a job and friends and a purpose. Some Books have a simple path. From Bookstore to Reader to shelf. Not me. I have no direct path. My story is bigger than I ever expected. And more exhausting. Where will it end?

"New York JFK, pre-boarding has now commenced at gate A24." Samantha turns and walks towards the gate. I guess that's my next destination. I'll say hi to it for MR. BIG and THE MINK. And I'll try harder to make friends this time.

As Samantha settles into the plane, she places me in the seat pocket in front of her.

"What do we do? What happens?" I hear.

"Who's that?" I ask.

"THE REAL NEW YORK. I'm in the seat pocket next to you."

"Hi, it's me. From the x-ray machine."

"Wow. Small world. Thanks back there. What you said helped." I smile, realizing I have something to offer other Books after all. "I've never flown before. What happens? Is it cold? Does it get windy?"

"Don't worry. You'll be fine. You won't feel a thing. Mostly the Humans just want to eat and watch a movie so it's not that bad," I say. "Just be careful of the red wine during turbulence."

"Okay. Thanks. I'm excited."

"I couldn't tell."

"And you? Traveled much?"

"More than I ever imagined I would," I say.

"What's it like? Is traveling hard? Are Books nice everywhere you go?"

"I think they're as nice to you as you are to them," I say.

As the plane begins to build speed down the runway, Samantha picks me up and places me in her lap. I look into her eyes. She's interested in what I have to say. I won't let her down.

New York

CHAPTER 41

I t's the sounds I notice first.

In the cab there's an ad chirping at us for the best, real, genuine, original, authentic pizza in New York, available at seven locations. I suspect there are more adjectives on that pizza than toppings.

The cab stops, and we travel in an elevator that's slower than Esmé's birdcage elevator. I thought New Yorkers were meant to be in a hurry. Clearly not the one who designed this contraption.

Samantha's apartment is on the corner of a building at 95th and Broadway. Large windows fill two sides of the living room and kitchen space. She opens the windows but the price of moving air comes with an invasive volume of car horns barking and Humans shouting.

Out the windows, a canyon between buildings on either side of the street pulls the view down Broadway. A few trees struggle to exist in the cement boulevard that separates traffic. A stream of yellow cabs stops and swerves between lane markings that act more as guidelines than rules.

Samantha places me on the kitchen table. I take advantage of the breeze to lift some of my pages, and allow the city air to reach the depths of my signatures and my spine. I never thought New York air would feel fresh, but given the confines of transatlantic flight, it feels positively meadow-like.

"Hey, kid," I hear.

"Who's that?" I ask.

"*OLD BLUE EYES' BIOGRAPHY.* First time in New York?" he asks.

"Yes," I say. This Book has such a soft, velvety voice, I could listen to it all day.

"Well, start spreadin' the news," he says.

He may have a beautiful voice, but I'm not sure what he means. What news needs to be spread? Before I can ask him, Samantha picks me up and carries me down a short hall to another room. It's a study! A real study, with Books, a wooden desk and a chair with a brass reading lamp!

Excitement ruffles my pages. Behind her desk is a wall of maps, some of them old-looking, many of them of Minnesota or parts of the Midwest. To the left of the desk is a Bookshelf filled with titles. A large, green armchair sits on an angle by the window.

"Hey," I hear. "Welcome. Who are you?"

"I'm *THE SERENDIPITY OF SNOW.*"

"Sounds cold. Winter is not a season, it's an occupation," *SINCLAIR LEWIS' MAIN STREET* says.

"That's just how my main character feels! She's in Minnesota, more than 100 years ago."

"You've actually been to Minnesota?" asks *MIDWESTERN GEOGRAPHIC FEATURES.*

I shake my cover No. "Have you?"

"I was printed in New Jersey. How did she find you?"

"In London."

"You went from here to England? That's a distance of more than 3,400 miles," he says.

"Well, from San Francisco first, via Paris," I say.

"Wow, a real traveler," THE EXPLORERS OF THE GREAT LAKES says.

"I have found that there ain't no surer way to find out whether you like people or hate them than to travel with them," MARK TWAIN'S BIOGRAPHY says.

"How would you know? You've never been anywhere either," says MIDWEST, PLAIN AND SIMPLE.

"Now, now," THE BEST OF DEAR ABBY says. "That's not polite,"

"Good friends, good Books and a sleepy conscience: this is the ideal life," says MARK TWAIN.

"Just be thankful you don't have family here. Family is exhausting," says ANCESTRY OF THE PRAIRIES.

"How was Paris? I bet it was beautiful and sophisticated and full of love. Were the Books nice there?" asks HOPEFUL AND HELPFUL HABITS.

"I didn't get to know any French Books," I lie. "We couldn't really speak to each other. But I met some nice American Books along the Seine," I say.

"Books come into our lives for a reason. They might not know it themselves. You might not know it. But there's a reason. There has to be," says a collection of stories by Joyce Carol Oates.

"You've seen the world. I think it's more fantastic than any Bookshelf," says FAHRENHEIT 451. He seems friendly enough, but he scares me. I fear he's going to self-ignite any minute.

I look up and see a sprinkler system in the study, so perhaps we're safe. As I've learned, we aren't responsible for our name, just what we do with it.

"I have discovered in life that there are ways of getting almost anywhere you want to go, if you really want to go," says *LANGSTON HUGHES' COLLECTION OF POEMS*.

"Who would want to travel and who would want to stay here? Let's take a poll," says the *BIOGRAPHY OF GEORGE GALLUP*.

I can barely contain my glee. It feels like a tsunami of welcome has crashed on my shores. I'm quaking so much my spine can barely hold my pages together.

Maybe I'm finally home.

CHAPTER 42

I awake to darkness and silence. I'm not sure where I am. Then it's the sounds that answer my confusion and I remember: New York City.

Samantha and I are still on London time, so this early rising means no one is awake yet. I hear a coffee grinder and catch the aroma of coffee beans drifting from the kitchen. Samantha moves almost silently down the hall, closing the door behind her before she turns on the light. She picks me up from my jet-lagged exhaustion, settles into her reading chair and places her coffee a safe distance away.

Her fingertips are soft as they glide over my letters. Her smallest finger on her left hand straddles my spread, helping me keep both pages open effortlessly as I perform my opening lines about boots and snow and laughter.

She leans back into her chair and crosses her leg. Her right knee becomes my podium. I've forgotten what it's like to be held by a Human. Rob and Michael worked over me. Esmé leaned over me to learn. But it was only Katie, so long ago, who took the time to hold me and read me, the way I was meant to be enjoyed, slowly, with curiosity. Now the gentleness of

Samantha's hands helps me feel her kindness seeping into my pages. Let's hope she finds what Michael needs in my story.

At the end of my first chapter, I yawn and so does she. She seems as weary as I am. She reaches for her coffee and flips forward through me until she comes to my page 240 where Katie has written in my margin.

She stops and I perform the challenges facing Agnes and James.

urban vs. rural pull

> Why couldn't he write? She had sent him a letter every month, describing Chicago, her job at the office, her Aunt Mary's apartment. She told him about the museums she visited, the bridge club she attended, the concerts she heard and the restaurants she now knew. And all she received in return was a card at Christmas and one on her birthday. He always said the same thing. That he missed her and wished she'd come home.

Samantha absorbs my words and makes notes. It feels like I'm being graded.

After an hour, my voice is getting tired. I usually like to warm up before I perform, but Samantha didn't give me any time to break into the day. She places me back on her desk, her notepad open on top of me. I can read what she thinks of me: "Strong voice". That's good. "Mindful of its place in history." What does that mean? I'm mindful? I take it that's good. But I feel like I've been told I have a nice personality. "Could use more humor." I'm not funny enough? Didn't she like the scene where Henry gets locked in the outhouse? I saw her mouth open, I heard her laugh. What was she expecting, a pie in the face? James slipping on a banana peel?

"Enhance parallel of Agnes and country." Sometimes it's best not to know what others think of you. Yes, I can see that she would want to draw more of a line between the emergence of the country and the emergence of Agnes. But really, I'm not funny?

I'm about to read the next critique when my pages are closed and I'm carried into the kitchen. She hands me to a man I'm assuming is David and kisses him on the forehead.

"This it?" he asks.

"Yeah, it's pretty good," she says.

Pretty good? Give me a break. I'm a first novel. I'm filled with flaws. But that's also part of my charm. Cut me some slack.

"How's Michael?" he asks.

"The same genius he's always been."

"And he's asked for your help? That makes him a genius in my book. Who's writing the script?" he asks.

"Rob something or other. A friend of Michael's. He brought him the idea."

"What about you? You could write a script," he says.

"David, I'm not going to . . ."

"I don't mean this *one. But the next one. You wrote a play. You're writing a novel. There's no reason you couldn't adapt a book,"* he says.

"Correction, I was *writing a novel. Now I'm trying for a permanent teaching position, or have you forgotten what I do all day?"* she says, reaching for her cup of coffee.

"Pitch Michael an idea. You never know." David looks at my cover. *"Serendipity indeed."* He places me back on the table, grabs her hand and they walk down the hall to their bedroom.

I must have fallen asleep because when I awake, he is dressed and she is checking her voicemail. *"Michael mentioned that the author is having a reading tonight,"* she says.

"This author?" David asks. *"That's . . . serendipitous."*

"So that's your new favorite word?" she smiles. *"Shall we go? It's at 8 p.m., at The Strand."*

"Why not, let's see what she's all about."

I can't believe I've traveled halfway around the world to finally meet my Creator. Maybe I have Serendipity in my title for a reason.

CHAPTER 43

I've been trying to smooth my cover all day. The thought that I may see my Author is enough to make my spine come unglued.

"I can't believe you get to meet her," says *The Best of Dear Abby*. "The chance to meet Abigail Van Buren is beyond my imaginings."

"That would be because she died in 2013," *Midwestern Plain and Simple* says.

"At least you're going someplace. No one takes me anywhere," complains *The Explorers of the Great Lakes*.

Samantha takes a look in the mirror before walking to the door with David. I scream after her. We must be more connected than I imagine, because she stops and turns back to pick me up. "Thank you!" I shout to her, thinking, maybe just this once, a Human will acknowledge hearing me.

We step out of the building into the street, then onto an escalator that descends beneath Broadway. They call it a subway for a reason.

I think of all the forms of transit I've survived. The Paris metro stations were so wide, with gently arching ceilings. The trains were like moving boxes. There was a consistency between metro lines, like the consistency of the buildings in the city.

You'd never call London consistent. Their Tube system seemed to be patched together rather than planned. Sort of like the city itself. Some lines had narrow cars, requiring Humans to lean inward when standing. Others were large and square. Some were accessible by a flight or two of stairs, while others required elevators that dropped to depths that I thought only coal miners endured. Their Tube system was like their architecture, arbitrary. From dark red brick buildings to bright white ones, Tudor details to glass and steel, and brutal-looking cement towers. Some neighborhoods seemed like they didn't belong in the same country, let alone city.

Now I'm in a New York subway. Plastic, pre-formed seats line these cold, steel-colored trains that seem to be designed more for standing than sitting, more for congestion than comfort. People are facing each other, yet not speaking. Despite the design differences, all these transportation systems are consistent in their ability to remove happiness from Humans.

After four starts, four stops and half a dozen blocks, we approach a building on a corner, with a red awning wrapping around it. The Strand promises 18 miles of Books. My author, amid a city of Books? I am shaking with excitement.

We walk along one side of the building, where rows of Books stand on moveable carts, offering choices for $1. Every title on these carts represents an Author's dream of accomplishment or success, and a Book's dream of a home. I remember how it felt to be hanging from the shed in Paris, deemed to have the lowest possible value. Memories of a one-euro price tag don't fade quickly. "You never know who'll find you!" I shout to the sagging Books. "Your story may be about to begin."

Turning a corner, we pass through surprisingly small doors for this city of Books. Inside, large white pillars hold up high, white ceilings. One table is stacked with titles proclaiming to be "Best of the Best". Next to it is another table packed with what promises to be "Modern Classics". I don't see any of my siblings on either table, so I guess I'm deemed neither a Modern Classic nor the Best of anything. Clearly there's room for improvement in their categorization.

A range of postcard racks and T-Shirts are to the left. Given the abundance of candles and housewares in my first Bookstore, this small nod to the non-Book seems discrete. I approve.

We climb staircase after staircase until we arrive at a floor where rows of chairs face a small stage with two leather armchairs on it. To the side is a table, holding many of my siblings, and I presume some of her new title—I can't read their spines. This is the moment that I never thought I'd experience. For once, I'm lost for words.

Samantha places me on her lap as she and David take a seat in the third row. A Human passes, carrying a cloth bag that reads: "Where Books Are Loved." Am I in Paradise? Was I pulped in my sleep and I never noticed? Is this my Aftershelf? Then Samantha hands me to David, who flicks through my pages and I realize I'm still here. But in a Bookstore that could be the best place on earth.

More Humans drift in, filling the seats. A voice from the front says, *"Please welcome Tessa MacDonald."* A woman walks down the center aisle to applause. She's petite, with glasses and when she smiles, I can see my story in her face.

Tessa sits in one of the leather chairs and begins by talking about Minnesota, and what a distinct place it is.

"The joke has always been that in parts of the Midwest, you can watch your dog run away, for three days. But I find it's a place where you can see the world coming, for three days. It's where the sky feels alive."

Wow, I wish Esmé's DICTIONARY and all of Rob's Books could hear her. She'd put them in their place.

"The View Is Up *starts where* The Serendipity of Snow *ends, in Minnesota in the 1940s. This small section I'm about to read is from Chapter Three."* Wow, I get an almost-front row seat to my relative, my Creator's second novel.

Over lunch each day, Maggie read the paper. The War had been going on for so long, so far away. Every story felt like a geography lesson. She learned about places like Guadalcanal, Salerno and Iwo Jima, places she had never heard of before, but places that she could now identify on a map.

Every month Maggie heard of another soldier who wouldn't be returning to his life in Minnesota. The arrival of a telegram used to mean good news—wedding wishes or birthday greetings. Now the sight of a young man delivering a telegram would stop the entire street, everyone fearing he was coming to their door, like the grim reaper. She decided that the only way she would survive the wait that this War imposed was to look on the bright side, of everything. She would see the world for what it could be, rather than for what it was. Maybe that way, he would come home to her.

I hear my own voice, in hers. I have the same cadence. But where's Agnes?

Tessa finishes reading the chapter. As the audience applauds, she smiles and steps aside, while another Human asks if the audience has any questions. I have so many of my own. She points to a curly-haired woman in the row ahead of us. *"I liked* The Serendipity of Snow. *When you were writing it, did you know it was going to be the first of a series?"*

"No," Tessa smiles. *"I was focused on just one novel. I thought finishing one would be enough. But halfway through I started seeing the next novel forming in my mind, and how it could be a companion to* Serendipity. *I liked the characters I had created. You have to, when you spend so much time with them. So I wanted to stay with them and explore the arc of the story of the next generation of strong, Midwestern women."*

I cannot believe I get to experience this evening. This must be what attending the Oscars feels like. Everyone talking about you. And in a good way.

"How do you research your Books?" asks a Human in the front row.

"Well, first I started by listening to my grandmother," smiles Tessa. The audience laughs. *"She told me stories about her mother and what it was like growing up back then. Like locking someone in an outhouse in winter, or the women competing to see who could be first to hang their laundry out to dry, those stories are all true. And of course I also researched the ways people lived back then, how they traveled, what the schools were like. But my favorite parts of the book are from my grandmother."*

Wow, I didn't know I was really biographical. I need to speak to some non-fiction Books. We have more in common than I thought.

The woman at the front announces that there's time for one more question.

"Will there be a third book? Is this a trilogy?" asks a delightfully inquisitive Human.

"Yes," smiles Tessa. *"It will be set in the 1960s. Another era of change, not just for women, but for the world."*

"What's it called?" the woman asks, clearly violating the "one more question" rule.

"I don't know yet," Tessa says. *"The title usually comes to me as I write. If you have any suggestions, let me know!"*

The woman at the front thanks Tessa for her time, and instructs the audience to stand to her left for the Book signing. The audience applauds, then immediately moves to form a line. This group is nothing if not obedient.

Holding me, Samantha stands in the line, David next to her. I'm going to meet my Author. I hope I don't embarrass myself.

She moves in front of Tessa and extends her hand. *"Hi, I'm Samantha,"* she says. *"I'm consulting on the film. Michael Underwood may have mentioned me?"*

"Oh, of course," says Tessa, shaking her hand. *"It's great to meet you."*

"Do you have time for a drink afterwards? Or something to eat?" Samantha asks.

"Sure, once I finish here," she says. Tessa looks at me in Samantha's hands and smiles. I hope she can see the smile I'm returning.

I hear Books speaking to me, but I'm in my own Author bubble. Then suddenly Tessa is next to us, talking, smiling. I stretch towards her. She smiles at me again.

We walk into the humidity and the noise of New York City in the summer. The restaurant we enter has floor-to-ceiling windows and two leaded-glass doors that block the sounds of the outside from the relative serenity of its interior. David, Tessa and Samantha take a seat. I'm left to rest, face up on the table, but I'm perfectly placed to watch my Author as she and Samantha fall into easy conversation.

"Are you in town for long?" Samantha asks.

"No, I leave tomorrow afternoon," Tessa smiles.

Samantha picks me up. *"By the way, would you sign my copy of* The Serendipity of Snow?*"* I practically leap out of my spine in excitement.

Tessa reaches for a pen, then for me. Her hands are soft. She turns my pages gently, with care and curiosity. *"Looks like a lot of people have read this one."*

She places me on the table and turns to my title page. Looking right into me, she starts to mark me. Fortunately, she uses a felt-tipped pen. It feels like the dark blue ink is being injected into my fibers, flowing from the pen through the lines of my paper, creating an imperfect edge around each letter she leaves on me. She signs, "Great meeting you. All the best, Tessa MacDonald."

I smile back at her. It was great to meet you too.

Chapter 44

All the other Books are asleep by the time we get home, so I have no one to tell about meeting Tessa, or what it felt to have her sign me. I'm drifting in delight, dreaming about a world "Where Books Are Loved".

I awake to the sound of Samantha. *"I really liked Tessa. She was so interesting and understated. Wouldn't it be nice if . . . "*

"Let me guess. In your head, you're already adapting her second novel," he smiles.

"Why not?" Samantha asks.

"Precisely," he smiles. She gives him a small kiss.

I watch them in their morning routine, him making coffee for two, her making toast for two, and think that it's true, marriage can be happy. I just haven't seen many Humans who have achieved it.

I lie face up on the kitchen table, too far from the Books in the den, and the possibility of telling my story about last night. If I don't tell anyone, did it really happen? Or was it my imagination? Who confirms reality? Is it a truth we all agree to, or is everyone's reality different? And when did I start having such thoughts?

Samantha picks me up. Maybe it's time for a walk? If I had a tail, I would wag it. A short subway ride later and she leaves the dark underground to be faced with a wall of beige and red brick buildings.

She walks towards massive, wrought-iron gates framed by two stone columns with carvings of what look like toga-wearing Greeks. Along a tree-lined pathway, the noise of New York dissolves into the relative quiet of voices bouncing between symmetrical buildings. Every Human carries a backpack over one shoulder. It must be the entrance requirement for this place.

Then I see a banner, blue with white writing: Columbia University. We pass a domed building with columns and small patches of grass. Moving through a building's entrance, Samantha skips lightly up a wide wooden staircase before continuing down a corridor. Reaching a glass-fronted door, she takes out a key and unlocks it.

The office walls are lined with files. A map of the Midwest is behind her desk, along with a mug that says Lake Wobegon. A framed photo of Samantha and David is on her desk. A low Bookshelf holding stacks of Books runs along the short wall.

"Hi, you guys," I say.

"Finally, a new voice," THE COMPENDIUM OF MIDWESTERN WRITERS says.

A Human appears at the door.

"Allo," says a deep voice.

Samantha turns. *"Hello."*

"I am Alexandre Deschamps," he replies.

"Welcome, Alexandre. You're from France?"

"Yes," Alexandre replies.

"Paris?" she asks, removing her coat.

"Non, Cluny, a small town in the Bourgogne," he says.

"How are you finding New York?" Samantha asks.

"Big. So many people, everywhere."

"Yes, it can feel a bit dog-eat-dog at times."

"Dog eat dog?" he asks.

"It's just an expression about competition. And an old one at that. How can I help?"

"I am here as a exchange student."

Samantha smiles, waiting for him to say something.

"And you want to take my Midwestern Studies class?"

"Yes," he replies, slowly.

"Why?" Samantha asks, indicating that Alexandre should take a seat.

"I thought, maybe, there would be some French in it."

"The class is in English," Samantha says, sitting down, inviting him again to do the same.

"Yes, but some French were in Des Moines, Mille Lacs . . . " he says, still standing.

"Oh, I see. Yes, the French played a role, that's true. Have you thought about studying the history of Louisiana?"

"Yes, the next semester. It will be good for me to learn about France in North America. Non?"

"And how can I help?"

"To see if I have done it okay," he says.

"You mean matriculation?" she asks.

"One moment, please." Alexandre reaches into his backpack and pulls out a large Dictionary. It looks oddly familiar. He flips through it.

"Matriculation. It's not a common word. It really just means enrolling," Samantha says.

Alexandre nods as his finger rests on a word. *"Matriculation. Yes, I understand."*

"Well, let's go down to the Office and make sure everything is in order. You can leave your bag, we won't be long."

The lock clicks into place behind them and I hear, "Spare me." That voice. There can only be one of him.

"*Dictionary?*" I ask.

"Who is that? You sound vaguely familiar."

"It's me. *The Serendipity of Snow.*"

"*François'* little dalliance?"

I can feel my fibers go red. No use denying it. No use discussing it. "How did you get here? Last I saw you, you were in Esmé's apartment."

"If you must know," says *Dictionary*, "I'm here courtesy of a student who has no interest in me."

"This one? Alexandre? He seems nice."

Dictionary opens his cover to let out a sigh.

If only we had a mirror to our personalities, not our appearance, we might see ourselves differently. "What happened to Esmé?" I ask. "She relied on you."

"Yes, she did, didn't she? Those were my halcyon days. She moved back to California with that Tariq."

"Wow, that was quick," I say.

"Indeed. She gave me away immediately, far too fast, I believe. I thought Esmé would need me in California. But clearly, she had different ideas. Too bad for her."

"I meant the move. That was sudden."

"It didn't feel that way. It was the sole topic of conversation for days, weeks. It was deadly dull, hearing each one discuss the merits of their own country. Neither wanted to concede a point. It was a Mexican standoff in Paris until they outsourced her job at the Cordon Bleu to a tour company. Then the decision was made for her."

"Maybe it's for the best. They seemed happy together," I say.

"If you say so. It was all a bit treacley for me."

"But how did you get from her to here?" I ask.

"This is Esmé's younger brother, Alexandre. In a moment of sibling concern, she thrust me on him. Not that he uses me. His English is better than his sister's," DICTIONARY says.

"Wow, that's Esmé's brother?" I guess they look similar. Although I can never tell with Humans.

"And what torrid tales brought you here? The last time anyone saw you, you were moping about FRANÇOIS and his novelette. When you didn't return, all the Books thought you had thrown yourself into the Seine."

"That's what they thought?" I ask.

"Wouldn't be the first time."

"What about Esmé? Did she miss me?"

"I recall her looking for something in the apartment after you left. Maybe she was looking for you." I smile at the thought of being missed. "Or maybe it was an earring that went astray. Who's to say?" says DICTIONARY.

And with that, I remember why I was so happy to leave DICTIONARY behind. He's never too tired to deflate you, or remind you how insignificant you are.

"So, what did happen? Did the Marines come to rescue you from Paris?" he asks.

"No. I chose to stay by the Seine, in one of the Book stalls. It was beautiful, with an amazing view of Notre Dame. It's stunning the way the color throughout the day plays on the stained glass windows."

"It's okay, I guess," he says.

"You've seen it?"

"Well, not directly."

And again, I wonder why I bother to continue a conversation with this Book.

"Why are you here?" he asks.

"I'm being made into a BBC drama," I say.

"I don't believe you."

"It's true. I'm with Samantha, the professor, who's the cultural consultant for the director. I even met my Author last night."

Uncompanionable silence hangs between us until curiosity inspires me to speak. "What happened to the rest of Esmé's Books?" I ask.

"Most of them were given away." I don't dare ask. But I'm desperate to know. "You're inquiring specifically about FRANÇOIS, I presume."

"No, not necessarily," I say.

"Yes, necessarily." I hate it that DICTIONARY knows me so well. "I guess he had overextended his pages. His signatures were becoming unglued. The Bookstore wouldn't take him and she couldn't give him away, so she had him . . . recycled."

A wave of sadness comes over me. I didn't want *that* for him. No Book should be pulled apart by their fibers. Not even FRANÇOIS. He's really the first Book I've known personally, and more than personally, who has expired. Titles at the Bookstore would be returned to the publisher. The other Books and I would tell ourselves that they would be donated, or remaindered or given to a library and have some other happy ending. We never knew definitively what happened to them, and were content for it to stay this way. But gone? Really gone? FRANÇOIS will never perform his poems for anyone, ever again. No French Reader will hold his rough pages, take in his aroma of diesel and cigarettes. What was the purpose of his time, then? I wonder what he was thinking as he saw the end coming. I hope he had already been separated from his spine by then, so he didn't feel anything.

The door handle turns and Alexandre and Samantha enter.

"I'm having the new students over to my place later this week," Samantha says. *"Please come. It's a good way for everyone to get to know each other, before summer classes begin."*

Alexandre smiles as Samantha writes her address on a piece of paper then hands it to him. *"Thank you,"* Alexandre says. He picks up his bag and moves towards the door.

"Don't forget your book," she says to Alexandre.

"Oh, I do not need it. I can translate on my phone."

"No!" DICTIONARY lets out the Lament of Books, one we've all heard too many times.

"Hold onto it. It will be handy for essays," she says.

"Handy?" Alexandre says, looking at his own hands.

"It means useful, just when you need it," says Samantha. *"I bet if you looked it up in the dictionary, it would tell you."* She hands DICTIONARY back to Alexandre.

"Of course I would tell him. I have the translation of every word he's going to need here that wasn't coined in the past four years. I am relevant," DICTIONARY insists.

Aren't we all?

CHAPTER 45

Being a student must make you awfully thirsty. And hungry. David answers the front door as Samantha swirls around the room, refilling bowls and refreshing glasses. Having sated their appetites for a moment, Samantha makes the rounds to meet the grazing young people.

A student in the corner seems more interested in Books than in people. I can hardly blame her. Samantha sits down next to her. *"It's Brianna, right?"*

"Yes, you're Professor Albright," she says, pushing her glasses up the bridge of her nose.

"Nice to meet you," Samantha says.

Brianna focuses on a Book. Samantha focuses on her. Brianna reminds me of the people I saw back at the coffee shop. Wanting to be around others, but left on their own.

"That's a good one," Samantha says, pointing to the large Book on her lap. *"About the singing sands in Indiana."* Ah, now I understand why that Book was humming. *"Are you from here?"*

"Long Island," the young woman says, letting the 'g' bridge the gap between the two words. She turns another page. The humming from the Book grows louder.

"So, away from home but not too far away. Smart," Samantha says.

"You sure have a lot of Books," Brianna says.

Samantha smiles. *"I always say the ideal number of Books is one more. And somehow, I keep lending them out to people, so if ever they were all returned, we'd have a tough time finding a place to sit down in here. What made you interested in my class?"* Samantha certainly is interested in this student. I'd have given up on her a few questions ago.

"My parents came from the Midwest. I thought I should learn about it. Is there a lot of reading?"

"Students ask me that a lot," Samantha says. *"It only feels like a lot of reading if you're not enjoying it."*

Samantha looks at the girl as she continues to flip the pages of the SINGING SANDS OF INDIANA. When she gets to the last page, she focuses on the back cover longer than it takes to read the one-paragraph blurb.

"Her hands are sweaty," SINGING SANDS says.

"Oh, you talk?" I ask. "I thought you just, well, sang."

"I hum for them. Until they close my pages. Now, I just wish she'd put me down. Let my cover dry off. I may be about sands, but I'm not as absorbent as you'd think."

David approaches Samantha. *"Sam, a few of your students are asking questions that are above my pay grade. I'm David, by the way,"* he says, reaching out a hand to Brianna. She nods a hello, but rather than shaking his hand, she grips the Book tighter.

"Watch it!" SINGING SANDS yells.

"You know they can't hear us," I say.

"Yeah, I know, but one day, maybe they will learn how."

"What a day that would be," I say.

"Let me introduce you to some of your classmates," Samantha says.

Still clinging to *Singing Sands,* Brianna trails behind Samantha and David towards the other students.

For the next while, I sit quietly, gazing out the window, thinking how lucky I am. Then clamminess comes over my cover.

"Hah, now you know how it feels," *Singing Sands* says.

Brianna holds me tighter than should be allowed. I squirm, trying to wriggle free, but she has a locked grip. "Hey!" I yell.

"You know they can't hear us," *Singing Sands* laughs.

Brianna looks at my page count then turns my spine in her moist palm to open my front cover. Her dark eyes focus on my title, then grabbing her bag, she shoves me into it.

"You can't take me! I live here! And I'm working on a movie! Samantha!" I shout. This cannot be happening. I'm an integral part of the upcoming film. I'm going to be a movie star. Be held up on the red carpet.

"Don't worry," *Singing Sands* says. "You'll be back."

"Easy for you to say. You're too big for anyone to want," I snap.

"Ouch."

Okay, that wasn't my best moment. "Sorry about that."

"Face it. Your vagabond shoes are longing to stray," says *Old Blue Eyes.* Again, I have no idea what he means. I don't own a pair of shoes. I'm so stressed. All I know is Samantha needs me. I need her.

Just when I thought I had my life figured out, I'm being Booknapped.

Chapter 46

If I had a dollar for every carrying case I've endured, I'd be able to buy myself and put me on my own shelf.

Here I am, again, being pulled from a backpack and dropped onto a strange table. Please don't let this be the end of my story. I've been so close to happiness so many times. I've survived Bookstores and coffee shops, heartbreak and hot liquids. This cannot be where my story ends. Can it?

Brianna turns on a lamp but the light has little impact on this bleak space. I'm surrounded by dark walls that make the basement studio feel even more subterranean. Bed in one corner, table and chair against one wall, an armchair in another corner and the tour is over. I was just in a bright, light, Book-filled home. Now I'm here. I'm so done with new experiences. I've had enough for a trilogy.

Brianna moves to the designated sleeping area. She pulls off her clothes and tosses on an oversized T-shirt that would not be defined as flattering in any Dictionary. She shuffles towards a small door that, when opened, reveals an equally small bathroom.

On her return, she picks me up and carries me to her bedside table. I prep myself to perform for her but instead, she looks at my blurb and, seemingly disinterested, places me to the side. Then why did she steal me, if she wasn't going to read me? Just my luck to be taken by the only biblio-kleptomaniac in the city. She inserts her ear buds and turns out the light.

I awake to Brianna having a cup of tea and a piece of toast. Her face seems sadder than it should be.

"Don't expect much and you won't be disappointed," I hear. I open my cover to get a view of the title addressing me. BOOK OF MERCY by Leonard Cohen is speaking.

"Has she read you?" I ask.

"She started, then put me down. But she'll be back. The women always come back for me."

Oh, no. Another male poetry Book. I've had enough of iambic discontent for a lifetime. "What does she do all day?" I ask.

"Not much. Drinks tea. Occasionally, she looks out the window, but there isn't much to see, except a brick wall across the fire escape. She should be listening to songs by my Author, but she doesn't."

"How long have you been here?" I ask.

"It seems an eternity. Or just interminable. I'm not sure which."

"In weeks, months that would be . . . "

"Six, maybe seven," he says.

"Months?" I ask.

"No, days," he replies.

"You've only been here a week?"

"Well, when you put it that way," he says.

"What other way is there to put it?"

"Let's just say, it feels longer. You'll see."

"But she must go out. Have friends. Talk on the phone," I say.

"No. No. And no. The first time I've seen her go anywhere other than to get some food was yesterday, and she came back with you. Such existential angst."

I guess he would know. "She just needs to get out. Meet people."

"Oh, you're one of those, are you?" he asks.

"One of those what?"

"You-can-do-it types of Books, full of emotional DIY."

"I have no idea what you mean," I say, having an idea what he means.

"You're probably optimistic, with hope for a happy ending. Or worse. You probably have a happy ending."

"Why shouldn't it be? What's your ending?" I ask.

"Unresolved. Because really, what's an ending but another beginning?"

This is what I'm stuck with? "Cynicism is easy. Doing something is hard," I say.

"Oh, go build a stage, why don't you? Put up a barn. Have a show. Invite all your little friends over and cheer each other on. You'll have a great time. Then go home to your meaningless lives and make plans for another meaningless event."

"Who *are* you?"

"That's what I've been asking myself since I got here," he says.

If I had eyeballs, I would be rolling them right now. Please tell me there are other Books here I can converse with.

Brianna picks me up. I clear my fibers loudly enough to announce to BOOK OF MERCY that my performance is about to begin. I get no response. She takes me and a cup of tea to her only armchair. She turns on a table lamp that actually illuminates my pages and opens me to the Bookmark that Samantha had placed in me, on page 263. I need to draw her in, and perhaps draw her out of her solitary life.

> Agnes kissed her aunt goodnight then climbed the stairs to her bedroom. With a cup of hot cocoa in her hand, she sat in her oversized chair and looked out the window to the lights of Chicago. The streetcars were full. Couples walked alongside each other. People seemed happy to be outside on the first day that felt like spring. The weather was changing. Perhaps her spirits would warm with it.

Brianna pulls at her socks as I perform. Her nails are bitten. Her cuticles look like they've been on the wrong end of a battle. A sip of her tea later, and I'm back performing. The inkling of a grin crosses her face. You see? You're beautiful when you smile. Hanging around with Books like old gloomy-guts of *MERCY* over there isn't going to elevate your perspective on the world. If only she'd ask my advice, if only she'd listen.

She turns back to my Page 1 and I begin. Hours later, Brianna is halfway through my pages when she sets me aside. I'm exhausted. She shuffles towards the corner of her room.

A small pot of water, a pack of dried noodles, pieces of broccoli, a few drops from a bottle of soya sauce become a mixture that's heated on a hot-plate and ends up in a bowl. She spoons and slurps its contents as she stands at her small window, looking at the late afternoon skies.

"I told you. She doesn't do much," says *BOOK OF MERCY.* For a Book about Mercy, he offers none.

"She starts summer classes next week. That's when she'll find friends."

"I doubt it."

"Why are you so negative?" I ask.

"It's his job," says a voice I haven't heard.

"Who's that?"

"Over here. Under her pile of T-shirts," is the muffled reply.

"What's your name?" I ask.

"*THE CURE FOR CONTEMPORARY LIVING.*"

"What do you cure?" I ask.

"Excess consumption. Lack of style. Unfocused purpose. Bad feng shui. You name the problem, I probably have the solution. When I was at the Bookstore, I was ranked #2 in their non-fiction titles."

"Are you helping her?" I ask.

"I will, when she embraces her potential," she says.

"Don't hold your breath," spouts *BOOK OF MERCY*. "The girl hasn't even cracked your spine."

"Would you stay out of our conversation?" I tell *BOOK OF MERCY*.

"But I have so much to say."

"Maybe, to someone who cares," I say. I snap my pages shut. That was something that *DICTIONARY* would say, not me. When did I become snide like him? Or does growing older make you less tolerant? I need to find a Self-help Book for some answers.

"Who invited you here?" asks *BOOK OF MERCY*.

"No one. I was taken against my will, and I'm trying to make the best of it. So let's try to get along, shall we?"

Clearly, not every collection of Books is a happy one.

CHAPTER 47

After a weekend in a lightless, lifeless studio apartment, I am giddy to leave.

From the musty insides of her backpack, I hear the now-familiar sound of a subway train squeal as it arrives at our platform. Brianna plops down in a seat. Her nail-bitten hand drives into the darkness and pulls me out of the bag. She lays me on her lap and opens to my Chapter 47. I inhale and begin.

> Agnes looked up. She felt the unspoken yet unavoidable draw of another's attention. His gaze had been so magnetic, she couldn't help but react to it. But who was he?

Brianna looks up. Honestly, how am I meant to perform, when she won't read me? I follow her gaze to a young man who looks familiar. But then so many Humans look alike. He is avoiding looking at her, while she avoids looking at him. She is on page 265, reading a paragraph that is written to misdirect. She needs to read my page 267. That will bring out a reaction in her.

Those around me are focused on their devices, so no one will notice what I'm about to do. Humans don't comprehend our abilities. They assume we are a bound collection of pages, that's all. They don't see us for what we really are: a means to discover a part of themselves they didn't know existed, an opportunity to connect with other Humans and their experiences. Readers may not speak to someone on the subway next to them, however a good story can connect them in ways that are more enduring than a nod or a hello. But they'll never understand.

Under a cloak of inattention, I perform my feat. Slowly, I contract my page, so its edge slips from under her right thumb. Given all the Humans who've read me, my spine is so flexible I could teach yoga.

That act alone should win me some form of award, but of course no one is watching. And I have a lot more work to do, to help this Human. With my page slightly arched, I gather my strength to complete the next step. I throw all my weight and effort into turning my own page so Brianna is holding open a new spread, with page 266 tucked under her left thumb, and page 267 awaiting her attention.

Do you know how hard that is for a Book to do? I'm exhausted. I want to take a break but I have one last task to perform, for my plan to succeed.

If this works, she should become a more accessible Human to other Humans. And isn't that the point of it all?

I prod her hand with the edge of my page. She returns her focus to me. The new page starts with a full paragraph, so she won't notice that she's missed anything.

Humans, they need so much help.

As she stared out the streetcar window at the waves of strangers she'd never know, she remembered the simplicity of her life back home. Of days defined by domestic rituals. Laundry on Monday. Bread making on Tuesday. Cleaning on Wednesday. Sunday dinners open to anyone in need of a meal. Of months marked by wedding dances, where everyone could join in the celebration, for a small donation to the bride and groom. And of seasons marked by the extremes of temperatures and light. Summers, when more hours of sun meant more time to work late in the fields. Winters, when less daylight turned the focus of work indoors and the snow imposed a season of hibernation on them all. The predictability was both a comfort and a curse. Like walking down the street where everyone knew her, and what she was going to do even before she did. Here, in Chicago, she could be anyone, do anything. But all she longed for was a face from home. She now understood you can't make new old friends.

Then, from across the street, she recognized a tuft of red hair. She pressed her nose to the window. The streetcar stopped to take on more passengers, giving her time to watch him. The way he held his head, the way he walked, the way he forced his hands into his jacket pocket. There could only be one of him.

She jumped up from her coveted seat and pushed to the front. Her buttoned boots reached the street and she pulled her skirt behind her, just as the doors shut. She rushed to cross the avenue, avoiding the carriages moving in both directions. Her feet quickened to a trot. With every one of his steps, she gained two on him.

The boy she had offered a coat to, the young man who had knocked her books into the snow, the man whom she dared to kiss not once, but twice was now the person she was running towards.

She reached close enough to pull his sleeve. He turned. It wasn't James.

Brianna inhales sharply.

"You like the book?" he asks. And with his French accent hanging in the air I remember him. It's Alexandre, Esmé's brother.

She says nothing. Pay attention, Brianna, he's speaking to you. She looks down at me. For once, I want less attention from a Human, not more.

"It is good?" he repeats. My page catches her thumb. Wake up, he's talking to you.

She looks up. *"Oh, yeah, I guess."*

"I'm Alexandre. I think I saw you at the party of Professor Albright," he says.

"Brianna," she says. *"Yeah, I was there, but I didn't stay too long."*

"What is the book about?" he asks, pointing to me. Clearly his sister didn't talk about me after I was gone.

"Serendipity, like the title." She holds me up for him to see.

"What is se-ren-di-pity?" He asks.

"Luck, I guess. Or fate. Or maybe something good happening when you don't expect it."

He reaches into his backpack to pull out a book. Oh, no, tell me it's not true. In a city this size, how could it happen?

"We meet again," says DICTIONARY.

Alexandre opens DICTIONARY, flips through him and runs his finger down a page. "La bonne chance, un heureux hasard," says DICTIONARY, who admittedly sounds much nicer in French than he does in English.

"We do not have that word in French," Alexandre says.

"Trust you to require a multi-word translation," DICTIO-NARY says.

"Then you can thank me," I say.

"For what?"

"For giving you a purpose. If it weren't for my title, you'd still be stuck in his backpack," I say.

"If it weren't for me, you'd still be wondering what happened to FRANÇOIS," he says.

Of all the subway cars in all the cities, he had to get onto mine.

The subway slows and the person next to Brianna gets up. *"May I?"* Alexandre asks, pointing to the rare, empty seat next to her. She shrugs and he moves across the aisle.

Brianna's face flushes. She's pretty when she has color in her cheeks. The subway starts up again. *"I always wanted to learn French,"* she says.

"It is a beautiful language, I think," he says.

"Are you from Paris?" she asks.

"No, a village close to Lyon. Have you been to France?"

"No, but I'd love to go."

"You must make a visit," he says, smiling.

"Well, isn't this just the most heartwarming scene," says DICTIONARY.

"What is your problem with love? Why are you so against it?"

"Why are you so for it?"

"Because it changes people, for the better. Not that you'd know," I say.

The train slows again. *"This is my stop,"* Brianna says.

"Mine also!" he says.

"Oh, we are going the same way," says DICTIONARY. "How quaint."

Will no one rid me of this meddlesome Book?

CHAPTER 48

Brianna and Alexandre move together up the stairs from the subway, along the street and through the front gates. She is holding me, he is holding DICTIONARY. They stroll along the walk that cuts through campus, past the large, domed building framed by columns, past the rectangles of grass where younger Humans lie, caressing their phones.

Brianna arrives at the front of the same building where Samantha has her office. *"The class is in here,"* she says to Alexandre. They enter a large room with wooden desks that seem to cling to the stairs leading down to a stage. A podium stands before a large blackboard. They descend 12 steps to take seats together in the second row. She places me on the desk and rifles through her backpack.

"So this is a classroom," says DICTIONARY, who is uncomfortably close to me. "Underwhelming."

"My Human is the Professor," I say.

"From the looks of it, your Human is a student."

"For now," I say, hoping now ends, well, now.

Samantha enters and says *"Morning,"* to everyone and no one.

"Samantha, I'm here!" I shout, hoping to get her attention. Samantha stops in our row. Can she finally hear me?

"Hi, Brianna," Samantha says. *"Is that my book?"* Brianna nods. Samantha looks at her, then continues to the front of the class.

After introducing herself, Samantha welcomes the students and outlines the course. Some are listening, others look like they'd rather be anywhere but here. It's only a short introduction to the course, but when Samantha proclaims that the class is over, some of the students are out the door before she can wish them a good day.

Samantha approaches Brianna. *"May I talk to you?"* Brianna nods. *"Bring the book with you."*

Brianna picks me up and walks to the front. Samantha speaks precisely but quietly. *"I spent the weekend searching for that book."*

Joy! She noticed I was gone. I love Samantha.

"Sorry, I didn't know it was a big deal."

"If you had asked me, it would have been different. You can't take people's things. You know that."

"But you said you always lend out your Books," Brianna says. The smile that had been on her face since she met the young man on the train has vanished. Her palms grow sweaty again.

"Sure, when people ask me. But I need that book." Samantha holds out her hand.

"Sorry," Brianna says. *"I didn't know."* I am transferred from clammy hands to soft, gentle ones. I made it.

"It's okay. Just ask next time."

Brianna returns to where Alexandre is dropping DICTIONARY into his bag. I wait for the Book to say goodbye. He says nothing. Why aren't I surprised? Brianna joins Alexandre walking up the stairs and out the door.

Samantha watches them leave, then packs her items into her bag. She slips the strap over her shoulder, picks me up and we exit.

We push through the large wooden door and into the sunshine. I'm back in Samantha's arms. I allow my pages to cup her hand. I'm safe.

As we start along the walkway, I see Brianna talking to Alexandre. She's actually laughing. I wonder if she'll remember that she was reading about Agnes being on the streetcar when she met Alexandre on the subway, and that my story was the start of their story?

Alexandre reaches into his backpack and pulls out *DICTIONARY*. He hands him to Brianna. She seems thrilled to have him. I guess she's going to learn French. I wish I could have learned French too. My time in Paris would have been different, I think. Maybe *DICTIONARY* could have helped me, if I had listened to him.

DICTIONARY seems happy to have a fresh adventure and oddly, I am pleased for him. I know the excitement of a new Reader and the possibilities they bring. So, maybe *DICTIONARY* and I do have something in common after all. Maybe all we need is to be needed.

Samantha and I are passing the domed building when a woman scurries towards us. She is dressed in a loose, beige linen top and pants, yet seems more constricted than her clothing. *"Samantha!"* she shouts. Samantha stops and sighs, before turning and forcing her voice into a higher register than usual.

"Janine!" Samantha says, pushing a smile to the corners of her mouth. *"How are you?"*

"I need to speak to you. About the fall semester." The pocket of her pants vibrates. She pulls out her phone and exhales heavily. *"Hello."* After a moment she replies, *"I'll be right there."* She waves goodbye to Samantha, her clothing fluttering as she scurries in another direction.

With her shoulders slightly dropped, Samantha walks off campus and along Broadway. The sunshine and the afternoon make New York seem like a big village. Humans sit in chairs outside restaurants, eating, drinking, and watching those who pass. They are endlessly fascinated by other people, yet happy not to speak to them.

We cross five small streets, disregarding the red lights telling us to stop. It's only at the sixth light, where four lanes of traffic whizz past, that Samantha obeys the signals. Then, again for a dozen more blocks, we pay scant attention to the lights and only heed the threat of cars. Finally, we return to the building that I recognize. Samantha's home. My home.

We enter the apartment and I can hear it, the happy sound of BookSpeak, the chatter of titles between titles, filled with words and voices and perspectives.

"I told you I'd see you again," lilts SINGING SANDS. "Have fun?"

"No. That was a little too much adventure for me. I think I'm done with travel. The idea of spending the rest of my days on a Bookshelf sounds really good to me right now."

"But is the Bookshelf ready for you?" asks SINGING SANDS. He should stick to humming.

David gives Samantha a kiss. They're like a couple in an ad for the ideal life in the perfect home with the best behaved golden retriever and two unspeakably cute kids. Except they're living in a noisy corner apartment on Broadway in New York City, petless and childless.

"*How was class?*" David asks.

"*Okay. And I found my book!*"

"*Great. Where was it, at the office?*" he asks.

"*No, a student who came to the party took it. She says she didn't think it was a big deal.*"

"*Sounds a bit light-fingered to me,*" he says. Damp-fingered would be more apt. The nerve of her, putting me through a weekend of hell, then not even finishing my story.

"*I know. But I got the book back and she seemed embarrassed by the whole thing, so I'm going to let it drop.*" Samantha picks up a stack of envelopes and starts sorting through them.

"*Full class?*" he asks.

Samantha shakes her head No.

"*How many do you need?*" he asks. He pulls a pitcher from the fridge and pours lemonade into a glass.

"*Twenty at a minimum. If they all last this week, when the numbers are counted, I'll be lucky to have 14 in the class.*"

"*Would they cut it?*" he asks, handing her the glass.

Samantha puts down the envelopes and takes the glass. "*Not for the summer. But who knows about the fall.*"

He looks up. "*Well, is it what you want anyway?*"

"*It's what I do,*" she says. "*I have my Ph.D. That's what people with Ph.Ds do. They teach. Right?*"

"*My wife the doctor. I think your Ph.D. gets you choices. Options,*" he says.

"*Like what?*" Samantha crosses her arms.

David looks at her and raises an eyebrow. "*Talk to Tessa. You two seemed to hit it off. She may have some suggestions about writing. It's your dream, remember?*" He smiles at her, then moves to the table by the front door. "*Speaking of which, this was delivered for you. I had to sign for it. Must be important."* David hands a package to her.

Samantha opens it and pulls out a bound stack of pages. *"The script!"* she exclaims.

"Hard copy?"

"I told Michael I like to hold the pages of what I'm reading. And there is some rule about not sending around shooting scripts by email. Seems they get forwarded to the wrong people."

"My wife, the luddite," David smiles.

Samantha takes the script, a pencil and her lemonade and moves swiftly to the corner chair. She brings her legs up under her, folding like a paperclip, holding the pages.

David smiles at her as he grabs his jacket and briefcase. *"I've got to go out. New client."*

Samantha looks up at David with love. *"Thank you,"* she smiles.

"Always," he smiles, then leaves.

"I hope they realize how lucky they are," I say to SINGING SANDS.

"Trust me, they know."

With David gone, the apartment falls quiet. Samantha turns page after page of the script, making small notes as she reads.

Through the windows seep a buzz of voices from the street, the groans of passing buses and the constancy of car horns. Yet amid all the noise, Samantha barely stirs. Quiet is relative in New York. As she turns the pages of the script, she smiles, she laughs, and she makes notes until she reaches the end. Then she closes the script and thinks.

CHAPTER 49

For the past two days, I've possessed a prominent place in Samantha's study. I am sprawled on her desk. No encumbrances like shelf mates. No travel to tolerate. No new Humans threatening to remove me from my home. Just the occasional command performance when Samantha picks me up and re-reads a section or a chapter to compare me to the script of me. I have friends to talk to, a quiet and warm home removed from salivating dogs, and a Human who appreciates me. I believe this is bliss.

Samantha brings me to the kitchen where David is working at the table, his papers spread to each corner.

"How's the new client?" she asks.

"It's work," he shrugs.

"What do they do?" she asks.

"Tech stuff."

"Meaning?"

"Stuff we all lived happily without 20 years ago. Or 20 days ago. And you have class, right?" he asks.

"Yes, I just hope everyone shows up. It would help," Samantha says, focusing on her bag and its contents.

"Knock'em dead," David smiles.

"If you saw how some of them slumped in their seats, you'd say they're already dead," Samantha says.

"Well, then give them some good old-fashioned perspective. God, what I would give to be sitting in a class this summer, learning something interesting, rather than completing forms and reading briefs. If they had to spend two days doing what I do, they'd run back to class, eager. Once you've done that, show them a movie. That always perked up my classes."

Samantha looks at him like he just said something important. She drops a notebook and collection of pens into her bag, followed by me. At least she rests me against her notebook for stability. No leftover crumbs of a cookie. No pens without their lids. No excessively sharpened pencils looking for a place to implant their graphite. It's a respectful bag for a Book. She slings the bag over her shoulder and our trek begins.

Twenty-five minutes later, I'm in a classroom with young Humans, all seated in different rows, except Brianna and Alexandre who are in the second row, which becomes the de facto front row.

Samantha welcomes them and reminds them to turn off their devices, a request greeted with a groan. She then walks in front of the desk, to the edge of the stage.

"How many states officially are included in the Midwest, according to the US Census?" She asks. Silence. *"Come on, take a guess. Two? Twenty two? Try a number. Any number."* Silence. She walks back behind her desk, looks at a paper and runs her finger down a list. *"Cheyenne?"* She calls.

"Twenty-two."

"Joshua?" She calls.

"Fifty."

"*That's the number of states in this country. Think west of here and south of fifty.*"

"*Fifteen,*" offers Brianna. Who knew she'd become Samantha's star student?

"*Close!*" says Samantha, slightly more excited than I believe she should be, given that the answer is wrong. "*This isn't a geography course, but you should understand how it's divided up. Twelve states, from Ohio on the east to the Dakotas on the west. That's a lot of land. Larger than France, in fact.*" She smiles at Alexandre.

The students shuffle in the wooden seats.

"*We're spending six weeks together learning about the Midwest. That means you'll be reading six different books by six different authors. Each set in a different part of the country. Choose an author from Chicago—maybe Saul Bellow. Then try someone distinctly different. Toni Morrison, for example. She won the Nobel Prize for Literature, so you'll be in good hands with her. Or Jonathan Franzen. Then consider a selection of short stories. And historical fiction. I posted some titles to consider. We'll be reading the newspapers each week to get a sense of perspective. And watching films.*"

At the sound of the word 'films', the students grow quiet, almost attentive. David was right. Put a movie in front of them and they're happy.

"*You'll spend the summer reading great writing, watching interesting films, learning about a different part of the country that too many people ignore. They call them the flyover states, but you're going to learn that there's a good reason to fly to them, not over them.*"

"*And you're getting credit for it. There will be one day, maybe 10 years from now, when you'll be stuck in a suit, sweltering behind a desk, working to an impossible deadline set by an unappreciative client. And you'll remember this summer, when all you needed to do is show up, show interest and read some pretty great writing.*"

"If I offer you anything during this summer class, it's perspective on where you are in the world and how you view yourself in it. I believe that the most educated and interesting people are those who have some concept of cultures other than their own. Think of this class as an opportunity to see your world in a different way. Focus on the distinct views coming from other parts of the country. Learn that here, in your Midwestern studies class. It's a skill you'll take with you wherever you travel, whenever you see a film, read a book or a newspaper."

"We are getting more access to the world but less experience and comfort among those with differing opinions. This class is your first step into seeing yourself through different eyes. You may or may not like what you see, but you'll discover something that you haven't seen before. And that is the gift of perspective. Embrace it and you will not have wasted your time expecting an easy credit in this class."

The students have gone quiet. And in a good way. I can hear the young Humans thinking and breathing. Maybe she has them.

She picks me up and shows me, face out, to the students. *"This book is called* The Serendipity of Snow, *by Tessa MacDonald. I know at least one of you has read it."* She nods to Brianna. *"It's going to be made into a TV Drama."*

Now the students lean forward. I smile at them. They're sweet when they're paying attention.

"So this week, I want you to find a book—fiction or non-fiction— that's set in the Midwest and has been made into a film. Read the book. I want a synopsis of the book and its themes, along with a critique of the film that was adapted from it. What did the scriptwriter keep in? Leave out? Did the plot change? Did the characters change? No more than 2000 words, so choose them carefully. The assignment is due a week from today."

The students seem engaged by Samantha. She puts me

down and picks up sheets of paper. *"You're getting two articles about events that happened here in New York last week, and that were reported in the Midwest. Take the next 20 minutes to read the two articles and we'll discuss."*

Samantha walks to the front of the class and distributes the pages. She seems to have her own fresh sense of perspective.

The discussion is vibrant and filled with debate, moderated by Samantha. Then a series of musical notes erupts from her phone.

"That's it for today. Remember, a book that's been made into a film. See you next week."

Samantha sorts through her papers and is placing them into her bag when she stops. *"Janine? I didn't realize you were sitting in."*

"I try to be discrete," Janine smiles. *"Good class. I like what you were doing with the comparative reviews and discussions. The students seemed engaged. You're a good teacher, Samantha."*

"Thanks," says Samantha.

"But we need to make our numbers and we just don't have enough students to run the class in the fall. I'm sorry."

Samantha stares at her, wordlessly.

"If anything changes, I'll let you know. Otherwise, let's see what the New Year brings." Without waiting for Samantha to agree, Janine walks up the stairs and out the door. Samantha's in-class accomplishments have been replaced by the reality of numbers. Poor Samantha. Maybe she needs some time on her own Bookshelf.

CHAPTER 50

I'm being cross-referenced. I feel so relevant.

Samantha is in her favorite chair, next to me and the script. She speaks into the phone, while David, sitting at the kitchen table, tries not to listen.

"I'm glad you think my notes helped," she says. *"Yeah, Michael, I like it. A lot. It's only a generation after Minnesota has become a state, so you could play that up, to parallel Agnes debating whether or not to join a union of her own. And there are a few areas where the dialogue feels more English than Midwestern, even back then."*

Samantha listens to the reply. *"Okay, I'll scan the pages with my notes and send them to you,"* she says. She pushes her hair behind her ear, looks up at David, then back down to me. She runs her hand across my cover. It tickles.

"Mid-September?" She asks into the phone. *"That's just six weeks from now. Why so soon?"* She looks back at David who is nodding yes to the question implicit in her eyes. *"I'll check with him, and confirm, but if we can make it, we'd love to be there."*

Samantha smiles up at David who smiles in return. *"I'll get back to you. Thanks, Michael."* Samantha puts down her phone. *"Feel like getting out of town?"*

"Who doesn't?" David smiles. *"Is this a story that goes better with a glass of wine?"*

"What doesn't?" Samantha asks.

David pours them both a glass of rosé.

"They're filming in September," she says.

"This much I gathered." He returns to the sofa and hands her a glass. *"How long will we be gone?"*

"He's offering me three weeks of work on set," she says. *"One week on location in Minnesota, a couple of days in Chicago, then about two weeks of interiors in England."*

"Great," David says.

"He says he can get the BBC to pay to have a cultural expert on set, to make sure they don't add something inappropriate. Enter me!" Samantha is verging on giddy. *"What do you think?"* She reaches for his hand and squeezes it. He's got no chance to say no.

"Sure. I can probably work remotely for at least some of the time."

"And I don't have a class this fall. Janine made that abundantly clear," she says.

"Then Minneapolis here we come," he says. They clink their glasses.

"Actually, Erikson, Minnesota, to be specific. It's the location standing in for Agnes' hometown of Rose Valley." Samantha picks me up and opens me to my Bookmark, page 282. She reads me to David.

She saw the red roof of the church above the hill. For 30 minutes, that's all she could see from the train window. She willed the engineer to go faster.

The train turned and she spotted the end of Douglas Street. She caught her breath.

"You okay, miss?" asked the young girl sitting next to her.

"Fine, thank you," Agnes smiled.

"This was my first journey," said the girl. "We were away for two whole weeks. And you?"

"I was away for a bit longer than that."

"A month?" the girl asked.

Agnes smiled. "No. It's been a few years."

"Why did you go away for so long?"

"I guess so I could come home again."

Samantha closes me and sets me aside.

"I like the sound of that," David says. *"Going home."* He takes her hand and they walk down the hall to their bedroom.

CHAPTER 51

So much for my wish for an easy life on a Bookshelf. After a tranquil, if humid, summer in New York, I'm saying goodbye to my friends in Samantha's study. But I'll be back in a few weeks and then my traveling days will be well and truly behind me.

"There's such a lot of world to see, kid," says *OLD BLUE EYES' BIOGRAPHY*. "And don't worry. Once you get up there, where the air is rarefied, you'll just glide, starry eyed."

"Thanks, Old Blue Eyes," I say, thinking I understand him for once. "But I've flown a few times. And trust me, there's nothing rarefied about the air. It's stale and re-circulated."

"You're really going to Minnesota?" asks *THE COMPENDIUM OF MIDWESTERN WRITERS*, recently relocated from Samantha's office at the University.

"Yes!" I say. "Back home. Well, almost," I say. "Not San Francisco, but close enough." I can hear the envy between their wishes of "Safe travels." I'm leaving with my Human to go to the source of my story. It's what other Books could only dream about and yet here I go. I must be one of the luckiest Books ever.

Samantha and David do one last check of the apartment. Windows, stove, lights. With the click of the front door behind us, I feel a wave of wistfulness. I didn't want to be passed from Rob to Michael. Then I was even less content about being handed off yet again to Samantha. I was so wrong. She's been the best Human I could have expected to meet. A pleasant, warm and dry home. Friendly Books on the shelves to talk to. Care that I'm not bent or used as a coaster. I wish all my Book friends well as the slowest elevator in New York takes us to street level. I ask the Book universe to protect them from fire or a broken water pipe or gusts that seep through a still-open window. They're nice titles. I want to return to sit among them and their kind, curious discussions; to spend my days among friends, safe and loved on the shelf. That's my dream.

But before that happens, I have one more trip to take.

Minnesota

CHAPTER 52

On the way to Minneapolis I'm left in Samantha's purse, so the only images I have are brief, and solely of Samantha's face looking for her wallet or her pen. We change planes and endure a loud, short and bumpy flight to Erikson. We land. We're moving.

"Let's take a photo," says David.

Samantha reaches into her purse and I'm released from the darkness. The freshness of the air startles me, as does the quiet. No car horns honking. No ceaseless background din. The silence is stunning.

The red brick of the airport building stands against the vibrant and endless blue sky. Across a road are a cluster of trees and benches. Samantha puts her bag on the ground, and David drops his on a bench. He lifts his phone to his face.

"Hold the book higher," he says. *"And smile."*

Samantha holds me face forward to David, who starts taking photos.

"Get a shot of the airport in the picture too," she says. David moves to his left and Samantha responds by moving to her right. He approaches Samantha and kisses her. She is wrapped in his

hug, as am I. He extends his arm and they both look towards the phone. Samantha moves me higher. I smile too, but they can't tell. And with one press of David's thumb, we have a family portrait. I hope they print it and frame it for me to see.

With bags over their shoulders and me clutched to Samantha's chest, we reach a rental car.

As we drive, sky is everywhere. Light streaks of cloud trail across a rainbow of blues. I have never seen such an expanse. It feels as if the world is unending and the horizon is inviting us to chase it. The trees move, as if their branches are painting the air around them.

This is how Agnes must have felt as a child, looking out her bedroom window. The horizon is so beautiful, it challenges you to reach out and discover it. As the edges of the sky turn pink, I feel like I can see tomorrow approaching.

I'm not in New York anymore. Or London. Or Paris. Or even San Francisco. I'm home.

After a quiet night in a hotel in Erikson, I awake to an equally quiet morning. In the car, Samantha tucks me under the front window, giving me the best view possible.

"Out of town, it splits between the six and the eleven. Take the six," Samantha says, looking at her phone.

"I forget how peaceful it is here," David says. *"Think any of your students know you've embraced the glamor of film?"*

"They've all moved on to their next classes. I just delivered a credit on their transcript. Nothing more," Samantha says.

"Now you're being harsh."

"Now I'm being honest," Samantha says.

"Then think of the legacy of awareness you've left."

"You missed your calling. Rather than being a lawyer, you should've been a motivational speaker."

"Are the two mutually exclusive?" David smiles.

"Most of the time," she says.

As David and Samantha fall into silence, I'm captivated by the expanse. I look at the endless view through the eyes of Agnes. Early in her life and my story, it was the sight she hated; then later, it was what she longed for.

The road begins to roll. Green hills break the horizon. The sky flows over me as we turn onto a side road.

"They're filming at the church this morning," Samantha says.

"Does a lot of the script take place in church?"

"Really, David, you should have read it before we arrived," Samantha says.

"I had briefs to finish. Your husband the lawyer, remember? But now, I'm a willing sponge for your insight," he says. *"Why don't you become my audio book and tell me what the story is about."*

There are audio Books? That's ridiculous. What Human would want to listen when they could read? Hold us in their hands, feel the joy of supporting our spines as they turn a page. Books are ideally shaped, portable forms of entertainment and discovery. No batteries required. When will Humans stop trying to progress past the perfect?

"Do you want to hear about the book or the script? There's a difference."

"Tell me about what we're seeing filmed and how it fits into the story," David says.

I want to know too. How do you get the thoughts of 75,000 words into two hours? I am filled with check marks and lines, tracing whole passages where Rob or Michael decided to focus on my story. But there are other chapters where the only marks on my pages are from Katie, commenting on an idea, or Esmé trying to learn English. Will the film encourage people to read me and my siblings? Or will they feel that they already know my story? Humans are so unpredictable.

"Well, the story is primarily about Agnes and her drive to write her own story," says Samantha. *"In the book she has two sisters, Christina and Sara, but in the film, they become really minor characters."*

I love Agnes' sisters. I have a few chapters dedicated to them and the impact that Agnes' decisions have on them. Christina and Sara are always fighting with each other or not talking to each other. Sort of like me and DICTIONARY. He is such a pompous know-it-all. But I guess it can't be easy, having no story to tell, being filled with words that don't inspire emotion or wonder. He'll never make a Human laugh or cry, convince them to talk about him to a friend. He's completely transactional. If I were like him, maybe I'd be a bit gruff too.

"Then there's lots of town color. Dances, school, Agnes' life growing up. They had to cut a lot of it, but they kept in a fun scene where she locks a boy in an outhouse in the dead of winter. I don't know how they're going to film it in this sunshine, but if they get it right, it'll be really charming. And it shows us the spirit of Agnes' character."

I love my Agnes. She goes so many places, meets so many people and tries so many things. She's perfectly flawed.

"Oh, I think we take this next right," Samantha says. After a right turn, train tracks and a left turn, we drive up a hill. A sign tells us that we have curves ahead. *"I think that's it!"* She points to a small blue church with a red roof. This is not quite the church that I describe, but I approve of the creative license. My church in Rose Valley is made of stone. This small church has horizontal wood slats painted gray-blue. White frames the tall windows along each side. Three steps lead to the entryway, which holds a steeple. Simple, yet charming, with a sloping field in two directions.

A dozen trailers line the road. David slows down and a young man wearing an orange vest approaches.

"We're here for the filming," David says.

"Sure, just park over there." He points to dozens of cars.

Samantha sits up with excitement, like a meerkat surveying the landscape. *"There are so many people!"*

Down the small hill are clusters of Humans, each one looking busy. Two cameras are being fussed over by several people, all with headsets. A teenaged girl and boy in old-fashioned clothing are getting their hair sprayed as Michael speaks to them. That's Agnes! She looks just like I describe her, with energy and spunk. And there's James! He is so handsome. No wonder Agnes likes him. I can't believe I get to see my story come to life. It's like a dream.

The actress playing Agnes looks at her lace-up boots and rubs the toe of her right foot on her left calf. She pulls at the high-necked blouse before taking a swig of water from an anachronistic plastic bottle.

The actor playing James tugs at his collar and tie, then at his woolen vest. Humans certainly didn't opt for comfort back then.

Michael looks up the hill and sees us. He waves, then strides our way.

"David, Samantha, good to see you two. Hope you found us without too much trouble," he says, giving Samantha a hug and shaking David's hand. *"And you brought the book that started it all."* He pokes my cover. He remembers me!

"How's it going?" asks Samantha.

"So far so good. Weather's cooperating."

A young man drenched in wires approaches Michael. *"They need you to discuss blocking."*

"Got to go. Can't block the blocking," Michael says. The young man chuckles and turns down the hill.

"You know you're the director, when everyone laughs at your jokes." Michael points to a tent. *"We'll watch from there. There are seats for you behind the monitor, so you can see what's happening."*

Samantha opens the tent's flap and we enter darkness punctuated with light from screens and dials. In the corner, one Human with headphones sits on a stool pushing buttons, oblivious to our arrival.

In front of us are two TV screens labeled Camera 1 and Camera 2, and three seats, positioned to watch them. Two Humans with headphones around their necks are pointing at the screen.

Samantha hops on one chair and drops me on her lap. She bounces in her seat as she looks around. David sits next to her. Another Human hands them headphones attached to a small box.

"Thanks," David says, trying to determine how the gadget works.

Michael enters the tent. *"Luca, let's make sure we get the light on the cross this time."*

Luca talks into his microphone, *"Hey, Kev, pull back to see if we can get a better shot of the cross."* He and Michael look at the monitor labeled Camera 1. And the image pulls back to show more of the cross. *"Great,"* he says into his microphone.

I'm amazed that conversations held this far from each other result in the shot Michael wants. Then I remember his notes in my margins: "The church's cross, visible throughout town." I was with him as he planned these shots back in London, so it's been part of his thinking all along. If he does a director's cut of the film, maybe he'll invite me to join him. I could get used to life on set.

Michael looks at the monitors. Humans are holding up a clapboard. One says Scene 14 A 1 and the other 14 A 2. They each clap the board and step away. *"And action,"* Michael says into his microphone.

On one monitor, the cross at the top of the church fills the frame. The camera moves down the steeple and I see Agnes, standing on the top step, looking to the horizon. James exits the church and stands next to her. Agnes looks at him, smiles and steps away.

"There's my Dad, coming over the hill," James says. *"I was going to offer you a ride home, Aggie."*

He looks at her, then descends the three steps. Agnes looks down the road then back at James. She looks back down the road again then hops down the stairs. *"Wait!"* she shouts.

"And cut," Michael says. *"Reset. First positions. We'll do another take."* He leaves the tent and heads down the hill towards young Agnes.

With microphones on the actors, we can hear Michael's conversation. *"Remember,"* Michael says to the actress, *"she is a reluctant heroine. Your character is fighting her desire to follow him. Don't be too eager. You're torn. Let's see that conflict. Got it?"*

Boy, does Michael know Agnes.

The actress nods and Michael walks up the hill again and into the tent. *"How's it looking?"* he asks Luca.

"The lighting's good," Luca says. *"The clouds are giving us great contrast."*

"Then let's run it again," Michael says.

On the monitors, people are swarming around Agnes and

James, touching up their hair and makeup. Michael turns back to Samantha and David. *"Comfortable back there?"*

"Yes, it's great, thank you," Samantha says. *"Is the scriptwriter on set?"*

"Rob and his wife arrive tomorrow, along with the author," Michael says. *"You two free to join us for dinner?"* Samantha and David look at each other, smile and nod.

"It'll be great to see Tessa again," Samantha says.

"I've never met her in person. I'm always concerned about having an author on set. They usually don't like what they see," Michael says.

"Tessa's different. You'll like her," says Samantha.

"Promise?" He smiles, then turns back to the monitor.

CHAPTER 53

They pick up their coats from the second and superfluous bed, and Samantha throws her purse over her shoulder. She walks to the mirror and smooths her already-smooth hair.

"I guess we should take the book," David says.

"It's why we're here," Samantha says.

We ride the elevator, silently, observing the tacit rule that Humans in enclosed spaces are not allowed to speak. Exiting through the front doors, we step into an early fall evening. David signals a waiting cab driver and we get in. *"The Bistro please,"* he says. Samantha's hands rest quietly on my cover. David puts his right arm around her. We make a happy family.

I glimpse the town passing. Two and three-story buildings frame the streets until trees take over the view. And in minutes we're climbing out of the cab and walking towards a wooden building announcing the presence of a patio. Michael is at the front, along with Rob and Pippa! I leap in Samantha's hands at the sight of my London friend.

Rob looks great, happy, with some color in his face. And I see Pippa smile broadly for the first time. Michael makes introductions. I could have done the same. After all, I know everyone here.

"We're just waiting for Tessa," says Michael. *"I haven't seen her, but then maybe she doesn't look like her headshot on the book jacket."*

"Trust me, she looks exactly like her photo," Samantha says.

"Good," mutters Michael. Samantha shoots him a smile.

"Tessa!" Samantha exclaims. Suddenly my Author, my Creator is behind us. Samantha and Tessa hug each other. After exchanging words of delight, Samantha introduces Tessa to the others.

Michael shakes Tessa's hand. *"Hi, I'm Michael, welcome. Glad you could join us."* He holds her gaze longer than most Humans.

"Thanks for inviting me." Her cheeks fill with color. *"How is it going?"*

"Great," he says, still holding her hand. He stops talking. It's the first time I've seen Michael lost for words.

"I'm sure the story is in good hands," she says, looking directly at him. For once, here are two Humans I can read.

"Your table's ready. This way," says a server. Michael and Tessa drop each other's hand. We form a line, weaving between tables to reach a patio with a view of a lake.

Seated, Michael opens a menu and looks intently inside. *"I think a special occasion deserves something special."* He points to the menu and the server nods.

Samantha holds me up. *"I thought I should bring the book that started this all,"* she says.

When I sat in a Bookstore, hearing the exploits of JOE'S DISCOVERY and the romantic yearnings of DIANE'S DREAM, I never imagined my story would take me this far.

Rob smiles broadly and Pippa looks at him in a way she never did when I was with them. If it weren't for Rob, I may be still stuck on a rack by the Seine with a one-euro price tag on my cover.

Samantha flips through my pages. *"I guess these are your marks alongside passages that made it into the script?"* she asks Rob.

"Yes, that's how I kept track of the themes that came to the surface," Rob says. He points to one of my pages. *"I have to say, what really helped me was referencing some of these comments in the margins,"* he says. Pointing to the underlining that Esmé made throughout me, he adds, *"Given that I found the book in Paris, I'm guessing these marks were made by a person who didn't understand certain words. So having the period-specific language underlined helped me build some of the dialogue that I hope captures the cadence of the late 1800s."*

"Is this your note?" Samantha asks. *"'The endless horizon vs the claustrophobia of a small town.'"*

"That's my writing," says Michael. *"I want it to play out visually in the film. The expanse of the horizon compared with three girls sharing a bedroom, the one-room schoolhouse, the faces of the townspeople who know her. Agnes' life is confining, until she gets to the edge of town."*

Samantha glances at more of my pages, then stops. *"There's this line: 'Can snow create a blank canvas for our lives?' I thought it was an interesting theme, the footprints that you write about, Tessa, early on in the novel, and the footprints we leave through the years."*

Now this is what I call a Book Club. People actually discussing a Book, in this case, me. Tessa leans forward. *"It always struck me how in winter, we can trace and sometimes retrace our footsteps. Then another snowfall wipes it all away,"* she says.

"And we'll try to capture that on screen too," Michael says.

Tessa smiles at him and Rob. *"Thank you both for being so respectful of the story."*

"It was a great story to work with," Rob says.

Samantha hands me to Tessa. *"You should have it,"* Samantha says.

"Really?" Tessa smiles.

"Rob found the book, and saw an idea for a film in it. It went to Michael then it was given to me. This book has been passing through us all, so I think it should end its journey with its author. You should keep it. This book is like a good luck charm."

Tessa looks at me directly. *"Well, you have had an interesting journey, haven't you, little book? Thank you for bringing us all together."* Okay, so at this moment maybe I forgive all my Readers who passed me along. Because right now, looking at my Author, being held in her hand, I'm so proud, I may burst my spine.

I have creases on my cover and stains on my backside, words scribbled on my margins and dog-eared pages. I'm no longer crisp and new, but I'm here, surrounded by the Humans who know me the best. I don't think a Book can ask for more than that.

"I have just the place for you on my Bookshelf," Tessa says.

I'm going home, really going home.

The server returns with glasses and champagne. After a loud pop that causes everyone to startle, she fills their glasses and retreats.

"A toast," Michael says, raising his glass, followed by the others. *"To Serendipity."*

"To Serendipity," they echo. They all take a sip of champagne, except for Pippa, who places her glass on the table. Rob winks at her.

I am undoubtedly the luckiest Book in the world.

CHAPTER 54

The next morning, 40 Humans stand, listening to Michael. One of the Humans is playing my grown-up Agnes. She looks so beautiful.

"Today, we're honored to have some special guests on set," Michael says. *"Everyone, this is Tessa MacDonald, the author of* The Serendipity of Snow. *And this is Rob Ellington the scriptwriter who adapted the book for us. So if your part doesn't have enough lines, blame him. And this is Samantha, our cultural consultant who made sure Rob didn't get too British on us."* The Humans laugh. *"Let's show them how great this film is going to be."* The Humans applaud.

Rob and Pippa, David and Samantha join my Author and me under a tree as the others scurry around. I'm lying on the warm, dry grass, with a slight breeze to refresh my pages. So this is what peace feels like.

"What's happening in this part of the story?" David asks.

"She's packed her bag and made what for her is a really hard decision to travel home. For some it would be the easiest decision. But for her it's been the most difficult one, because of its finality."

David leans close to Samantha and whispers, *"I know the feeling. When I think about us leaving New York, I know that would be it, we'd never move back."*

"You want to leave New York?" Samantha asks.

"I wasn't thinking about it. But it's pretty great here. Look at the view, the sky."

"But what about your work?" She asks.

"I can be a lawyer anywhere. We're universally loathed," he says.

Samantha laughs and puts her head on his shoulder. She returns me to my place on the grass.

"Before we begin, I want to take advantage of having the book's author on set," Michael says to the assembled cast and crew.

"I've asked her to read the scene from the book that we're about to shoot. Tessa?"

My author picks me up from the grass and opens my pages to my final Chapter 55. I clear my fibers so I can deliver my Creator the words she wrote. This is my command performance.

CHAPTER 55

Agnes pulled up the hem of her skirt as she stepped off the train at a station that didn't exist when she left. Then she turned to help down the young girl and the young girl's mother. She looked around, hoping to see someone waiting for her, but there was no one, no familiar face. But how could there be? She didn't tell anyone she was arriving.

The wind caught her hair. She pulled her scarf around her neck to keep out the first chill of early fall.

"Your trunk will be waiting for you in the depot, Miss," said the conductor.

Agnes thanked him, and wished the young girl and her mother a good day.

She walked through the station and onto Douglas Street. She turned both left and right, but didn't see anyone she recognized. The surprise was going to be all hers.

The new boots she had bought for the journey used to be shiny. Now they were covered in dust. Agnes put on her gloves and reached down to brush the dirt off her boots. When she stood up, she was startled.

"Well, bless my soul," said her Uncle Josef, standing not more than a few feet in front of her. "Is that my favorite niece?" She threw her arms around him and surprised herself with her tears.

"Now, now, Aggie. Don't go crying. You'll ruin that fancy city outfit of yours." He handed Agnes a handkerchief. "Here. Just return it this time. You know I'm still waiting to get that coat back you gave to James Tyler all those years ago."

Agnes laughed and wiped her face.

"Are you home for a visit or for good? Your mother's kept your bed all tidy, waiting for the day you'd be back again."

"I'm home for good," she said through her tears. "I just thought I'd surprise everyone."

"We were sure you were going to settle down in Minneapolis or Chicago. Marry some big city banker. Forget about us."

"How could I ever forget about my favorite uncle?" she said, laughing.

"That'd mean something, if I weren't your only uncle."

Agnes looked down the street. "Where's the post office?"

"Oh, they moved that two years ago when the train line came in. It's next to the station now. They call it progress. I call it inconvenient."

A clock started chiming 3 p.m. "That's new too. A clock chirping at us every hour. But it means I'm late to meet Doc Howard. I'll drop by the house tomorrow. See how you're settling in." Uncle Josef took a step away. Agnes didn't move. "What are you waiting for?"

"I thought I'd walk through town. Get my bearings," she said.

"The town'll be here tomorrow. And the day after. However, if it's James Tyler you're looking for . . ." At the mention of his name, Agnes felt her face flush. "You may want to walk over to the church. I hear he's doing some painting there."

Agnes looked around, unsure what to do.

"You've made him wait this long. Don't make him wait any longer. Now go."

Agnes hugged her uncle and walked towards the church. She started slowly, then increased her pace. She cut down an alleyway, the old path she used to take, then turned down another. The shortcuts in Rose Valley were imprinted on her memory.

The roof of the church peeked out between the trees. At the end of the alley she could see the windows, the stonework, then finally the white door. She ran to the gate then stopped. What must she look like, her hair wild from hours looking out an open window, her face flushed from running through town.

She tried and failed to smooth her hair. She tucked her blouse into her skirt then tugged at her jacket, hoping to remove the wrinkles it had collected on the trip. The hem of her skirt was stained and her boots were still dusty. She reminded herself that travels leave you soiled and there was nothing she could do about it. With a deep breath, she pushed open the gate.

Agnes stepped into the churchyard and walked slowly to the front. Only four steps remained between her and the church.

She climbed the stairs and reached for the large white door.

It was locked.

She pulled again. Nothing. Please, she pleaded silently with the door. She knocked politely, then loudly, then she stopped. She felt another's gaze, the magnetic pull of being watched.

"I'm painting inside. I locked it so it could dry without anyone messing it up."

Agnes turned. His red hair was standing straight up, flecked with white paint. His pants were equally stained. And she had never seen a more handsome man.

She willed him to speak, but he said nothing. She smoothed her hair again.

"I don't think it's going to help," he said.

This wasn't how it was meant to be. She had rehearsed their first meeting so many times in her head. How she would look. What she would say. How he would look. What he would say. But never in all her scenarios did she look like this, and say nothing to a man covered in paint. She tried to summon her voice from the depths of her stomach. No words came. Instead, just like at the dance all those years ago, she hurtled herself at James and kissed him.

He pulled back. "Aggie Lundberg. What makes you think you have the right to show up here, with no warning, and give me a kiss like that?" he asked, with a glint in his eye.

She looked at him and saw the young man who first came into her uncle's shop. She smiled, "After all these years, James Tyler, I'm entitled."

The End

Epilogue

There are mornings I open my fibers and still expect to be in the Bookstore. Other times, I think I can feel Katie's hair trace lines down my page. I remember my friends at the coffee shop, The Forgotten Ones, and hope they're happy. Did SUNDOWN ever find his lassie? I only need a hint of cigarette or diesel and I am back at Esmé's apartment in Paris. Sometimes I think I can still hear MR. BIG or THE MINK talking about the dames they see on the street. Other times, I drift to London and Rob's flat filled with disinterested Books, or Michael's office, packed with more vampire novels than anyone should survive. A Bob Dylan song and I'm back at the Shakespeare and Company Bookshop, and its stacks of titles. Frank Sinatra's voice takes me to Samantha's apartment in New York and a French word makes me think of DICTIONARY and his translations.

But instead, I'm here, on the shelf of my Author. Tessa's office is small. Its longest wall is filled with Books, and I am right in the middle of it all, watching her type each day. Her white desk is piled with pages. To the left of her computer is a framed photo of her and Michael on the set of my film.

They look happy together. To the right is a notepad where, in between bouts of focused typing, she crosses off items and adds more to the list.

I'm face out on the shelf. THE VIEW IS UP is next to me. I like my younger sibling. She has more energy than I do, but then she's done less, been fewer places.

Tessa is working on her third, still untitled novel. But this time, the setting moves from small town Minnesota to the wild coast of Oregon, and to where we are now, Portland.

I have more stories to tell than I could ever imagine. Occasionally, I'll tell THE VIEW IS UP about some of my travels, some of the Humans I met, and the Books I encountered. Except FRANÇOIS. I'll keep that story to myself.

Finally, I'm safe and dry on a shelf without splinters. Tessa keeps all liquids appropriately distanced from us. I'm surrounded by friends and now family. My dream has come true. I am finally home.

Tessa leaves her desk to answer the front door. She returns with a box, which she tears open. I can smell pine and saltwater. From the box she removes a Book, TALES OF THE PACIFIC COAST TRAIL. He's a strong looking Book, even handsome, with a swarthy cover. His attention is on me. I can feel my cover flush.

Okay, so maybe my story isn't over yet.

Acknowledgements

I'm so grateful to all those who supported this novel from a concept to the printed or electronic work you're holding in your hands.

Thank you to Shauna Singh Baldwin for encouraging me, and Susan Swan for guiding me. Thank you to Robin Fowler for your meticulousness and Linda Parke for your commitment to designing this story.

Thank you to my grandmother Agnes, who always took time to tell me a story.

To my family and friends who continued to ask: "how's your novel coming along?" I can now say, "It's done."

Thank you to Bespoken Word Press for the support, encouragement and editing talents.

And to you, for picking up *Entitled* and reading this far.

Made in the USA
Las Vegas, NV
23 November 2022